D1599824

WHAT BECKONING GHOST

'What beckoning ghost along the moonlight shade
Invites my steps and points to yonder glade?'

ALEXANDER POPE

To the Memory of an Unfortunate Lady

WHAT BECKONING GHOST

by

Douglas G. Browne

DOVER PUBLICATIONS, INC.
New York

To

GWEN

This Dover edition, first published in 1986, is an unabridged and unaltered republication of the first edition, as published by MacDonald & Co., (Publishers) Ltd., London, 1947.

Manufactured in the United States of America
Dover Publications, Inc., 31 East 2nd Street, Mineola, N.Y. 11501

Library of Congress Cataloging-in-Publication Data

Browne, Douglas G. (Douglas Gordon), 1884–
What beckoning ghost.

Reprint. Originally published: London : Macdonald, 1947.
I. Title.
PR6003.R49W4 1986 823′.914 85-25304
ISBN 0-486-25055-5 (pbk.)

CONTENTS

PRECURSORY: TUESDAY, WEDNESDAY

PART ONE: WEDNESDAY, THURSDAY

PART TWO: FRIDAY

PART THREE: SATURDAY, SUNDAY

PART FOUR: MONDAY, TUESDAY

EXORCISM: TUESDAY, WEDNESDAY

PRECURSORY

Tuesday, Wednesday

"The subject of Natural Magic is one of great extent, as well as of deep interest."

Sir David Brewster
(Letters on Natural Magic)

CHAPTER I

POLICE NOTICE

No. 68.

METROPOLITAN POLICE

Body Found

Where . . .	The Serpentine.
When . . .	6.9.47.
Sex	Male.
Name . . .	Wallace Arthur Whichcord.
Apparent Age . .	65.
Height . . .	5 ft. 7½ in.
Complexion . .	Sallow.
Hair . . .	Grey.
Eyes	Grey.
Peculiarities and Marks	None.
Dress . . .	Raincoat, grey flannel suit, brown shoes, cotton shirt striped blue, grey woollen scarf, leather belt, vest, drawers, grey socks.
Now at . . .	Paddington Mortuary.

Dated this 6th day of September 19. .

CHAPTER II

THE *Morning News* RECALLS AN OLD STORY

THE HYDE PARK GHOST AGAIN

SERPENTINE FATALITY

(From THE *Morning News* Staff Reporter, JAMES FENNE)

Wednesday.

"AFTER seven years, the Hyde Park Ghost has walked again. It has been seen by Wally Whichcord, one of the three witnesses to its materialization in September, 1940. But this time we have his account of it only at second hand. For yesterday morning poor Wally was found drowned in the Serpentine.

"Have these seven troubled years obliterated memories of the ghost? I was the first to record the story in these columns, and I may claim to know as much about it as anybody outside the small circle intimately concerned. Let me briefly recall the facts. In March, 1940, H.M. Submarine *Narwhal* was lost in the North Atlantic with all hands. Her commander, Lt. F. H. Demarest, was the only child of Mrs. Hugo Demarest, of 7a Lancaster Terrace, W.2. Compelled, as months went by, to abandon hope of her son's survival, Mrs. Demarest, like other bereaved women, turned to the comforts of spiritualism. She became convinced that she had spoken to her lost one across the gulf, and that in certain circumstances he would reappear to her. And one September night she slipped out of her house in obedience to a summons imparted through the medium whose séances she was attending.

"It was midnight, an air raid was in progress down the Thames estuary, and the streets were deserted. The household at 7a retired at night to the basement, and there Mrs.

Demarest's companion, Miss Plimsoll, was awake, listening to the gunfire, when she heard the front door close softly. She rose to investigate, found the maid asleep but Mrs. Demarest's bed empty, and ran upstairs to the dining-room, a window of which looks down Lancaster Terrace to Bayswater Road and the parks. By a full moon and the beams of searchlights she saw Mrs. Demarest standing with a shadowy figure at the street corner. Then the mysterious form walked noiselessly away across Bayswater Road. It seemed to melt into the shadows of the trees in Kensington Gardens. After a brief hesitation, Mrs. Demarest followed.

"Miss Plimsoll donned a coat and ran out. Mrs. Demarest was on the pavement across the road, calling distractedly to her son, and even stretching her hands through the park railings. For this was 1940, long before the railings were removed. The park gates were closed, and down the length of Bayswater Road not another soul was in sight. Mrs. Demarest declared that the figure, in the act of crossing the road, suddenly vanished. But it was indeed her son, in naval uniform, whom she had met and talked with face to face.

"Now we come to Wally Whichcord. Wally was one of those waifs who pick up a living somehow. He spent many of his nights in Hyde Park, for it was easy to lie low in some shrubbery when the gates were closed. He liked sleeping in the open, and he felt safer there after bombing started. Readers will remember the warm, dry nights of that September, and on this eventful one Wally was under a tree near the Cockpit, a few hundred yards from the Serpentine. Like Miss Plimsoll, he was listening to the gunfire and watching the searchlights. Suddenly a dark figure appeared near him. It made no sound, but he saw it clearly, for a searchlight was overhead. It was dressed like photographs he had seen of submarine officers, in high boots with light stockings turned over them, brass-buttoned reefer coat, and peaked cap. It wore a dark beard. Its pale, unearthly face turned this way and that as it stood still for several seconds. Then noiselessly it walked away towards the Serpentine. It passed behind a tree. Wally watched for it to come into view again, along the waterfront.

But it did not reappear. He got up and looked round. The figure had vanished into air.

"Wally was puzzled, but did not then give the matter much thought. Hyde Park was full of A.A. gunners and others in uniform. But in a day or two, when he was having his pint in a local bar, a queer story came to his ears. Mrs. Demarest talked freely of her occult experiences, to friends and before her maid. Miss Plimsoll told how she too had seen the apparition. The tale was soon all over the neighbourhood, and when Wally heard it, he talked of what *he* had witnessed that night.

"It was a change from air raids, anyway, and it was still a nine days' wonder in Paddington when a bombing incident took me there. I got Wally's version from his own lips, and saw the scene of his adventure in Hyde Park. With what I learnt about Mrs. Demarest's meeting with the ghost of her dead son, it made a good story.

"That was seven years ago. Yesterday, being in Paddington again, I heard that the ghost had reappeared, and to Wally Whichcord, of all people. Mrs. Demarest is dead, but Wally was still about, and still sometimes sleeping in the park. There, a fortnight ago, he saw the ghost again, at or near the same spot. Once more it vanished before his eyes. But when I tried to track Wally down, to get this new story from him, I was too late. His body had been recovered from the Serpentine that morning.

"How he got into the water, and was drowned where it is only a few inches deep, looks like remaining a mystery. A more perplexing mystery remains—the mystery of another man who was drowned, seven years ago, and who was seen again by three people, and by one of them twice. 'Dead men', wrote Swinburne, 'rise up never. . . .' But if any reader of *The Morning News* sees the Hyde Park Ghost, I should like to know."

PART ONE

Wednesday, Thursday

"*A thoroughly good hostess is one who is herself able to enjoy, without anxiety, the dinner she is giving to her friends.*"

Mrs. Beeton.

CHAPTER I

MR. AND MRS. TUKE DINE OUT

HARVEY TUKE, under protest, was accompanying his wife to dinner with the Clifford Reaveleys. Under protest, because he knew neither of them, and Yvette Tuke had only met Mrs. Reaveley, and that in the most casual manner, at a committee empanelled to collect toys and comforts for the orphaned children of the Côte d'Or, from which region Yvette herself came. Reminded that Mrs. Reaveley was rich, and the committee short of funds, Mr. Tuke commented caustically on the unscrupulous methods of charity, especially when in the hands of women. He added that the wine would probably be frightful. His wife, taking this for acquiescence, merely smiled and pointed out that it was only dinner, and he need not take a bottle of his precious sherry, as he had been known to do when on a visit.

So here he was, driving the Delage under Burton's Gate at Hyde Park Corner, and along the Serpentine Road. The afterglow still hung in the west, and was reflected in the mirror of the lake. Along Knightsbridge and Park Lane and Bayswater a ring of brightness encircled the old Manor of Hyde. In the haze of autumn mist the undulations of the park, the embowered habitations of rangers and policemen, took on a fairy-like opalescence. As the Delage swung into the Ring Road its powerful lamps played for an instant upon the classic front of the Magazine, which shone like some temple—a temple to Flora, rather than to Mars. Mr. Tuke had seen all this before, and he was unaware, on that Wednesday evening, of any shadows thrown by past or coming events upon these glades and waters. It was just Hyde Park.

It was ten minutes to eight when the car drew up in Gloucester Terrace. Though numbered 7a Lancaster Terrace, the Reaveleys' house had its front door round the corner.

Its situation at the junction of the two streets, and its pronounced bow, gave it windows looking in three directions —across Lancaster Terrace, down the short arm of this to Bayswater Road and the parks, and up it to the triangle of green at the head of Sussex Gardens. So much Mr. Tuke was able to observe, though not very clearly, for Paddington, like Fanny, is still seen darkly by gas-lamps. The pervading gloom, pierced by a few gay windows in the block of flats on the opposite corner of Gloucester Terrace, became unmitigated blackness on the side beyond the door of No. 7a, suggesting bomb-damaged and empty homes.

In a queerly shaped drawing-room on the first floor, queerly furnished in a style wavering between Mr. Osbert Lancaster's Vogue Regency and Curzon Street Baroque, the Tukes were welcomed by their hostess. Corinne Reaveley was a young woman with an impudent, elfin prettiness, of medium height and extremely thin in the modern manner. Her green frock, like the Empress of Austria's riding habit, might have been sewn on her. Thick chestnut hair was piled high above high cheekbones and long slanting eyes which seemed to take their colour from her frock and her jade earrings. These, and a gold bangle, were her only jewellery. She gushed over Mrs. Tuke, and then the green eyes took in Mr. Tuke's mephistophelian features, and became faintly amused.

"Are you hating it already?" Mrs. Reaveley said. "We won't bother with introductions till you've had some sherry. *Not* cocktails. Am I right? . . . Hi, Cliff . . . !"

A tall, powerful young man, whose broad shoulders and narrow hips were displayed by the cut of his dinner jacket, came to join them, bearing a tray with glasses. His eyes, very blue in a fresh-coloured face, blunt-featured and undistinguished, expressed the right appreciation of Mrs. Tuke, elegant in black and silver. Clifford Reaveley had curly yellow hair and admirable teeth, which he showed frequently, for he smiled a good deal in an easy, good-humoured way. Mr. Tuke, wondering whether the high forehead implied that his host was more intelligent than he looked, put him down as in the mid thirties. His wife, according to Mrs. Tuke, was several years younger.

"Nice of you to come," Reaveley said. Mr. Tuke, making a perfunctory reply, sipped his sherry suspiciously, like a cat. He had an agreeable surprise. The sherry was good.

So were the dinner and the wines which accompanied it, when presently the company trooped downstairs to a dining-room of similar triangular shape to the drawing-room above, though its furniture, far from being Vogue Regency, was solid Victorian. Introductions had been of a casual kind, and it was only when all were seated that Mr. Tuke was able to sort out his fellow guests, all of them strangers to him. There were nine, for the small vivacious dark girl whose name was Kay Kittredge appeared to be a member of the household, and, from her watchful supervision of the two maids and her frequent air of taking stock, also responsible for the management of the dinner. A youngish man with a tooth-brush moustache proved to be Gordon Cartwright, the novelist. On his right sat an elderly lady, a Miss Plimsoll. There was a Squadron Leader Garroway, with his wife, another colourless married couple whose name remained uncertain to the end, a girl called Dolly, a very young man with long fair hair who cast looks of dog-like devotion at Corinne Reaveley—he was Peter Warrener—and finally a Mr. Gervase Coverdale. About Clifford Reaveley's age, Coverdale was handsome in a full-blooded way, with almost black hair, a predatory nose, and full red lips. Everything about him was a trifle overdone—his slight swagger, the length of his shirt-cuffs, the waist of his dinner jacket. His dark eyes were intelligent, and his share of the small if frothy beer which was the staple of talk was uttered in a surprisingly soft and pleasant voice.

Excepting the Misses Plimsoll and Kittredge and the novelist —who occasionally glanced at Mr. Tuke in a speculative manner—these people were of a type the latter seldom met. He was reminded, though the difference in period and manner was immense, of the dinner parties at the Veneerings'. So slender was Yvette Tuke's acquaintance with Mrs. Reaveley

—this was the true Veneering touch—that she had been of small help in placing Corinne and her husband beforehand. The husband, she thought, was in a ministry, a supposition confirmed by jokes at his expense. Others between him and Coverdale implied that at one time they had worked together. As for the rest, most of them were obviously Corinne Reaveley's friends. Even Coverdale, whatever his link with his host, was on quite another sort of terms with his hostess. In this company Gordon Cartwright seemed out of place; he was there, Mr. Tuke conjectured, mainly on account of Miss Kittredge, upon whom he kept a humorously protective eye, which she met, from time to time, with a smile of understanding. In another category, of one, was Miss Plimsoll, who appeared to belong to a past shared by both the Reaveleys, and indeed, of the two, to have known the husband longer.

If the latter was plainly outside the orbit in which his wife and her friends moved, he made an admirable host. Corinne, at her end of the oval table, chattered ceaselessly in a high voice. Sometimes Mr. Tuke, on her right, found her slanting green eyes appraising him with amusement. He was used to that; his resemblance to a stage Mephistopheles invited it. She appeared genuinely to admire Yvette's good looks and *chic*. Mr. Tuke assessed her as a thoroughly self-centred young woman, not without brains and a somewhat malicious sense of humour. He suspected that she might have a temper, too.

She was drinking freely, and a little flush appeared on her high cheekbones. Her high voice rose a tone. Some of her guests—the Air Force couple, and the girl Dolly, and Peter Warrener—had been drinking a good deal too, and before long were talking rather loudly. Clifford Reaveley kept them company, but his blunt, good-humoured, somewhat wooden face, his ready smile and quiet, easy speech remained unaffected. Only his blue eyes were perhaps less well controlled than before; it seemed to Mr. Tuke that they dwelt more often and longer than mere friendliness demanded on the piquant face of Miss Kittredge, who for her part declined to meet them, betraying a faint discomfort as she talked rapidly to someone else. And at these times Gordon Cartwright's eyebrows went up a shade, and he glanced thoughtfully from the girl to their host, like a man who has made a disagreeable discovery. His air of detached amusement deserted him. If this byplay was apparent to Corinne Reaveley, chattering hard all the time, she ignored it; but Mrs. Tuke, when later consulted, held the view that the long green eyes missed little, and that Corinne, unlike the novelist, was secretly and maliciously amused.

These illusive undercurrents apart, if continuous talk and laughter were any guide, the dinner might be deemed a success up to the time when the sweet came in. Even Mr. Tuke, stimulated by curiosity about these strange people, eluded boredom. But it was now, upon this animated scene, upon the coloured frocks and the gleaming silver and the shaded lights and wine-dark mahogany, that a sort of chill wind blew suddenly with the first mention of the ghost.

It was Miss Plimsoll, in her prim voice, who interjected the discordant note. She turned to Corinne Reaveley.

"Dear Corinne, have you heard about that poor man Whichcord? I read the notice about him yesterday, outside that oddly rural police station in Hyde Park. It gave me quite a shock. After his seeing the ghost again, you know. I believe it's in the papers now. . . ."

Mrs. Reaveley was raising her glass. Mr. Tuke saw the movement arrested, and her long fingers tighten round the stem. He could not see the glance she flashed at her husband, but Yvette, beside their host at the other end of the table, caught a flicker of green lightning, as she afterwards described it, and was considerably startled. Whatever the meaning of that lambent glance, Clifford Reaveley was outwardly quite unperturbed by it; he merely smiled his attractive, boyish smile, showing his white teeth. And already Corinne, her jade earrings swinging, was emptying her glance before she replied rather curtly to Miss Plimsoll.

"Yes, Kay told me."

She turned away to Mr. Tuke. But the ghost, once evoked, was not to be so readily exorcised. There was a foolish babble from the Squadron Leader's wife and the female half of the nameless couple, and young Mr. Warrener, upon whom the excellent wine had wrought powerfully by now, clamoured for the story. Corinne, who seemed herself again, shook her chestnut head.

"Nothing doing. I'm not going to have that silly old tale raked up."

"Come on, Miss Plimsoll," Warrener urged. "*You* tell."

"No, indeed," said that lady, who seemed to regret having raised the topic. "Let us talk of something else."

"I want a ghost story!" Warrener insisted, with the mulishness of the slightly intoxicated.

Corinne's glass had been refilled. As she half emptied it once more, a tiny frown appeared between her plucked, slanting brows. She rapped on the table with a spoon.

"Shut up, Peter! And that goes for everybody," she added, as the girl Dolly seemed about to join the chorus.

The well meaning, led by Miss Plimsoll and Kay Kittredge, began to talk energetically. Mr. Tuke turned to his hostess. But in the midst of these diversionary tactics, Gervase Coverdale, who had been frowning to himself, suddenly clicked a thumb and finger.

"Of course, the papers!" He looked round the table. "Evidently nobody here takes the *Morning News*. I don't, but I read bits in other people's in the train. I've just remembered. I saw a heading this morning about the Hyde Park ghost. Don't tell me, Corinne, it's turned up again?"

Mrs. Reaveley's irritation was now more marked. Another lambent flash from the green eyes flickered from Coverdale to her husband, and back to Coverdale.

"Oh, drop it, Gervase!" she said sharply.

Coverdale looked blandly surprised. "But we're all naturally interested. It's a very old story now, Corinne—a mere echo from your blameless past. I don't remember much about it myself, though Whichcord sounds familiar too. . . ." Wine, perhaps, had loosened the man's tongue, and there was a spice of mockery in his suave voice as he added: "Of course I'm sorry if I've touched a nerve. I scarcely thought, after all these years. . . ."

Green lightning, in Mrs. Tuke's phrase, was now playing about him. As he met it with the same look of polite surprise on his florid features, Corinne leaned forward, her fingers tightening again round the stem of her glass; and for an instant Mr. Tuke even wondered (so suddenly and melodramatically had the tempo of a convivial evening changed) whether she would throw it in Coverdale's face.

"Gervase, *darling*! I said, *shut up*! Do I have to repeat everything three times before it gets into your thick head? Or remind you"—her voice was menacingly sweet—"that some people have pasts a damned sight less blameless than mine? People who're lucky at finding things, for instance . . .?"

Coverdale's jaw dropped. No man ever looked more taken aback. Then his full-blooded face began to crimson. He stared venomously at Corinne, as white with temper as he was flushed, her jade ear-rings swinging, smiling wickedly as she watched him. The rest of the company sat dumbfounded, until Clifford Reaveley broke the appalled silence with an air of authority.

"What the deuce is all this? Pipe down, Gervase! You look positively apoplectic. Anyone can pull your leg, but you ought to know Corinne by this time." Reaveley grinned in his infectious way. "Did a long shot go home, old man? Who cares about your ruddy past? Can it, there's a good fellow. And less of your peculiar brand of humour, Corinne," he added to his wife. "It bounces off me, but some people don't like it."

"Humour . . .!" Corinne muttered in a smouldering way.

"Oh, chuck it! If you don't like old songs, we won't have them. It's your party."

He turned to Mrs. Tuke, while most of the guests again plunged into rather feverish talk. Coverdale sat with a face like thunder, and Corinne's oblique eyes were still slits of green fire in a white mask. She emptied the glass she had conceivably just stayed herself from throwing. And then, as once more it was refilled by an expressionless maid, there was another abrupt change of mood. Mrs. Reaveley laughed, apparently with genuine if malicious amusement. She raised the glass to the scowling Coverdale.

"You *do* go purple when you're cross, darling! As if I should ever give you away! Damn all pasts, anyhow!"

The man's face was still dark with anger, but after giving her a sour look he forced a smile and lifted his own glass before he tossed it off and began to talk to Kay Kittredge. Conversation, if also a little forced, became general again, and as Coverdale's colour ebbed, and Corinne prattled artlessly to Mr. Tuke, the tension in the room lessened and passed.

Yet a feeling of constraint remained. A very ordinary dinner party had for an instant been thrown violently out of gear; and to Harvey Tuke himself, who had his fancies, the spectres conjured up by Miss Plimsoll still haunted the shadows about the glittering table. For that prim looking lady, with her air of some trusted companion or governess, had innocently loosed more than the Hyde Park ghost, whatever that might be. There was the ghost of someone called Whichcord, and the phantoms of those pasts Corinne Reaveley had damned—quite a company of bogies for a social evening.

CHAPTER II

MR. TUKE HEARS AN OLD SONG

CLIFFORD REAVELEY closed the door behind his wife and her ladies and took Corinne's seat beside Mr. Tuke.

"My wife," he said with his amiable grin, "is very vague about her friends' husbands. I always have to ask them what they are. You look as if you might be a lawyer."

"I am what I look like."

Reaveley grinned again. "We're a mixed bag," he went on, sliding the port towards his guest. "Coverdale and I are engineers. Garroway's another, in civil life—aero-engines. Warrener's a budding economist, though you'd never think it. Or would you? They all let their hair grow now. Shows intellect, or politics, or something. A few years ago Cartwright would have had the tresses."

"I know his books," Mr. Tuke said, glancing at the novelist, who seemed to be finding the Squadron Leader rather heavy in the hand. "This is excellent port, if I may say so. Cockburn?"

"Yes, 1912. Glad you like it."

"One doesn't often meet a cellar like yours in these days. That Latour was admirable."

"My cousin Hugo laid the stuff down," Reaveley said. "He was the older generation of course. Luckily it's carried us through the war. You're a bit of an authority on wine, aren't you? Doesn't your wife come from the Côte d'Or, or somewhere?"

"From one of the greater Burgundies. Clos Garay."

The ready smile came again. "Good for Cousin Hugo! I might have been giving you awful stuff." Reaveley looked at his other guests, some of whom were treating the 1912 Cockburn with less respect than it deserved. "Most of us wouldn't know the difference. We're been practically living on gin for six or seven years."

Mr. Tuke shuddered. "I haven't."

From this topic the conversation strayed to others. It came out that Reaveley had been in the army, and had campaigned in Italy. He referred casually to his ministry, which was that swollen growth arisen from the old Office of Works. Coverdale, he said, was with the L.C.C., while the nameless man—Jones or Jenks was the nearest Mr. Tuke got to his unmemorable patronymic—belonged to another mysterious profession, road transport. It did not occur to Harvey himself to enlarge on his own occupation; he was accustomed to company where his name was known, and, where it was not, his peculiar position in the legal world was nobody's business. Once again, however, he caught a glance from Gordon Cartwright which suggested that as to this the novelist might be better informed than the rest.

The subject of the ghost had not been resurrected. Coverdale, if now and then looking moody and thoughtful, seemed almost himself again. Young Mr. Warrener, a little flushed, a lock of his long hair over one eye, brooded darkly and refilled his glass whenever the port came within reach. Clifford Reaveley glanced once or twice at his watch; and some ten minutes having passed, he said to his guests:

"Shall we go upstairs?"

The seven men trooped up accordingly, to find Miss Kittredge setting tables for bridge in the drawing-room. Corinne Reaveley, in her shimmering green sheath, swam up to Harvey.

"I expect you're a wizard at bridge, Mr. Tuke."

"On the contrary," said Mr. Tuke baldly, "I don't play cards." He had the grace to add: "Sorry. My wife should have warned you that I have no social accomplishments."

Yvette made a small gesture of apology to her hostess.

"I have been meaning to explain," she said in her attractive English. "He has none whatever, Mrs. Reaveley. Unless you call being the rudest man in the Department of Public Prosecutions an accomplishment. He is rather proud of that."

"In the *what?* . . ." said Corinne, looking rather startled, though the default of an expected bridge player perhaps accounted for her brusque manner. Squadron Leader Garroway guffawed, and with a pointed stare at Mr. Tuke's satanic features achieved a sort of wit.

"You've been entertaining a devil unawares, Corinne."

The girl Dolly laughed shrilly. "I didn't like to say so before, Mr. Tuke, but you *are* the very *image!*"

Corinne's narrowed green eyes flashed to her husband, standing in the doorway.

"We shall have to rearrange the tables. Kay, you'll have to come in."

"Help," said Miss Kittredge. "Well, you know I'm no good, Corinne. Cards are work to me, not play."

The man Jenks or Jones hove up beside Mr. Tuke with the air of coming to his rescue.

"Same here, you know," he said in a bluff fraternal manner which Mr. Tuke vaguely associated with Rotarians and similar bodies. "But one must do something in the evening."

"Must one?"

"Give me outdoor sport, anyway. You a golfer?"

"No, I don't play golf, either."

"Tennis, I expect?"

"No."

"A hunting man, I expect. Lots of you lawyers hunt."

"I am one that doesn't."

A little baffled, Jenks (or Jones) persisted. "Do a bit of riding, though, eh?"

"No, I hate horses."

As no Englishman can hate horses, this was taken as a joke. With a fraternal laugh the haulier tried once more.

"Shoot or fish?"

Tired of this *questionnaire*, Mr. Tuke lived up to his reputation and replied in his grimmest tones:

"Neither. I do nothing."

At this his fellow guest abandoned him to his fate. Mr. Tuke moved away to where Miss Plimsoll had seated herself on a sofa of vaguely Spanish design, its ends, edged by leather studded with brass nails, being attached to the body by leathern thongs. The rest of the upholstering was later described by Mr. Tuke as of good Waring material.

"As one outside the pale, may I join you?" he inquired.

"Do sit down, Mr. Tuke. *I* do not play bridge, either. A nice game of bezique, now," said Miss Plimsoll, who in her dove-grey dress and tight little grey curls might have walked straight out of *Cranford*. "I am very fond of bezique. I used to play with dear Mrs. Demarest in this very room."

"Who was Mrs. Demarest?" Mr. Tuke asked idly, feeling for his cigar-case.

"Why, she lived here," said Miss Plimsoll, rather surprised that anyone should not know this. "I was her companion here for twenty-five years, from the time of Mr. Demarest's death. Yes, do smoke, Mr. Tuke. I enjoy the aroma of a good cigar."

"Would Mr. Demarest be Mr. Reaveley's cousin Hugo?"

"Yes. Mr. Hugo Demarest. Actually, the relationship was very distant. Then, after poor Felix was lost with his ship, Mrs. Demarest left this house, and half her money, to dear Corinne."

Mrs. Tuke once remarked that her husband's degrading profession induced a tendency to see skeletons at every feast. But in this oddly-shaped house, which had been Mrs. Demarest's, and was now dear Corinne's, ghosts, if not skeletons, had fairly thrust themselves upon his notice. He would not have been human—he certainly would not have been Harvey Tuke—if he had not felt curious about the background to the suppressions and *crises de nerfs* at the dinner table. While he carefully lighted his Larranaga, and the card players settled themselves beneath a central cluster of writhing baroque candlesticks, he was reflecting that a well of information sat beside him. No one could know more about the family history than this elderly pattern of decorum who had lived in the house for twenty-five years.

"Who was Felix?" he inquired.

"Why, Mrs. Demarest's son," said Miss Plimsoll. "Her only child. He was lost with his submarine in the Arctic in the first year of the war."

"He would have inherited her property, I presume, had he lived?"

The late Mrs. Demarest's companion gave him a sharp look.

"Naturally," she replied.

"But as things fell out, half of it has come to Mrs. Reaveley. Is she another relative?"

Miss Plimsoll raised her eyebrows. "No," she said, with the air of dismissing the topic.

Mr. Tuke grinned. When he chose, he could transform his dark and forbidding features by a smile which was none the less engaging because it was still rather diabolical.

"I do like stories about families. And," he added, "I like ghost stories even better."

"We agreed, I think, to say no more about *that*," said Miss Plimsoll. "I wish I had never mentioned it."

"But apparently one has only to buy a copy of to-day's *Morning News* to read about it."

Miss Plimsoll made small clucking sounds of disapproval.

"Yes. I have seen the paper. *Most* deplorable. It's that dreadful man again," she added, in the style of Mr. Handley. "He positively pestered us all at the time of the first—er, manifestation. A person named Fenne. But that is seven years ago, this very month, and one did hope it had all died a natural death——" Miss Plimsoll tut-tutted again, and shook her neat grey head. "Dear me, that is not a very happy way of putting it, after what has happened to that poor man Whichcord."

"Ah, Whichcord," said Mr. Tuke. "You mentioned him at dinner, and his having seen the ghost again."

"It is all in the paper, Mr. Tuke."

"So you may as well tell me. At this time, seven years ago, I was abroad, so if there was an earlier story in the papers then, I didn't read about it. Who is Whichcord, which is he, and what happened to him?"

They had kept their voices low, for bridge is indeed taken as seriously as work, if not more so. No one paid them the least attention. As Miss Plimsoll pursed her lips, it was not difficult to read her thoughts. Her distinguished if satanic looking companion, who plainly belonged to the class of which she approved, unlike some of dear Corinne's rather flashy friends, would in fact find the whole story in the paper, and in a garbled form. It was surely better he should be given the authentic version beforehand.

"Of course, I don't want you to get a wrong idea," said Miss Plimsoll, thus capitulating with her conscience. "It is quite natural that dear Corinne should wish to let sleeping dogs lie. To be in the papers *again*. . . ."

"Mrs. Reaveley figures in this new press story?"

"Well, not yet. But you never know what they will drag in. Her connection with Felix, you see. . . ."

"One moment," said Mr. Tuke. "Where does this Felix Demarest come in? What had he to do with a ghost?"

"Why, it was *his* ghost, Mr. Tuke."

"Oh, indeed? And Mrs. Reaveley . . .?"

"Corinne and he were to have been married," said Miss Plimsoll.

Mr. Tuke looked at his hostess, a shining emerald figure, gleaming chestnut head bent over her cards, intent on the game.

"Indeed?" he said again. He turned back to Miss Plimsoll. "Now tell me all about it."

Miss Plimsoll was now nothing loath. This tale of midnight sorceries, in which she had played a minor part, was a highlight in her sheltered and unadventurous life. It was, in fact, in itself a very queer story; and as elicited and glossed by the arts of a trained legal mind it became even queerer. That she was being lured on to tell or imply far more than she intended Miss Plimsoll herself remained unaware. During that long session on the Spanish sofa the conversation often wandered. It was interrupted when from time to time the bridge players, as they became disengaged, gravitated to the fireplace of blue glass and chromium beside which the sofa was placed. A little fire burned, for the September evening was cool, and Corinne Reaveley, all skin and bone, of the salamander type. She herself paid several visits, and was the polite if casual hostess. She was restless, smoked cigarettes ceaselessly, and usually had a glass in her hand. Often her thoughts were obviously elsewhere. Sometimes her slanting eyes seemed to wonder what Mr. Tuke and his companion found in common. It so happened, however—though Miss Plimsoll failed to note the coincidence—that whenever Corinne joined them their talk had gone off on a tangent. They would be discussing books, London, post-war difficulties, anything but ghosts, and 7a Lancaster Terrace, and the Demarest family. But sooner or later some casual and insidious question would bring them back to the main theme.

Another visitor observed with surprise (as she later remarked) that her husband did not even look as black as he was painted. Mrs. Tuke had expected him to be bored and taciturn, instead of lamb-like and polite. She, too, wondered what he was up to, conferring so contentedly and so long with this little elderly woman whose remark at the dinner table had stirred up undercurrents of feeling which made Yvette herself repent of her too casual acceptance of Corinne Reaveley's invitation.

Reaveley came over, and chatted in his pleasant, easy way, apparently without a care in the world; and Coverdale, quite recovered from his temper. The little squabble with Corinne seemed to be forgotten, and they chaffed one another with the allusive intimacy of old friends. Jenks (or Jones) was hawky and Rotarian, and the Squadron Leader guffawed more loudly than ever. As for young Mr. Warrener, his long hair rumpled and his face flushed, though on occasion he laughed as boisterously as anyone, he was given to fits of sulks and scowling. Once, when he was dummy, he cornered Miss Kittredge, who was also free at that moment, and though she soon rather summarily shook him off, Mr. Tuke saw the young economist grinning to himself with the solemn satisfaction of the slightly sottish.

Gordon Cartwright, who drank in moderation and had brains, also came to the fireside. His gaze was inclined to wander thoughtfully after Kay, who when not playing was busy among the guests or absent from the room. She returned from the last of these excursions to announce that she had been putting the maid to bed. The Clifford Reaveleys were not exempt from current domestic problems; only one maid slept in, and she, said Miss Kittredge acidly, had to be handled like a hothouse bloom. It appeared that most of the excellent dinner had been cooked by Kay herself.

"I'm housekeeper and everything else," she explained to Mr. Tuke. "When I came out of the Wrens I blew my gratuity on domestic science, and Corinne asked me to run this house for her. I'm really learning now. One of the troubles with these scientific cookery places is that they teach you to use about ten times as many saucepans as any household ever had."

This was just before another rubber ended. Corinne, Coverdale, and the man Jones (or Jenks) moved to join the players already released, who were grouped by the three long windows in the bow of the room, where decanters and glasses were set out on a pseudo-Venetian table. Mrs. Jenks (or Jones), the girl Dolly, Garroway and Cartwright were still playing. Mr. Tuke looked at his watch. The time was twenty-three minutes past eleven. As Mrs. Tuke came to the sofa, his raised eyebrows suggested that it was time to go home. Miss Plimsoll had been pumped almost dry, though she was happily unaware of this, and he saw no further source of entertainment. Yvette herself, who played bridge as a social duty, had not only had enough of it but was vaguely ill at ease, being still conscious, as she admitted later, of uncomfortable nuances lingering in the party atmosphere; and Corinne presently drifting up, glass in hand, Mr. Tuke got to his feet as his wife began a little speech of thanks and farewell.

"Oh, but it's *early!*" Corinne cried. "You can't go yet. We're having another rubber." But she seemed to be in one of her abstracted moods, her mind on something else. She shivered suddenly. "My God, I'm cold!" And setting down her glass to stretch her hands to the fire, which had sunk low, for even Mr. Tuke thought the room by now rather warm, she exclaimed irritably: "The damned weather's changing. It's going to rain. I always know."

"Our little barometer," laughed the Squadron Leader, who was dummy. "I was at the Air House this afternoon, and the forecast's lousy." He turned to Coverdale, who had joined the group. "But it all goes down the drain, doesn't it, old boy? You know a bit about it. I remember that yarn of yours. Nasty experience, eh? I'd rather run *my* risks up above."

Clifford Reaveley had come up. "Oh, for God's sake," he said quickly, "no old shop here. Where's Peter? I've got a bone to pick with him over that last hand."

Corinne, bending over the fire, looked up at her husband. "Getting jumpy about the weather again, Cliff? *Why?*"

Her tone was suddenly barbed; and in an instant the sense of tension which had followed the scene at the dinner table was revived. Reaveley's blunt face twisted for a moment with some emotion that might have been anger. Then he showed his teeth in his usual grin and replied easily enough:

"Who isn't, in this country? I'm running up to the Midlands tomorrow. Where the devil has Peter got to?"

Young Mr. Warrener was not in the room. The others reacted to an awkward moment by beginning a hasty *post mortem* on the game. Corinne, with a little frown, the dull fire colouring her elfin face and making her green eyes lambent, was still watching her husband.

It was at this juncture, amid a good deal of talk, that in swift succession every light in the room went out.

CHAPTER III

HOAXES ARE DANGEROUS

SOMEONE uttered a little squeal, and Coverdale exclaimed:
"Hullo! Fuse blown?"

The drawing-room was by no means in darkness, for the fire cast a carmine glow on the high ceiling, but the group standing before it acted as a screen, and their magnified shadows were projected upon the opposite wall and the door in it. As eyes grew accustomed to the sudden gloom, the outline of the doorway, with its handsome moulding, could be distinguished. The door itself was wide open.

The landing beyond was dark. Suspended in the black rectangle of the doorway hung a dim face. A lock of hair was plastered over the forehead. From the face came a high reedy voice.

"*Did anybody ask for Whichcord?*" it piped.

The girl Dolly screamed. There were quick gasps and ejaculations, and then Corinne's voice crying shrilly: "Oh, my God, *no*! . . ." And then a figure was leaping across the room, there was a scuffle at the door, a click, and the central cluster of lights came on again. Mr. Tuke, himself half way to the door, found Reaveley before him, one hand on the light switches, the other gripping Peter Warrener.

Warrener laughed foolishly. He had reversed his dinner jacket to conceal shirt front and collar; his long hair was damped and dragged over his eyes. It flopped absurdly up and down as Reaveley, who had him by the shoulder, shook him with a vigour that showed his own considerable strength and choked the younger man's laugh in his throat.

"Steady on, Cliff!" Warrener gasped out. "You're *hurting!* It's only a joke——"

"I'll hurt you all right," Reaveley said through his teeth. "Blasted idiot! . . ."

He seemed in a passion of rage, but the scuffle was interrupted by an outcry from Corinne.

"I can't stand any more! Christ, what an evening! Well, I'm through! . . ."

Her frock flashed like green fire as she broke from the group by the hearth and brushed blindly past Mr. Tuke. Her husband dropped Warrener to put out a hand to stay her, but she clawed at him like a wild thing.

"Don't dare to touch me! You devil! . . ."

The slanting green eyes blazed at him, the jade ear-rings swung, there was another flash of the green frock, and she was gone. Those in the room could hear her running footsteps up the stairs.

Clifford Reaveley's back was to Mr. Tuke. The very set of the broad shoulders betrayed the anger that still possessed him. For an instant no one spoke. Peter Warrener, looking merely ridiculous in his reversed dinner jacket, stood gaping and getting his breath. He brushed the hair off his forehead, and edged away from Reaveley. Mr. Tuke had the impression that the latter had already forgotten him. As, somewhere upstairs, a door slammed, Reaveley regained control of himself, and as he turned to his guests with a creditable imitation of his usual easy smile, only the heightened colour and taut lines of his rather wooden face, and a hard glitter in his blue eyes, spoke of the anger he had stamped under.

"Sorry about all this," he said. He was still breathing a little fast. "Corinne flies off the handle sometimes. She's done it in the middle of a party before now. It doesn't mean a thing. Just nerves—too many long nights and short drinks. She'll be down again in a few minutes, full of apologies. All the same, Peter"—there was a vicious edge to Reaveley's voice as he threw a disgusted look at the culprit—"you've made a nice mess of things. Blistering ass! What on earth possessed you to do it? You know Corinne. You might have scared someone badly, for that matter."

"He did," said Dolly, with an uncertain laugh, which became a slightly hysterical giggle as Warrener sulkily got out of his jacket and resumed it right way on.

"Well, let's try to forget it," Reaveley said.

He crossed the room to Mrs. Tuke, to whom he offered special apologies in the charming, boyish way that was his normal manner. Mr. Tuke, looking again at his watch, again glanced meaningly at his wife, but she gave him a little shake of her head. In the unimaginable circumstance of her behaving as her hostess had done, she would assuredly pull herself together with the utmost speed and rejoin her guests to make amends; and courtesy dictated that Corinne should be given the chance. Nobody else, for that matter, made any move to go. No doubt they felt the same, or, from longer experience, considered a few tantrums neither here nor there. The remaining bridge four continued their rubber. The group at the table in the window bow was chaffing Peter Warrener, now looking shamefaced and unhappy as he poured himself a drink. Mrs. Tuke was being sympathetic to her host. Kay Kittredge, after hanging in the wind, her eyes on the door, came to the fire, where Mr. Tuke had rejoined Miss Plimsoll, who was making determined conversation about trifles.

A wryly humorous smile on her attractive face, Kay murmured to Mr. Tuke:

"Clifford's quite right. Please don't take our little upheavals seriously. Corinne *is* just like that. I've known her all my life. We're cousins, you know. She's always up or down. She'll probably come flying back, full of contrition. Miss Plimsoll will confirm."

"Dear Corinne," said Miss Plimsoll guardedly, "has always been a little un*dis*ciplined."

The bridge rubber was breaking up. Cartwright, coming across, caught the gist of this conversation. He glanced at the group by the window.

"That young fool wants kicking," he said.

"The practical joker," Mr. Tuke agreed, "is a public menace."

"Oh, I'm rather sorry for him now," Kay said. "It was an idiot schoolboy's trick, of course, but he's had far too much to drink. He came and pestered me about Whichcord, but

I never dreamed. . . . He's quite soppy about Corinne, you know," she added to Mr. Tuke. "They all are, for a time. I bet he's feeling he'd like to drown himself now."

Miss Plimsoll tut-tutted to herself. "It is I who am to blame. I should never have introduced that most *unfortunate* topic at dinner."

Clifford Reaveley joined them, looking at his watch.

"I'll go up and be matey," he said to Kay. He still looked rather strained, Mr. Tuke thought, and the smile he gave the latter was mechanical. "I've apologised to your wife. Corinne will be doing it in a minute. I shall probably find her thoroughly simmered down, and putting on fresh make-up."

"My dear fellow, don't worry," Mr. Tuke said.

Reaveley shrugged. He turned and went out of the room. As the door closed, Kay said in a low voice to Cartwright:

"This sort of thing isn't exactly fun for him. It's happened before, as he said."

Perhaps there was the faintest suggestion of rebutting some unspoken criticism. The novelist, at any rate, seemed less sympathetic.

"As he pointed out, it's her party. All the same," Cartwright added, "I thought he was going to scrag young Warrener."

Kay nodded seriously. "Yes, I've never seen him so angry." She looked round the room. "Well, in the absence of host and hostess, I'd better be doing my stuff. Curse those women! Look at them. It will be all over Bayswater to-morrow."

She walked away to where the Squadron Leader's wife and Mrs. Jenks (or Jones) had their heads together. A good deal of loud talk and laughter was coming from the window bow, the shrill voice of the girl Dolly rising above the rest. Peter Warrener was drowning his sorrows in dejected silence. Mrs. Tuke joined the little group of her husband and the novelist and Miss Plimsoll; and a remark to Cartwright about his books had led to a discussion of modern fiction in general when Squadron Leader Garroway came over from the window.

"Where's Reaveley?"

"He has gone upstairs to see how Mrs. Reaveley is," Cartwright explained.

"He's been gone some time," Coverdale said.

Mr. Tuke looked at his watch again. It was now five minutes to midnight: Clifford Reaveley had been absent for over ten minutes.

At this moment, however, he came into the room. In a little silence, as everyone turned to look at him, he showed his white teeth in a rather rueful grin.

"She's coming down," he said. "But she took some persuading. Let her down lightly, folks, and for God's sake don't mention ghosts. As for me, I need a drink."

He made for the table in the window. Mr. Tuke observed that he was breathing a little fast. The blunt-featured, nondescript face was still taut, and somewhat flushed. Persuasion, no doubt, had been hard work. As Reaveley passed a mirror, he paused in mid stride, straightened his black tie, and put a hand to his fair hair. He looked himself up and down before he moved away, wiping his hands on his handkerchief, to be welcomed at the table with Rotarian bonhomie by Jenks or Jones, and with shrill exclamations from the girl Dolly. He did not look at Peter Warrener as he poured himself half a glass of neat whisky and drank it at a gulp.

The rest of the company made conversation once more. It occurred to Mr. Tuke that they were continually covering up awkward moments that evening. An ormolu clock on the mantelpiece chimed midnight, and he automatically checked it by his watch. It was three minutes fast. He hoped his hostess would soon reappear. His interest in the party had evaporated, and he wanted to go home.

He did not have to wait long. But his hostess failed to reappear, after all. Some minutes having passed, during which Reaveley took more time over a second drink, the young engineer turned abruptly from the table, threw a glance and a shrug at Kay Kittredge, and strode out of the room once more. The flush had gone from his face, and some of his normal colour with it. There was determination in his set jaw and stiff back, and he closed the door behind him almost violently.

Kay was looking embarrassed again. She murmured to Gordon Cartwright. Yet another uncomfortable interlude was dragging along when suddenly the girl started, and frowned. Somewhere downstairs a door had slammed. Mr. Tuke heard her perplexed whisper to the novelist.

"That was the front door!"

Nobody was pretending any longer that this was a normal party. Others had heard that door slam. Conversation almost ceased as the guests waited for whatever was going to happen next. The girl Dolly hiccupped, and giggled foolishly. Miss Plimsoll heroically started a monologue on the advantages of Bayswater as a residential quarter. And in the middle of it the drawing-room door opened again.

Clifford Reaveley merely put his head in.

"Kay, come here for a moment, will you?"

Miss Kittredge joined him hurriedly, and the door closed upon them both. Miss Plimsoll doggedly resumed, Coverdale rallying to her aid, and Mr. Tuke, who detested Bayswater, helping to keep the ball rolling. Looking at the ormolu clock, he had just calculated that the correct time was three minutes past twelve when the missing pair returned.

Reaveley's face was at its most wooden. He contrived a smile that was purely automatic.

"Sorry," he said, his blank blue eyes taking in the expectant company. "Corinne has changed her mind. She's going to bed. Wants me to grovel, and say good night to you all for her, and so forth. Bad show, I'm afraid. Sorry, again."

Mr. Tuke was looking at Kay Kittredge. She was biting her lip, her eyes bewildered and a little scared. There was no time, however, for speculation: Miss Plimsoll rose and took the lead in making for the door, and then amid conventional expressions of sympathy for Mrs. Reaveley, Kay was accompanying the ladies to the room on the same floor where they had left their wraps. The men followed Reaveley downstairs to another oddly shaped room below for their hats and coats. Their host hardly spoke, and in an awkward silence they drifted into the hall.

Mr. Tuke and Gordon Cartwright were together as Kay

came running down the stairs and beckoned to the novelist. He went up to meet her, and they were still murmuring together when the ladies began to descend. Amid final good-byes in the hall, with the sobered guests emerging into the ill-lighted emptiness of Gloucester Terrace, and an un-autumnal chill entering through the door, Cartwright caught up with the Tukes. Mr. Tuke asked him where he lived.

"Across the park. In Clareville Grove."

"Have you a car?"

"Not here. I'll walk over the park. I rather like it at night. Making scrap of the railings was one of the few useful by-products of the war."

"Why not let me drive you? We go more or less your way."

In spite of his liking for Hyde Park at night, the novelist accepted the invitation—even readily, Mr. Tuke thought. But he did not speak until the long black Delage turned down Church Street. Then—he was sitting beside Harvey—he said abruptly:

"I know who you are, of course. I'm a bit worried. About Miss Kittredge. She's an old friend of mine."

Mr. Tuke said nothing, and after a moment the other went on:

"I know you'll keep this under your hat. I oughtn't to mention it, I suppose. But there's Kay. . . . And I dare say you've guessed it. It's all bunkum about Mrs. Reaveley going to bed. She did a bolt. When we heard the front door slam."

"Well, I wondered," Mr. Tuke said. "Though it seemed a little melodramatic."

"She's done it before, apparently. Rushed off in a temper to some friend. Once quite late at night. Extraordinary woman. She must have diddled Reaveley when he went up the first time—unless he had his doubts, and that's why he went up again so soon."

"How was it he didn't meet her, or hear her, on the stairs?"

"There are back stairs," Cartwright said. "She must have been nipping down them just as he left us the second time.

Well, the point is, he asked Miss Kittredge to back him up in pretending Corinne had gone to bed. One can understand, of course, but Kay doesn't like it. Because it's bound to come out. Half the people there guessed, and those silly women will revel in it. Anyway, I thought you ought to know."

"Why?" Mr. Tuke inquired.

But the novelist did not seem very clear about this. Probably he wanted to share his anxiety for Kay Kittredge, which it appeared ante-dated this evening's events, though the prior cause was not very clear either. He was determined, he said, to get her out of that house.

"Difficult house to run," Mr. Tuke agreed. "In every sense, I dare say." He grinned diabolically as the car turned east at St. Mary Abbot's. "I should have liked to witness that scene upstairs—from a safe distance."

Mrs. Tuke reproved him. Cartwright, for the first time, seemed amused.

"Yes, I gather Reaveley had a sticky time."

"Did you note that in addition to his slightly dishevelled appearance when he rejoined us, his shoes were wet?"

The novelist laughed outright. "No. But Kay says Corinne was having a bath, and she flung a sponge at him."

They left their passenger at his little house in Clareville Grove. As they drove on to Westminster and their flat in St. Luke's Court, Mrs. Tuke remarked that she had had a lesson. She had adopted the free and easy ways of the English, but *les convenances* had their value, after all.

"If I had been to that house before, if Mrs. Reaveley and I had exchanged visits, *comme il faut*, I should have known. There is something wrong there, Harvey. It is a bad house."

"Don't repine," said Mr. Tuke. "I thought it quite an exhilarating evening. A ghost, ructions, a midnight flitting—what more could one ask? And no doubt this little fracas will fizzle out, as similar ones seem to have done before, and all will be domestic felicity again—till the next time."

This opinion was afterwards to be of some use to Mrs. Tuke. Whenever in future her husband showed himself too dogmatic, she was able to hold it against him.

PART·TWO

FRIDAY

"The Department of Public Prosecutions
Handles crimes and their solutions:
Cases of thaumaturgy
Are better left to the clergy."

SIR BRUTON KAMES.

CHAPTER I

THE *Morning News* ASKS QUESTIONS

THE HYDE PARK GHOST

ANOTHER VICTIM?

(From the *Morning News* Staff Reporter, JAMES FENNE)

Friday.

"WHAT NEMESIS pursues the little group of people linked with the seven-year-old mystery of the Hyde Park Ghost? At dawn yesterday, close to the spot where Wally Whichcord was found drowned on Tuesday morning, a second body was discovered awash in the Serpentine. This new victim has been identified as Mrs. Clifford Reaveley, of 7a Lancaster Terrace, an address our readers will remember. For only on Wednesday, when I gave the exclusive news of Wally Whichcord's death, I retold the old story of the Hyde Park Ghost—the ghost of Lt. F. H. Demarest, R.N., which appeared to his mother, and later to Wally himself, during an air raid in September 1940. I told how, after seven years, Wally saw the ghost again, a fortnight before his body was found in the Serpentine. Is it merely another coincidence that Mrs. Reaveley should meet the same fate two days later?

"If so, it is a strange one. For 7a Lancaster Terrace, once the home of Mrs. Hugo Demarest, is not the only link between a young and beautiful woman, rich, happy, popular in society, and the mysterious events of seven years ago. Lt. Demarest, when he sailed on his last voyage, was betrothed to Miss Corinne Laura Shefford, who in 1941 married his cousin, and became Mrs. Clifford Reaveley. She and her husband have lived ever since in the house in Lancaster Terrace, and there, last Wednesday, they gave a dinner party. From there, at midnight, Mrs. Reaveley fled into the street, not to be heard of again till news was brought to her distracted husband that her body had been found in the Serpentine.

"As Hamlet said, there are more things in Heaven and earth than are dreamed of in our philosophy. Did Corinne Reaveley, too, see some dread spectre before her death? What fearful thoughts racked her as she fled from her beautiful home, deserting husband and friends for the last time? What fatal impulse drew her to the dark solitudes of Hyde Park? How did she, like Wally Whichcord, come to end her short life in the cold waters of the Serpentine? What secret destiny drew together these two victims, the wealthy young wife and the waif of the streets?

"Some of these questions may be answered today, when the inquest on Wally Whichcord opens at Westminster, or on Tuesday next, the 13th, when that on Mrs. Reaveley's body will be held at the same court. At present, only one known factor connects the two tragedies—the Hyde Park Ghost. In this atomic age we seem to be back again among spells and sorceries. Dim shades of dead men flit among the leafy glades of Hyde Park, and the waters that echo by day to the splash of oars and the laughter of young and old lap furtively by night about the drowned victims of phantoms and enchantments."

CHAPTER II

PRO AND CON HOKUM

SIR BRUTON KAMES, the Director of Public Prosecutions, seized his spectacles, one sidepiece of which was represented by an arrangement of wire and adhesive tape, jammed them crookedly on his large nose, stared pointedly at the clock, and still more pointedly and protuberantly at Mr. Hubert St. John Wray, the Assistant Commissioner (Crime).

"That all, Wray? Hope so. I'm busy."

"There's one more thing," Wray said. "It's really Tuke I want to see, but it's a rum story. It'll interest you. There's a ghost in it."

"My God, what next——?" Sir Bruton's prominent eyes became thoughtful. "D'you mean this Lancaster Gate affair?"

"Ah, you've heard of it?"

"I read the papers, don't I? And not only *The Times*, like Tuke. My man showed me the *News* this morning. Besides, I knew Hugo Demarest," added the Director, who knew everybody. "He was a member of the Senior Universities. Died years ago. Well, what's it got to do with you, Wray? And Tuke?"

"Tuke was at this dinner party on Wednesday."

"The deuce he was!" Sir Bruton unhooked his spectacles, the better to scowl at his senior assistant, who was extended in the only comfortable chair in the room, the Director's excepted. "Why didn't you tell me, Tuke?"

"You were not here yesterday," Mr. Tuke reminded him, for it was now Friday afternoon. "And since when were my social engagements of interest to you?"

"Since your hostesses took to skipping in the middle of 'em," the Director retorted. "And look what's happened now. Or wasn't it in *The Times*?"

"There was a paragraph this morning. It induced me to buy the *Morning News* at lunch time."

"Much more juicy, eh?" said Sir Bruton with relish. "I liked that bit about the shades of dead blokes flitting among the glades of Hyde Park. Bit of style about it. Makes your flesh creep."

"Yours must creep easily," Mr. Tuke said. "Try zinc ointment, or an alcohol rub."

"It's no affair of ours at present," Wray remarked, "and probably never will be. But when I read the local station report this morning, and found Tuke had been at the party, I thought I'd get his views. Bit of trouble quite early, at dinner, wasn't there, Tuke?"

"A temporary awkwardness. Have the maids been talking?"

"Maids or guests, I suppose. Wasn't the rumpus about the family ghost?"

"Partly. Mrs. Reaveley didn't want it discussed. It was the first I'd heard of it."

"I remember the story," Sir Bruton said. "There was talk about it at the club, because Hugo Demarest had been a member. You were roistering in Cairo or somewhere, Tuke."

"Who and what was Hugo Demarest?" Mr. Tuke inquired. "He seems to have had money, and he left a very good cellar."

"Jute? Nickel? Dunno," said the Director. "Something in the City. His father made the money."

"Well, what about this party?" Wray said. "Why did the late Mrs. Reaveley rush out of her house, leaving you all *planté là*? She'd changed into a coat and skirt, but apparently went off without a handbag or even a hat."

Mr. Tuke shrugged. "I can only tell you what happened."

His account of the dinner party omitted nothing of relevance. Wray, a dapper man with reddish hair and freckles and a strong general resemblance to a fox, smoked his Turkish cigarettes and from time to time cracked his bony fingers, a trick which irritated Sir Bruton, who glared at him with pop-eyed malevolence. As he said, the fatality might prove to be no business of his, but all cases of unnatural death were matters of routine interest to his department. And it was not often that their preliminaries were attended by a witness of Harvey Tuke's calibre and training.

"Bit of luck you were there," Wray commented at the end, though rather grudgingly, for the pair were old opponents, and seldom met without bickering. "You'll be a star turn at the inquest. I'll see to that. The Paddington court having been blitzed, it'll be on your doorstep."

"Now let's hear all about the spook," said Sir Bruton. "That's what interests *me*. And what about this bloke Whichcord? Also drowned in the Serpentine. Forgotten him, Wray?"

"No, I hadn't forgotten him. No more than a coincidence, probably. It may have put ideas into Mrs. Reaveley's head. These imitative cases are common. Would you say she was a suicidal type, Tuke?"

"How can I tell? I never saw her before. She drank a lot. She was neurotic. She was on edge all the evening, and young Warrener's clowning sent her over it. Before that, she shied off the family ghost, and she was touchy on the subject of pasts. So was her friend Coverdale, as I told you. My wife thinks there was some undercurrent of feeling between her and her husband. As she ran out, she called him a devil. It may have been no more than the backchat of married life, and he may have been right when he passed the whole thing off as a case of too many long nights and short drinks. Apparently she'd behaved in this way before. . . ." Mr. Tuke recrossed his legs. His dark, satanic face looked dissatisfied. "But suicidal . . .?" he said. "No, I shouldn't have thought so."

Sir Bruton, fiddling with his spectacles, caused the mended sidepiece to come apart, and swore sulphurously. He gave the Assistant Commissioner a truculent glare.

"Imitative cases are common, eh? Neurotic women, suggestion, suicide—yes, that's all very fine. But you've got a link between these two cases. The bally spook. I haven't seen Wednesday's *News*, with the rehash of the old story. Don't remember the details now. But the thing's turned up again, hasn't it? In other words, there was some thundering hanky-panky seven years ago, or someone was telling whopping lies, and now they're at it again. And a couple of drownings follow this time." With his prominent eyes and turned-down lips the Director was the picture of a soured old fish as he turned his glare on Mr. Tuke. "You say you had quite a pow-wow about it with this governess woman, Tuke. Cough it up."

"Ex-companion. Miss Plimsoll. Yes, we were together for a couple of hours."

"Poor creature. Her, I mean. Well, what's her tale?"

Wray cracked his fingers impatiently, but Mr. Tuke nodded. The old fish might like ghost stories, too, but as usual he had put his own finger on the spot.

Miss Plimsoll's tale of strange midnight happenings at Lancaster Gate seven years ago, as elicited during that symposium on the Spanish sofa, had filled out the story in Wednesday's *Morning News*, which none of the trio had read, though two of them could remember the brief notoriety of the Hyde Park Ghost. To Mr. Tuke himself, as he had said, it was all new. Old enough to have served in an earlier great war, in September, 1940, he was with the Judge Advocate's branch in the Middle East. It had taken the Director two years of intrigue and bluster to get his senior assistant back from Syria, where he was enjoying himself immensely.

When the latter now finished his recapitulation, to which even Wray listened with attention, Sir Bruton, who seemed to have forgotten that he was supposed to be busy, absently tipped cheroot ash into a bowl of paper clips.

"Yes, it comes back now," he said. "Must have made Hugo Demarest turn in his grave. Anyone less psychic you never saw. Well, whaddayou make of it, Tuke?"

"My mind is open. See *Hamlet*, quoted by your stylist."

"Open, heh? Detached, scientific attitude, and all that? Balderdash!" said Sir Bruton violently. "Credulous old woman. Mrs. Hugo, I mean. All worked up about her son. *And* she'd been to this fool medium. What's the name? Know anything about her, Wray?"

Wray, who had a remarkable memory, was grinning foxily.

"Madame Varché? Bond Street crystal gazer. We had our eye on her, but I haven't heard of her for some years. An out and out fraud. The whole thing reeks of hokum."

"But rather unusual hokum, don't you think?" Mr. Tuke said. "Let's consider the evidence. Because there *is* evidence. At least three people have alleged that they saw this apparition come and go in very peculiar circumstances—one of them twice over. Mrs. Demarest not only saw it, but spoke to it, at close quarters. She definitely recognized her son——"

"Pooh!" said Sir Bruton. "In the dark. So did Lady Titchborne, in broad daylight. And Orton wasn't any spook. He was fatter than me."

"You're catching up," Mr. Tuke said. "Anyway, in this case the son hadn't been absent for a quarter of a century. It was his voice too, or so his mother said. And though she may have been credulous, I'm told she was no fool. And she wasn't old. She was fifty-four. Her close sight was fair. Nor was it a dark night. There was a clear sky, a full moon, and searchlights. Nor again was it hallucination. My friend Miss Plimsoll saw it. Miss Plimsoll is a good witness. You won't shake her."

Sir Bruton puffed out his lips. His prominent stare was puzzled.

"What are you getting at, Tuke?"

"I'm considering the evidence. If someone was playing a trick, how was it done? Both women watched this figure walk away from the west corner of Lancaster Terrace across Bayswater Road, towards the end of Kensington Gardens. The two parks join just there——"

"I do know a few bits of London," Sir Bruton grunted.

"Not always the nice bits," Mr. Tuke said. "Well, Miss Plimsoll says that in the conditions of light she could follow the figure till it was almost across the road. Then it came into the shadow of the trees of the Gardens, and she lost it. From the window where she stood to the park railings is about three chains—sixty-six yards. Are those railings among the bits of London you remember?"

It was Wray who answered. Information about park railings fell among the many things he had cause to know.

"The height, you mean? Nine feet, with or without a brick base."

Mr. Tuke nodded. "And from my recollection only a cat could have got through them. An athlete might climb them, I suppose, but it would take time, and he'd land among bushes, and could hardly avoid making a bit of a noise. But Mrs. Demarest followed the figure within a few seconds. However gullible she may have been where her affections were strongly concerned, any *sounds* would have made her think—afterwards, if not at the moment. She heard nothing, though there was no gunfire just then. She looked up and down Bayswater Road, and saw no one. Her statement therefore bears out Miss Plimsoll's. During the time it took her to make up her mind and cross the road, the figure had disappeared without making a sound."

While Wray watched him with his sandy eyebrows drawn together, and Sir Bruton with querulous perplexity, Mr. Tuke took out his cigar-case and extracted a Larranaga. He was feeling in his pocket for matches as he went on.

"Now we come to the late Mr. Whichcord. Miss Plimsoll had refreshed her memory by reading the rehash of the story in Wednesday's *Morning News*. At the time, she heard all about it through local gossip, besides seeing Whichcord's original statement to this man Fenne, of the *News*. She thinks Whichcord saw his ghost, which by the law of probability must have been the same one, *after* it appeared to Mrs. Demarest and herself, but while the raid was still on. She is one of those rare witnesses who use their watches. Mrs. Demarest, she says, left the house just after midnight, and the All Clear went at 12.40. So some time before that we have Whichcord, half a mile away in Hyde Park, seeing a naval officer, who walked away behind a tree and thereupon vanished. Was his knell rung by fairy hands, like Thomas the Rhymer's in similar rural surroundings? One would think it improbable, but when Whichcord followed, and looked about, there was nothing beyond the tree but bare grass and the Serpentine. The same technique, you see, as in Bayswater Road. Again assuming a trick, how was it done? And how did the naval officer get there at all? We're up against the difficulty of the railings again."

Mr. Tuke carefully rotated his cigar as he applied a match to it. Wray uttered his little neighing laugh.

"Fairies?" he said. "It ought to have been Kensington Gardens. Barrie would have loved all this."

Mr. Tuke looked at him before blowing out his match.

"Sometimes you talk sense without meaning to, Wray. The *locus in quo* may be significant. Why that particular spot? The thing started across Bayswater Road towards the Gardens, but turned up in Hyde Park. It chose the same spot, or near by, for the repeat performance the other week. Why this haunting of Hyde Park, in fact? Why, for that matter, did it cross the road at all?——"

"Like the chicken," grunted Sir Bruton, bent over repairs to his glasses, "it wanted to get to the other side. Whadidyou think it would do? Go through the pavement?"

"Given a gift for disappearing, the *locus* wouldn't seem to matter."

"Are you taking all this seriously, Tuke?" Wray asked.

"I always take evidence seriously."

"So it seems," said the Director with heavy sarcasm. Testing his improvisation of wire and tape, he raised his spectacles and peered through them, so magnifying his prominent eyes that his likeness to a large disgruntled fish became quite startling. "Gone to a lot of trouble over this tomfoolery, haven't you?" he added. "Chains, and all that. Did you use a theodolite?"

"I measured the distance on the 25-inch Survey."

"May one ask why?"

"Certainly, if one asks civilly. I thought the distance would be greater than in fact it is, and I doubted the reliability of Miss Plimsoll's eyesight. But as this seems to be good, with a full moon and searchlights she would still see a figure quite clearly at fifty yards or so."

"The most puzzling thing," said Wray, who had been

thinking back and now spaciously dismissed the other conundrums, "is this repeat performance a fortnight ago, after seven years. If it happened, of course."

"Well, this bloke Whichcord won't talk any more," Sir Bruton said. "Neither will your wealthy and lovely hostess, Tuke. Wonder if *she* had something to talk about?"

"Any ideas about that?" Wray inquired of Mr. Tuke.

"None. I only know of Warrener's impersonation, if you mean that sort of thing. It will have occurred to you that everything seems to have come to a head within the last few weeks. The family banshee bobs up again, after seven years. Two interested parties are eliminated, by identical means——"

"There's a third one left," said the Director. "Your pal Miss Plimsoll. Does *she* believe in the banshee?"

"I think, like me, she believes in evidence. She remarked once, speaking generally, that there is a strong case for the supernatural, which you can take as you like. She added that she had known young Demarest since he was a baby, and that having been closely associated with his mother all that time, she was perhaps *en rapport* with Mrs. Demarest's mind——Yes?"

For Sir Bruton appeared to be struggling for speech.

"*En rapport!*" he roared. "Are we a legal department, or are we the flaming Society for Psychical Research?"

"The phrase is not mine," Mr. Tuke pointed out. "Now, if you'll stop blowing off, we'll get on. You'll agree that Miss Plimsoll saw this apparition? That's evidence. On the other hand, while she described what she saw quite objectively, without any reservations, I think something happened, outside her own experience that night, which gave her cause, not for doubt, perhaps, but for uneasiness. She was keeping something back."

"Oh, she was, was she?"

"The reservations began when I asked her what Mrs. Demarest and the apparition talked about. She skated neatly away from the subject. I could hardly press her——"

"You surprise me," said Sir Bruton.

"Then I tried to find out why this interview was held in the street. It seems inconsiderate of the astral plane to drag an elderly invalid out of doors at midnight, with a raid going on. And if the whole thing was a trick, one would expect it to be worked in the medium's room, with all necessary paraphernalia handy, and not at a street corner. But Miss Plimsoll was far from explicit about this, too. Some sort of appointment had been made—though she did not use that word—at a séance. On similar occasions Mrs. Demarest had received what purported to be messages from her son. She was not entirely convinced by them. She had her doubts of Madame Varché. It was this final meeting in the street, when she saw the boy, and spoke to him, that persuaded her."

"Persuaded her of what?" Sir Bruton asked.

"Yes, one would like to know, and what those messages were about. Miss Plimsoll left the subject in the air, rather abruptly. It was suggestive, as I said, of something she was not altogether happy about. She let out, by the way, that at the ghostly interview itself, the apparition warned Mrs. Demarest not to follow when it left her. She disobeyed. But then what mother would not have disobeyed in the circumstances?"

The Director, who had put on his spectacles, peered over them.

"She was expected to follow, eh? You may have got something there."

"Meaning that every trick needs an audience?" Mr. Tuke tapped the ash off his cigar, and recrossed his legs. "Which brings us back to the old snag," he said. "If it was a trick, how was it done? And what's more important, why was it done?" He turned to Wray. "A bit of routine never does any harm. If all this goes back seven years, it might be worth while to dig into the preterite. There's money in the case. The Reaveleys came into a lot of Mrs. Demarest's. Or rather, Mrs. Reaveley did."

Wray, who was fidgeting again, stopped to stare.

"I didn't know that. I assumed it had come to the husband. He's a relative, isn't he?"

"Only a distant one. The money, with the house, was left to his wife, who wasn't even his wife at the time, still less a family connection. But she had expected to become a close connection. She had been engaged to young Demarest."

"Oho!" said Sir Bruton darkly. But he was scowling reflectively. "Look here. Young Demarest. Suppose he isn't dead, eh? They still keep turning up—prisoners, survivors from ships, and so on. Some of 'em with their memory gone. Some half batty, poor devils. Starvation, exposure, and all that. No knowing what they might do."

Mr. Tuke considered this novel idea. "The Admiralty doesn't often make mistakes," he said. "And there wouldn't be many chances of survival near the Arctic Circle. Are you suggesting that if Demarest did survive, and somehow got back to England, he'd be capable of playing a particularly cruel hoax on his mother?"

"It would explain her thinking she saw his ghost."

"It wouldn't explain the vanishing trick. Or his turning up again seven years later, still in uniform. Where has he been all the time?"

"You want waxworks," said Sir Bruton. He rolled his cheroot from one side of his mouth to the other and leered over his spectacles at Wray. "Well, what about it, Wray?"

"Sounds weak to me."

"Ho, it does, does it? I didn't mean that, anyway, so sucks to you! I mean whadderyou going to do about the whole holus-bolus? Anything?"

Wray shrugged his well-tailored shoulders. "I may look into it. But it's not our pidgin at present. I wanted to hear Tuke's story. He hasn't given me anything to act on. We'll see what comes out at the inquest on Tuesday. Whichcord's was on this morning, but I shall be surprised if they turn up anything. Man without home or background, confirmed loafer and cadger, falls into the water, and there you are. There are hundreds of cases every year."

Mr. Tuke's black brows had gone up. "And there you are," he repeated. "Just as simple as that. Mrs. Reaveley also fell in the water, and there you are. But you aren't, are you? The case is altered."

Wray stared angrily. "What do you mean? You know

quite well that it's all one to us whether a case comes from Lancaster Gate or Rowton House—if it *is* a case. I've just said I have no reason to think so with either of these affairs, so far."

"Calm yourself, Wray. I was merely thinking how despicably human we are. I am, if you like. If I had known Whichcord, should I be moralising over him? And if Mrs. Reaveley hadn't been a wealthy young woman in a smart frock, and my hostess, should I be feeling shocked by her end—as I am? The answer, in both cases, is probably no."

The Director, giving his assistant a sour look, began to paw ostentatiously among his untidy papers.

"If you've done with this introspective tommy-rot," he grunted, "I've got some work to do. So've you. So's Wray, I hope."

"Yes, I'm off." Wray gave Mr. Tuke his foxy grin as he got up and collected brief-case, hat and gloves. "Of course, having been almost in at the death, it must have come as a bit of a shock."

Mr. Tuke seemed already to have forgotten his moralisings.

"By the way, you used the phrase 'fell in the water', just now," he remarked. "How does one fall in the Serpentine?"

Wray shrugged again. "How do I know? People do. There are fatalities there from time to time—most of them suicides. They throw themselves off the bridge, I suppose, or just walk in."

"E.g., the first Mrs. Shelley," said Sir Bruton, looking up from his papers. "Harriet Westbrook. Woman who wrote *Frankenstein*."

"What is the depth?" Mr. Tuke inquired of Wray.

"I believe there are holes nearly twenty feet deep."

"But not round the margin, where the bodies were found. There can scarcely be a current, and they wouldn't float. The *News* used the phrase 'awash'. And Mrs. Reaveley, certainly, had only been in the water a few hours."

"Probably the inquests will clear it all up for you." Wray smiled in his foxy way, showing his gums. "No, it's no go, Tuke. Don't try starting one of your hares. I agree the whole set-up is damned rum, however you look at it. Especially the family ghost. But ghosts, thank God, can still loiter with intent. We've enough trouble without them."

The Director looked up again with a howl.

"Oh, *hop* it!"

The Assistant Commissioner hopped it.

CHAPTER III

A WALK IN THE PARK

THE DOOR had no sooner closed behind Wray than Sir Bruton abandoned all pretence of being busy.

"I could do with a bit of exercise," he said.

Mr. Tuke affected to be startled. "Exercise? You?"

"See the flowers, and all that."

"What flowers?"

"Don't they still grow 'em in Hyde Park? Got your car?"

"No. Besides, you want exercise. Why this sudden interest in Hyde Park?"

"Ghosts," said Sir Bruton. "Wrong time of day, but we could have a look at the *locus spiritus*. By taxi."

"If you want a walk, you can start now," Mr. Tuke said firmly. "I'll stand you a tea, if we can get one there."

The Director was levering himself out of his chair. Having removed his spectacles, and begun to brush his waistcoat in a sketchy manner, he paused to give his senior assistant a shrewdly prominent stare.

"Don't much like all this bugaboo, do you, Tuke?"

Mr. Tuke replied without hesitation. "No. Of course, I was almost in at the death, as Wray pointed out. It has left a nasty taste. There is something very wrong with that house. Yvette felt it too. Though it may be largely the period—there are whole streets in Lancaster Gate and Kensington which one feels are *capable du tout*."

"Getting fanciful, aren't you? And what about Ashley Place?" said Sir Bruton, who lived there. "Reeking of popery as well. But you may have tumbled on something. You would. Regular Jonah—people'll get shy of asking you to dinner. But mind you, Tuke, keep out of the papers this time. No more dragging the department into the limelight."

"You're an optimist. Remember the inquest."

"Blast . . . ! I don't see," Sir Bruton added illogically, "why you should have it all, anyway. I'll come as a distinguished member of the public. Make Akers stare."

"Two of them, you mean," Mr. Tuke said.

From Devonshire House, to which the vicissitudes of wartime had translated the Department of Public Prosecutions from its Regency home in Richmond Terrace, the two walked along Curzon Street—Mr. Tuke lean and diabolical, a sort of nocturne in dark greys, the Director, his black jacket strained across his globular middle, an ancient felt hat over one prominent eye, trailing acrid cheroot smoke and swinging, to the public danger, a malacca cane with a dog-toothed bone handle and a hole for a tassel. The day was overcast and cool, but the rain foretold by the Air Ministry, as reported by Squadron Leader Garroway two evenings before, had not yet fallen on London. Turning into Stafford Street, the pair entered Hyde Park by Stanhope Gate, and crossed to where ten paths and roadways converge on the Dell and the broad end of the Serpentine. Beyond the water, along what had been the Route du Roi when William III planted a street of lamps to light him to Kensington Palace and keep the footpads at a distance, a few riders were cantering. In the Serpentine Road children fed the swans and ducks and their elders exercised dogs. Passing the Royal Humane Society's lodge and the boat-houses, the investigators paused to look up and down the waterside, Sir Bruton leaning on his cane, Mr. Tuke's dark face sombre and thoughtful. For somewhere about here, in the grey light of dawn two mornings ago, Corinne Reaveley's body was found awash. Three days earlier again, poor Wally Whichcord, without home or background to lend him glamour, had been dragged ashore. It was a natural if trite reflection that on this ill-omened spot two diverse lives were levelled and conjoined; journey's end for the London waif and the wealthy hostess was the same. In Paddington Mortuary they lay side by side.

There were boats on the Serpentine, and laughter rang over the water. Only one or two passers-by, readers perhaps of *The Morning News*, stopped and pointed and whispered. A nursemaid looked over her shoulder as she hurried her charges past the placid scene. Sir Bruton shifted his weight on his malacca and rolled an inquisitive eye at his companion.

"Rum business, eh?"

"Very rum," Mr. Tuke agreed.

He turned about. Across the roadway the ground rose to the Ranger's Lodge and the police station in their rustic setting, over against the Ring Tea House on the knoll once called the Tour, when the *monde* rode and drove there and Mr. Pepys came to see the fine ladies. There are plots of ground in London—Tyburn, and Tower Hill, and Execution Dock—where, if anywhere, ghosts should walk; and here was one more, for on other cold dawns men had died in duels under the trees of the Ring. But Mr. Tuke had never heard that the Tea House was haunted. It was not functioning now, though he did not remark on this to Sir Bruton as the latter came more deliberately about, scowled at the wide but unhelpful prospect of turf and trees, and said petulantly:

"Why didn't that fool reporter say where Whatsisname saw his ruddy spook?" The malacca described half a circle, and Mr. Tuke dodged. "Come on."

They went on, towards Rennie's bridge and the Magazine. On their right hand the amphitheatre of the Cockpit curved among trees. Where the road began to rise to the bridge, the usual cars stood ranked, bonnets inwards, their occupants absorbed in the curious pastime of staring solemnly at the water. The Director flourished his cane.

"Let's go up there, eh?"

They crossed the road to the Cockpit. The slope of this is quite steep, and Sir Bruton halted on the crest to draw breath and light a fresh Trichinopoli. It was then that a voice spoke behind them.

"The vultures gather! Well-timed, gentlemen! I can show you the very spot—the authentic tree. School parties catered for, services in uniform half-price, the Department of Public Prosecutions free of charge. Though naturally a *quid pro quo* would be acceptable."

Mr. Tuke had turned; Sir Bruton, less agile, swivelled one

prominent eye over his shoulder at the man who had approached unheard across the turf.

"And who the flaming blazes are you?" he demanded.

"The name is Fenne," said the newcomer. "You read the *Morning News*? Obviously. Only one thing could have brought the mountain to Mahomet. My exclusive story . . ."

Mr. Fenne's words trailed off as he realized that he might have chosen them better, and Mr. Tuke concealed a smile, for the Director's eye seemed likely to start from its socket.

"Damn your blasted impertinence!" he roared.

"Sorry, sir, sorry," the reporter said hastily. "Nothing personal intended, I assure you. A mere figure of speech—intended as a compliment. Comes from composing in clichés. . . ." He grinned suddenly, sobered as he met Sir Bruton's eye again, and went on in a tone of sweet reasonableness: "I apologize for butting in, but look at it from my point of view. It's my business to know who's who. Well, here you are, the D.P.P. and his *alter ego*, his *éminence grise*, scouting about within a stone's throw of where my old pal Whichcord saw his ghost. And Mr. Tuke was at the Reaveleys' dinner party two nights ago. *And* he's got a reputation for extra-departmental activities. You can't blame me for putting two and two together. It's how I make my living."

Mr. Fenne grinned again placatingly. He was a loose-jointed man of perhaps forty, with a long nose, untidy dark hair turning grey, and very sharp eyes behind horn-rimmed glasses. Hatless, he wore an old tweed jacket, its pockets pulled out of shape by notebooks and other impedimenta, and flannel trousers equally in need of cleaning and pressing. His movements were jerky and rapid; in a second he had fumbled in a pocket, produced a cigarette between nicotine-stained fingers, popped it in his mouth, dived again, fished out a lighter, flicked it, and blown a cloud of smoke.

Sir Bruton had revolved impressively on his axis. Leaning on his cane, he gave Mr. Tuke a baleful look and a growl. "*Your* reputation!" Then he regarded Mr. Fenne, his turned-down lips and wrinkled nose giving him the air of detecting an unpleasant smell. He seemed to have forgotten how recently he had complained because the very information now offered was lacking.

"And what are *you* doing here?" he growled.

"Well, dash it, it's a public park," the reporter replied reasonably. "And this is *my* story, you know. I dug it out seven years ago. I was hunting Whichcord again all last week-end. When I did find him, he was on ice. I was at the inquest this morning. It's adjourned, if you haven't heard. All over in ten minutes. Dr. New, their woman pathologist, did the p.m. Cause of death, drowning. No signs of violence. Identification by deceased's sister. Not a word about the ghost. Bags of discretion displayed by the coroner—it was old Akers, and he's a downy bird—and by everybody else. In view of another inquest on Tuesday, perhaps? Or is it just a coincidence about Mrs. Reaveley, do you think . . . ?"

Mr. Fenne's inquisitive glance, from behind his horn-rims, underlined a suggestive pause. Mr. Tuke was taking a cigar from his case. Sir Bruton continued to stare in a nauseated manner. Neither spoke, and the newspaperman shrugged jerkily, but without rancour.

"Well, you gentlemen are here," he said with a grin. "I take it you agree with me it's a queer show. And the queerest part is the ghost. It's the only one *I've* ever come across, and I've been about quite a bit. Now I've heard Whichcord on the subject. He took me to that tree over there where he was sitting when the thing popped up in front of him. That's seven years ago, and I haven't been here since. But now he's seen it again. Then he gets drowned, and the ghost's ex-fiancée has a brain-storm or something and gets drowned too. In that same bit of water. . . ." Fenne jerked a hand towards the Serpentine, shining below them, thinly transmitting to them like a sounding-board the tinkle of laughter and the splash of sculls. He looked curiously at Mr. Tuke. "*You* saw the beginning of that," he said. "I've only heard the maids' version, and one or two of the other guests'. But do you wonder I'm here too? It's my story, and there's something big in it. Midnight's the witching hour, of course, and I'll come then, probably. That's how it's got me."

Mr. Tuke was lighting his cigar. He said through the smoke: "You talk a lot. Where is this tree?"

"You're fairly warm." Fenne pointed. "I'll show you."

He began to lead the way with a long, loose-jointed stride round the lip of the Cockpit. Mr. Tuke went with him, and Sir Bruton, after a moment, grunted and followed. The reporter took a line in the direction of the Ranger's Lodge, on the slope below the police station. He halted beneath a large old tree.

"This is it," he said.

It was a plane, one of several thousand in the park, a well-grown specimen perhaps a hundred feet high. Its leaves were turning and beginning to fall. Round hairy seed containers dangled from the branches. Yellow patches showed where the old bark had flaked off the trunk, which, near the ground, two men's arms would scarcely have spanned.

"After seven years, can you be sure this is the same tree?" Mr. Tuke asked.

Fenne shot out a finger and laid it on the bark. There, faintly discernible, were engraved initials, W.W., interlined.

"Wally Whichcord, his mark. He liked this spot. The tree fitted his back, or something. And he had a good field of view, and he could watch the water. He liked looking at the water. And he ended up in it." Fenne pointed again. "Just down there, where he used to look."

Sir Bruton had come up and was staring in his pop-eyed way at the initials on the tree. They were, in a sense, evidence. They were all that was left behind by Wally Whichcord, who had no known home but the park and this old tree from America or Asia.

The Director seemed to have put by his annoyance when he turned to the newspaperman.

"It was about here the bloke saw his spook the second time, a fortnight ago, eh?"

"According to some versions of the story," Fenne said, "he was under this tree again. I've talked to a dozen people *he* talked to about it. Anyway, it was just round here. He was a creature of habit. They get like that. Look. . . ."

Before them the grass sloped to the Serpentine, two hundred yards away. Across the water, almost opposite, were the bathing huts, with the chimney-pots and pinnacles of Knightsbridge rising over the trees beyond. Half left, on the near shore, the Humane Society's lodge and the boat-houses stood near the eyot. Close at hand, a little to the observers' right, ten or a dozen big trees, grouped together, crowned the eastern end of the Cockpit; and, immediately in front, half-way down the slope, rose a solitary ash, the only tree within a considerable arc between that by which they stood and the flat waterside below.

Fenne, who had whipped out another cigarette, was talking while he lit it from the stub of the old one.

"When Whichcord first saw the figure, seven years ago, it was standing among those trees." With one action the reporter threw the stub away and pointed to the clump above the Cockpit. "He'd had a doze, but for some minutes he'd been awake, watching the gunfire down the river. The figure moved, and caught his eye. There was plenty of light—full moon and searchlights, one of 'em overhead—and when the figure came out into the open, *there*, he saw the naval officer's rig—long boots, turned-down stockings, reefer and peaked cap. And beard. It walked quite slowly down the slope, and passed behind that tree." With another of his swift gestures Fenne indicated the solitary ash. "It never came into view again," he said. "That was the end of it. Wally watched for some time. He could see the whole shore almost as clearly as we can now. But the thing had just gone out like a light. Or, as he put it, it seemed to have walked into the tree. It got him so puzzled that after a while he went down there to have a look. Perhaps the chap was still behind the tree. But he wasn't. There was nothing there."

"How long after was this?" Mr. Tuke asked.

"A matter of a few minutes, I gathered. Wally was as nosy as a ferret, especially about anything that went on in here in the park. I wouldn't put it past him to do a bit of mild black-mail on the side, and he bragged about having been useful to the police. A lot of queer things happen here, you know."

"So it seems. Had Whichcord seen anybody else about?"

"Not a soul. The guns were over by Park Lane, you'll remember. This was a nice quiet spot. Well," Fenne went on, "I suppose you read my article in Wednesday's *News*? The rehash of the old story?"

"I acquired a copy yesterday," Mr. Tuke admitted.

"He only takes the *Times* and the *Law Journal*," Sir Bruton explained.

Fenne grinned. "His loss. Well, I pointed out that Wally wasn't thinking of bogies at the time. It was only later, when Mrs. Demarest's story of *her* ghost passed into general circulation, through friends and servants, that he began to wonder. That was when I came in——"

"Yes, yes, I've read it," Mr. Tuke said. "Do you know whether Whichcord's adventure took place before or after Mrs. Demarest and Miss Plimsoll saw their figure?"

"Oh, after. Mrs. D. ran out of the house about midnight, you know. Wally said his man popped up not long before the All Clear, and that went more than half an hour later."

"In these versions you've heard of the reappearance, a fortnight ago, is there any indication of how the figure vanished again? Behind that tree, for instance?"

"They were all too damned vague," Fenne said regretfully. "That's the worst of second-hand stories. The general idea seemed to be that everything happened as before. I took that with a grain of salt. But it happened round about here again. They all agreed on that."

Sir Bruton seemed to feel he had been in the background long enough. In his new mood of amiability he leered benevolently at the reporter.

"You did your best with your material, Mr. Fenne. I read your last article. Good bit of writing. Imaginative touch about it. Style, too."

"Nice of you, sir," said Fenne with a bow. "Are you one of our regular readers?"

"I will be. And on the look out for your stuff."

Revolted by this fulsome flattery, Mr. Tuke walked away down the slope towards the tree which had, once at least, swallowed up a phantom. It proved to be just an ash tree, its long narrow leaves beginning to change colour, seed wings now and then parting from a branch and spinning and drifting on the breeze. There was no other tree within sixty or seventy yards, and none at all between the ash and the waterside. It was of fair girth—thick enough to have concealed a figure behind it. But the figure Wally Whichcord saw had not remained behind it; when he came to investigate, it was gone. Mr. Tuke looked back up the slope to his companions by the plane tree, and then turned about and surveyed the stretch of turf falling gently to the water. It was unbroken; only a path crossed it. On the strip of grass beyond this were one or two chairs. Then came the Ring Road, and then the Serpentine. There was a complete absence of any apparent aid to a vanishing trick. The figure might, of course, have walked straight on into the water, keeping the ash in line between it and the watcher above. But that was absurd. . . .

When he climbed to the plane tree again, the reporter was still talking about Wally Whichcord. Sir Bruton, leaning on his malacca, was listening with every sign of respectful attention.

"This was his only address," Fenne was saying. "Though he spent his nights here from choice, as often as not. Gypsy blood, he said—though that may have been all my eye. But the point is, he wasn't one of the down and outs. He'd sleep out here, and scrounge with the best, but he always had a bob or two in his pocket. He'd have a bit on a horse, or on the dogs. God knows what he did—I gathered he hadn't had a job for years—but it came out this morning, at the inquest, that he'd kept in touch with his sister——"

"Ah, the sister," Mr. Tuke interrupted. "It seems that Mr. Whichcord had some sort of background, after all."

"She was a most respectable old body," the reporter said. "A Mrs. Boyle, from Camden Town. A widow, with a bit put by, I should say. She shook her head over brother Wally—he'd touched her in other ways—but she obviously had a weak spot for him. He was a likeable little chap."

"What did the pathologist say about his general state of health?"

"Good enough. Nothing organically wrong."

"Was his sight good?" Mr. Tuke asked, measuring the slope to the ash tree with his eye.

"It was, seven years ago," Fenne said. "I checked it."

"Did you honestly believe his story, Mr. Fenne?"

"He was telling the truth as he saw it," Fenne replied without hesitation. "That's why I thought it worth working up. He spoke of seeing this figure, you know, before Mrs. Demarest's tale got about—in a pub the next morning. He was wondering where it had got to, and what the Navy was doing there, anyway. Later he may have embroidered a bit—the spectral face, for instance—but he saw something, or somebody, all right."

Sir Bruton had suddenly recalled the passage of time. He took out a gold hunter and snapped it open.

"We'll have to be pushing along. Thought you were in a hurry, Tuke? Come on. Where's that cup of tea?" He turned an unctuous leer on the newspaperman. "Delighted to have met you, Mr. Fenne. A most interesting conversation. I look forward to reading more of your instructive articles. A bit of literary style's rare enough nowadays. H'm. I can rely on you, I'm sure, not to refer to this very pleasant meeting in print, eh? It wouldn't do, you know. The department has to be very sticky about that sort of thing. Mr. Tuke's got into the papers once or twice, and haven't I rubbed his nose for him! *And*, of course"—the smile was less ingratiating, the lips were turned down, the Director's prominent stare was daunting—"the department has its powers, and not a little influence. . . ."

"Are you trying to browbeat a free and enlightened press, sir?" said Fenne with a grin.

"Not a bit of it. You know better." Sir Bruton was all geniality again. "We understand one another, Mr. Fenne. Not a word about this, and—well, you never know. Good-bye to you. Good-bye!"

He waved the malacca as he began to trundle over the turf

in a northerly direction. Sardonically silent until out of earshot of the reporter, Mr. Tuke then gave rein to his feelings.

"One of your most revolting exhibitions of blarney and bullying. Afraid of it getting about that you've got a streak of vulgar curiosity, are you?"

"I'm thinking of the department, which is more than you do," said Sir Bruton with dignity.

"Well, where are you taking me now?"

"We want tea, don't we? We're in the middle of this howling great park. If we can't get tea in Bayswater Road, we can get a taxi."

"I thought so. All right, I'll show you the house."

"Who said anything about a house? Is that fellow following us?"

"No. The press is less interested in you than you think."

Cars were spinning along the carriage road to Victoria Gate as the pair headed for this exit over the undulations where once Wyatt's rebels had skirmished in the rain. But near the gate Sir Bruton crossed the roadway and turned left by the dogs' cemetery into Kensington Gardens. They passed Wren's Alcove and emerged into Bayswater Road by the small gate immediately opposite the end of Lancaster Terrace, in the trough of the dip representing the old bed of the Westbourne, which, indeed, still flowed almost beneath their feet.

"Where's this house?" Sir Bruton inquired without further pretence.

Mr. Tuke pointed. "The one with the bow, on the left, at the first corner. That's Gloucester Terrace. Miss Plimsoll watched from the first floor window."

"And the other woman talked to the spook across the way there?" The Director waved his cane at the nearer corner facing them. "And then it trotted over here, eh?"

"Roughly towards where we're standing, I assume. And vanished *en route*."

Sir Bruton turned to stare at the two-foot brick base which, seven years before, had carried railings another seven feet high. Mr. Tuke was still gazing across Bayswater Road. Two figures had come round the corner of Gloucester Terrace—a man and a girl in black, who wore no hat.

"You're in luck this afternoon," he said. "Here are some of the *dramatis personae*. Miss Kittredge and her novelist. And they've seen us."

CHAPTER IV

THE BAD HOUSE

Miss Kittredge and Gordon Cartwright, in fact, had begun to stroll down Lancaster Terrace when the girl suddenly put a hand on her companion's arm. They both stood looking across the main road to where Sir Bruton and Mr. Tuke lingered by the park gate. Then they came on again more quickly. The traffic lights at that end of the Terrace halted the flow of traffic at this moment.

"Now's our chance," said Sir Bruton.

Mr. Tuke's expression spoke volumes, but was wasted, for the Director had started to cross the road. With a shrug, Harvey perforce followed.

The two couples accordingly met on the very flagstones which had been the scene of Mrs. Demarest's midnight encounter seven years before. Kay Kittredge's attractive and intelligent face was sobered and pale. Its pallor was accentuated by her black frock, and there were violet shadows beneath the rather wide eyes that seemed to be wondering what had recalled the guest of two nights ago to this haunted street corner. Mr. Tuke left the fact to speak for itself.

"We are taking a little exercise," he said baldly. "Miss Kittredge, this is Sir Bruton Kames. Sir Bruton—Mr. Gordon Cartwright. You know his books."

"How-de-do, ma'am," said Sir Bruton, replacing his ancient hat and waving his cheroot and cane together in a spacious gesture. He liked to call himself a lawyer of the old school, and he reserved for women—especially pretty ones—certain vaguely Victorian courtesies. A prominent eye was rolled at the novelist. "Of course I know Mr. Cartwright's books. Flattered to meet you, sir. We're having a literary afternoon. Muses all over the place. Nice change from major malpractices, eh, Tuke?"

Though by now Miss Kittredge was no doubt aware of what Mr. Tuke did for a living, her curious glance at the Director suggested that his name had meant nothing to her. Cartwright, who was himself looking harrassed and preoccupied, was again obviously better informed; and from the speculative way he eyed the newcomers the coincidence of their walk ending at this particular spot in all London had not escaped him.

"Fact is," said Sir Bruton, taking charge in his unscrupulous way of the situation he had engineered, "fact is, Tuke saw you across the road, and thought he ought to offer condolences, and all that. Felt I might be allowed to butt in too. Sad business—responsible one for a young gal. Got a pack of nieces myself—act *in loco parentis*, so I know." By the Director's own account his nieces were extremely self-sufficient young women who used his house as a hotel and drank all his liquor, but such discrepancies were swept aside in another large gesture as he turned to scowl at The Crown public house on the opposite corner—naturally closed at that hour—and then peered with a disgusted air up and down Bayswater Road. "Well, well, Tuke, you've done your duty. Don't outstay your welcome. Can't see any place along here, though, can you?"

"What are you looking for?"

"A tea shop. I want my tea. I want to sit down. This part of London's a howling desert. Your friend Tuke," Sir Bruton explained to Miss Kittredge, "lured me out with a promise of tea. And look where he's brought me."

Mr. Tuke caught Cartwright's amused glance as the shameless manœuvre came off.

"Will you let me give you some tea?" Kay said, after no more than an instant's hesitation. "I haven't had mine yet. I'm alone in the house, except for a maid. Mr. Reaveley is staying at his club."

"Reaveley always does the correct thing," the novelist murmured, and received an annoyed glance from Miss Kittredge.

"Hardly think we ought to inflict ourselves," said Sir Bruton, with insincerity so patent that it would not have deceived a child of two. "Eh, Tuke?"

"No doubt you will do the incorrect thing."

"Yes, do come," Kay said with a little smile at Mr. Tuke. "It will do me good. It isn't exactly a cheerful house just now, if you don't mind that." She flashed a look at Cartwright. "I'll be seeing you, Gordon."

And with a nod to him she began to lead the way up Lancaster Terrace, the Director, without more ado, falling in beside her. As Mr. Tuke followed, he exchanged a smile with Cartwright, left there at the corner, and the novelist's was the more sardonic of the two.

No 7a, as they approached it, could now be studied by daylight. It was a typical Victorian tower of a house, with a basement and five storeys, and was the more towerlike owing to its bow. Its numbering, and the rather insignificant front door round the corner, suggested that originally 7 and 7a had been one dwelling. Once in Gloucester Terrace, it became apparent that every house on that side, between the Reaveleys' and Lancaster Street, was blasted and derelict, or demolished. Lancaster Street itself, a short cross road into Lancaster Gate, appeared to have vanished altogether, and the church opposite had lost half its spire.

"We'll have tea in the study," the girl said as she opened the door. "I hate the drawing-room, and my sitting-room's up eight flights of stairs."

The study was that room behind the dining-room where, two nights earlier, the men had left their coats and hats. Mr. Tuke could now appreciate its queer proportions. Like the other rooms he had seen, it was wedge-shaped. This unorthodox plan, due to the position of the house at the obtuse corner of two streets, had at some time been carried to its logical conclusion by the filling in, with extra domestic offices, of a small triangular rear courtyard at basement level. The study, half of which was built out over the extension, came almost to a point. The angle was all glass, with a door giving on to an iron stair; and, the ground here dipping steeply, it gave a view across a hollow congested with a nexus of stablings. Beyond rose the tall backs of the houses in Lancaster Gate. Mr. Tuke, whose usual curiosity took him at once to the window, realized that he was looking down upon the old bed of the Westbourne, and determined to explore these sunken alleys, which were new to him.

He turned his attention to the room itself, while Sir Bruton made conversation with Miss Kittredge, who seemed to be keeping up her end only by an effort. Hoping to gain some insight into the character of Clifford Reaveley, whose retreat this was, Harvey did not find the study very helpful: equipped in the modern manner, it was bright but unhomely. Tubular steel chairs and overstuffed rectangular divans may merely mean that a shop or an interior decorator has been given a free hand. Pictures there were none—only some photographs of rock peaks and faces and snow cornices, suggesting that Mr. Reaveley liked mountaineering, a deduction confirmed by the bookshelves, which held many volumes on the subject, with bound series of *The Mountaineering Journal* and *The Rock and Fell Climber*, mingled untidily with others on constructional engineering, drainage, and geology. Fiction, apart from A. E. W. Mason's *Running Water*, was represented by sensational stuff of a crude type. It appeared from this literary pabulum that Clifford Reaveley was a serious reader only of works bearing on his profession or recreations. Mr. Tuke had scarcely expected him to be otherwise.

A maid whom Harvey remembered, and who obviously recognized one of the guests at the ill-omened dinner party, brought in tea with the air of being still in the presence of death, disaster and woe. And once the cups had been filled, Kay Kittredge abandoned all pretence of playing the polite hostess. In the strong light—the big angular window faced south—her charming face was suddenly aged and haggard. Mr. Tuke, though he professed to know little about women, knew a good deal about human nature in general. He had seen that some cause of difference had arisen between the girl and Gordon Cartwright, and he guessed that this had keyed her up to forget or control her deeper distress of mind. But now, with strangers, as sometimes happens, she was able to relax and remember. She sat drooping at the tea-table, her fingers working together in her lap, staring before her with a tragic face. There were those who denied that Harvey Tuke knew the meaning of finer feelings, but he would have been cursing Sir Bruton for inflicting the pair of them on this unhappy young creature had he not felt that the intrusion was, after all, perhaps the best thing for her.

The Director, who also had his perceptions, was gazing at her with pop-eyed sympathy from the overstuffed divan on which he sprawled.

"Drink up your tea, my dear," he said suddenly in an avuncular manner. "Cold tea never did anyone any good. Got any brandy in the house?"

Miss Kittredge woke from her melancholy trance with a start.

"Yes, of course. Would you prefer it?"

Sir Bruton chuckled. "Who wouldn't? But it's you I'm thinking of. Put a dollop in your tea. Pull you together."

"I don't need it, thank you. I'm perfectly all right."

But the girl's eyes had gone to a cabinet in the corner, and Sir Bruton waved a hand like a flipper.

"Stuff and nonsense! There you are, Tuke. We'll all have some. Nothing like making oneself at home."

"No, you're an authority on that," Mr. Tuke said with feeling as he rose.

In the cabinet there was quite an array of bottles, including Martell 1904, which doubtless came from Hugo Demarest's cellar. Miss Kittredge's tea, under protest, was liberally laced. These high-handed proceedings brought a faint smile to her pale face, and there was even a little colour in her cheeks when her cup was emptied.

"That's more like it," said Sir Bruton, who had not stinted himself. "Done me good, too. Tuke must have led me miles. Now have another."

"*No*, thank you."

"See to it, Tuke. And pass me one of those cakes."

Kay positively flushed. "I'm awfully sorry. I'm not looking after you a bit——"

"We can look after ourselves," said the Director truthfully. "Had a bad time, haven't you?"

The girl shuddered. "Dreadful! Yesterday was a nightmare. But at least one felt stunned. One couldn't think. Now. . . ."

"Haven't had much sleep, I dare say?"

"Sleep?" she echoed, in a tone Macbeth might have used. "No, I haven't had much sleep. . . ." She shivered again and leaned back in her chair, her eyes closed. Mr. Tuke took the opportunity to refill her cup and add brandy. She did not even notice what he was doing. Then she was erect again, her eyes wide. "I can't believe it!" she cried. "Corinne, of all people! *You* saw her, Mr. Tuke. Oh, I know she flew off in a temper, and she's talked of it before, but lots of people do. It doesn't *mean* anything. It's like saying you could murder the grocer, or the food officer, or someone. . . ."

Since repressions were coming out, the more that came out the better, Mr. Tuke felt, and he prompted her gently.

"You don't think it was an accident?"

"How could it be? What was she doing in the middle of Hyde Park, without even a handbag or a hat?"

"Would you care to tell us what did happen that night, after the rest of us left?"

Kay's rigid pose relaxed a little. She sipped her tea mechanically, picked up a cake, and put it down.

"Will you pass me a cigarette? In that box."

Harvey passed the immense glass cigarette-box, weighing several pounds, and struck a match for her.

"Yes, of course," she said more quietly, when she had exhaled a cloud of smoke. "Gordon Cartwright says he told you, when you took him home, that Corinne hadn't gone to bed. She went down the back stairs while Clifford was going up the second time. When he called me out, he said he couldn't tell all those people—he'd say she *had* gone to bed. He asked me to back him up. It wasn't the first time she'd done it, and when everyone had gone we could start telephoning. . . . Well, I could see his point. Anything to get them away. I don't mean you and your wife, Mr. Tuke——"

"Why not? We were almost complete strangers."

"You're different. We were thinking of those silly gossipping women. Anyhow, I agreed. I hadn't time to think it out. And of course neither of us ever dreamed of what Corinne had in her mind."

"Most of us would have acted in the same way," Mr. Tuke said. "What actually took place when Reaveley went upstairs the first time? He was away ten minutes or so."

The girl was already more herself. Her face was less haggard and white, her eyes were brighter, she looked nearer her age. She sipped her tea again.

"Corinne was having a bath," she said. "She was still in a tearing temper. She was fed up with everything, and she was going to bed. They had a long argument, Clifford said—if you can call it an argument. He was trying to calm her down, and she kept flying out at him, and splashing water about. . . ." Kay's lips twitched in a faint involuntary smile. "She threw her sponge at him."

"Rum idea," said Sir Bruton. "Having a bath, eh? If she was going to do away with herself."

"Oh, she can't have been even thinking of that *then!*" Kay exclaimed. "And she was always having hot baths. She said they calmed her nerves. I told her she'd make them worse. Anyway, in the end Clifford talked her round, so she can't have been thinking of—of doing what she did. She said she'd come down again. I suppose she *might* have been pretending, but he believed her. So he came and told us. You remember, Mr. Tuke, he waited a bit, and then, as she didn't come, he went up a second time, just as she slammed the front door. . . ."

Kay drew on her cigarette, frowning a little in an effort of concentration. She went on to Mr. Tuke:

"Well, then you all left. Clifford started telephoning at once. There are half a dozen people Corinne might have gone to. The friend she ran away to before, and—and others," the girl said, and continued quickly: "I ran up to her room and looked round. I could hardly believe it. But of course she *had* gone. Then I saw she'd left her handbag, with her keys and everything in it. Her small dressing cases were there too. All that was gone was the tweed coat and skirt they—they found on her. She'd actually put them on over the underclothes and stockings she'd been wearing that evening, which shows the state she was in." Kay made a bewildered gesture. "Unless, of course," she said, "Corinne had really started to dress, to come down, and then changed her mind, because of the brain storm, or whatever it was. It's all dreadfully puzzling, and horrible to think of. . . ."

"We'll drop the subject, if it's too painful," Mr. Tuke said.

"There isn't much more to tell. Clifford couldn't get any news of her. Then he began to worry, because though Corinne did mad things, she never forgot her comforts. He thought of the car, and ran out to the garage at the back there." Kay gestured towards the window and the old stablings below. "But the car was in. Then—oh, we talked and talked. He spoke of the police. Then he found it was after one o'clock, and said I must go to bed. I didn't want to, but what was one to *do*?" Her hands made another little gesture of helplessness. "I *was* dreadfully tired. Before all this I'd had the dinner to arrange, and cook, partly, and everything else to see to. So in the end I went. Clifford made up a drink for me, and I'm ashamed to say I went off almost at once, and slept for hours. I only came down yesterday morning just as the police sergeant brought the news. . . ."

She leaned back, the cigarette she had forgotten smouldering between her fingers. An electric clock on a bracket above the let-in radiator chimed five, and Mr. Tuke automatically checked it by his French chronometer. He took out his cigar-case, and seeing the Director's hand move to his pocket, hastily passed him a Larranaga. When they had lighted up, he turned to the girl again.

"If Mrs. Reaveley went off without even a handbag, how did they know so quickly who she was?"

Kay came out of her unhappy thoughts with a start.

"The policeman knew her," she said drearily. "He came from the police station in the park, and Corinne had seen him there about a clip she lost." She ground out her cigarette. "Well, that was yesterday morning," she repeated. "You won't want to hear any more about that. It was an appalling day. Clifford was half off his head. He had to go and identify her. A dreadful persistent newspaperman, called Fenne—

I expect you know about *him* by now—came and pestered us. He seemed to think he'd a right to, because it was what he called *his* story. Something to do with that silly old business about a ghost. As if there was any connection! *I* told him off," said Kay, with a wan smile at the recollection.

"Try to forget it," Mr. Tuke said. "We'll talk about something else."

But she was not now in a mood to talk about anything else. She went on as though she had not heard.

"What distresses Clifford so is that he thinks *he's* to blame. That he should have let her go to bed, instead of wrangling with her. He thinks that set her off. . . . It's horrible for him. And people don't *understand*," said Kay, a quick flush rising in her cheeks. "They think he doesn't really *feel* it. Of course, he and Corinne didn't always hit it off. They weren't in *love* with one another any more. But they went their own ways, and got along all right. Corinne having all the money made it difficult, as she wasn't even a relation, while he was. She was awfully generous, really, only sometimes when they had a tiff she used to drag this in. I know Corinne's good points—she was very good to me, and I was fond of her—but living here I've seen a lot. Clifford was in a rotten position. . . ."

If this was a trifle incoherent, it emerged clearly enough that for people who did not understand one should read Gordon Cartwright. And the impression Kay somehow gave of delivering her apologia for Clifford Reaveley as much to herself as to her audience reminded Mr. Tuke of the looks that young man had cast at her across the dinner table, and Cartwright's obvious annoyance. Too loyal consciously to admit it, the girl herself had no doubt found life in this household rather difficult. Sir Bruton, in his shrewd way, dotted her *i's* for her.

"Uncomfortable position for you too, eh? Thin ice, and all that?"

Kay coloured again. "It has been, sometimes. . . ." Leaving it at that, rather abruptly, she repeated: "People don't understand. Things are bad enough without Gordon—Mr. Cartwright—being cross because I won't go and stay with his mother. I can't run away like that. Clifford's gone to his club, as I told you, and *someone's* got to see to things."

"Mr. Reaveley's a stickler for the correct thing, as Mr. Cartwright remarked?" Sir Bruton queried.

"Yes, I suppose it was partly that. . . ." Playing nervously with a tea-knife, Kay went on hastily again, as if more thin ice had appeared: "He'll be in presently. I don't wonder he wanted to get out of this house. It seems more dreadful than ever now. And the next few days are going to be ghastly. I'm dreading the inquest. The police sergeant came again this morning with a summons for me, or whatever it is, adjuring me in the most solemn language to do this and that. . . ."

"Tuke'll hold your hand. They're getting him too."

Kay, who had rallied a faint smile, turned it on Mr. Tuke. Some of the latter's acquaintances would have been surprised by her ready acceptance of him, at their second meeting, as a confidential friend. Sir Bruton, when in a benign mood, was at least every inch the uncle—and there were many inches; but his senior assistant was accustomed to people being intimidated by satanic features and an astringent manner, but was less aware, perhaps, how much these were ameliorated towards the relatively few whom he liked. And he liked Kay Kittredge, who was charming as well as intelligent, and who had been rather left in the lurch by Clifford Reaveley, that stickler for the conventions, who had, in fact, run away.

"Besides holding your hand at the inquest," he said, "is there any other way in which one could help? I know that my wife, for instance, would be only too glad if she could do anything."

"It's nice of you," Kay said. "And of Mrs. Tuke, because I'm sure she would. She's lovely, isn't she? But really I can cope, though it *is* a help to feel one's got friends in the background. I've been out of London so long that I haven't many here. Miss Plimsoll has offered to stay with me, and she's a dear, but I can manage by myself. I feel much better already, just for talking things out."

Sir Bruton eyed her critically. "You look it. But give brandy its due. Anyway, at a pinch there's always Mr. Cartwright's mother, eh?"

Kay gave him a queer look. "I won't be *run* by anybody," she said. She added, more slowly: "At least, not yet."

The Director chuckled, and scattered ash over his waistcoat. His prominent gaze was roving about the bright but somehow comfortless room. He asked suddenly:

"Whaddayou mean by this house being more dreadful than ever now? What was wrong with it before? Seems all right to me." He waved a large hand. "Light and cheerful and all that. Rum shape, of course." He chuckled again. "So am I, eh? Better than having none."

Kay, who once more was brooding, perhaps on Gordon Cartwright or his mother, looked up in slight surprise.

"The house?" she said. "Oh, you don't know it. You can't go by one room. I've come to hate it. It grows on one—in a bad way. It isn't that it's just fusty and inconvenient and gloomy—though you should see the basement!—there's something else about it that gets one down. It makes me think of a coffin. And then I think that there are whole streets like it—streets of grey coffins, with grey, dead, fusty people in them. . . . Light and cheerful!" Kay repeated bitterly. "You haven't seen the rest of it. It's always *dark*. If it wasn't for electric light, one would go mad. Yet our grandfathers seem to have been perfectly happy, groping about behind thick lace curtains in perpetual twilight. Perhaps they did go mad? . . ."

"Not they," said Sir Bruton. "Insensitive lot. Too busy making money and putting up a show. Creeps were unknown to 'em. They came in with nerves—about 1920. But if you feel like that about the house, you'd better get out of it."

"I'm going to," Kay said, "as soon as I can. Do you know, I've even made a sort of arrangement with Gordon Cartwright, so that when I feel I can't stand it I can ring him up, and he'll meet me in the park, among the grass and trees and *openness*, where I can breathe again. Though naturally," she added, with her elusive and charming smile, "I haven't told him why. I just say I'm out for a walk."

Mr. Tuke had been recalling his wife's words, which now seemed prophetic, about this house.

"Did your cousin ever feel as you do?" he asked.

Kay looked at him quickly. "Corinne? It's odd you should ask that. I used to think she liked the house. It was *her* house, you see, and she'd never owned much before. We were all poor in the old days. I am still. Anyway, lately Corinne has talked a lot about getting rid of the place, and taking a flat. She's been very restless. . . ."

Sir Bruton was flapping ash off his waistcoat.

"Tell us about the old days," he said.

CHAPTER V

SOMETHING IN A CUPBOARD

KAY SHOWED no particular surprise at this request. She seemed to accept as a matter of course her visitors' interest in her affairs. She was perhaps too tired and preoccupied to wonder at it.

"But there's nothing to tell," she said. "Only the short and simple annals of the rather hard-up. When Corinne and I were quite young I lived in London, and we saw a lot of one another. Then my mother went to Bournemouth for her health, and I got a job there. Then there was the war, and I became a Wren rating, and Corinne joined the M.T.C.—she had an old car—and drove generals about, and had a marvellous time. She would, you know." Kay smiled without envy. "That was when she met Felix Demarest somehow. Then both our mothers died, and Felix was lost at sea, and she married Clifford. And that's about all."

Sir Bruton conscientiously rubbed cheroot ash into the carpet with a No. 10 shoe. He looked up to inquire:

"What was Mr. Reaveley in those days?"

"What he is now," the girl said. "A civil engineer. He was with the L.C.C. then. He joined the R.E.s. For a time he had a queer job in the Lebanon, teaching troops to climb mountains. He's keen on that. Then after a couple of years some friend in the ministry got him pulled out, to do whatever it is he does—he calls it plumbing—at new camps and factories. I know he was still away a lot. Corinne didn't see much of him, after the first year, and she went on driving staff officers about, and having a good time, instead of settling down. I think she would have," said Kay, frowning at her own thoughts, "if Clifford had been at home. They were crazy about one another at the beginning. Corinne used to write to me. But as it turned out . . ."

Her clear voice trailed away as she relapsed into a reverie, her small clever hands twisting lightly together. Except for the shadows beneath her eyes, she appeared almost her normal self. This inquisition, like a homœopathic cure, had exorcised the worst of the horrors with which for two days she had been living.

Sir Bruton continued his avuncular probings.

"Crazy about one another, were they? What about the other poor feller? Demarest? I knew his father."

"Oh, did you? . . ." Kay came back to earth again. "I know very little about that. I wasn't in London then, so I never met Felix Demarest, or his mother. I was only in this house about twice, until I came out of the Wrens and Corinne asked me to run it for her. . . ." She hesitated. "If you really *want* to know," she said, "I don't think Corinne was ever crazy about Felix Demarest. She liked him, and he was rich, or would be, and she hated being poor——"

"But the poor feller was keen on her, eh?"

"I suppose so. Well, he must have been. Miss Plimsoll says so, and she was here. I don't," said Kay, with sudden earnestness, "want you to think too hardly of Corinne. . . ."

"That's all right. Don't you worry." Sir Bruton waved his cheroot spaciously, and more ash flew. "Only I heard Mrs. Hugo left the gal a packet, and I wondered why."

"Because her son made her promise to look after Corinne if anything happened to him. Mrs. Demarest doted on him, and there were no other near relations. If he'd lived, Corinne would have been a very near one."

"Reaveley himself was a relative, though?"

"Only a cousin half a dozen times removed," Kay said. "Mrs. Demarest divided the rest of her property among her family, and Clifford got a legacy."

Miss Kittredge was not to know that the Director, as his senior assistant put it, seldom acted from unsullied motives, but she had become slightly defensive at this point, and Sir Bruton, rolling a significant eye at Mr. Tuke, effaced himself behind a smoke-screen, in the manner of the cuttlefish, which in some ways he resembled. The pair had worked for so long as a team that Mr. Tuke could always take the words from his senior's mouth, and with a sardonic glance at the smoke-screen he inquired of the girl:

"Could Mrs. Reaveley do what she liked with the property left to her? Leave it wholly to her husband, for instance?"

Kay's eyebrows rose a trifle. "Yes, I believe so. Well, I know, of course. She and Clifford each made a will in the other's favour."

"And her will still stands?"

"Corinne used to talk of altering it when she was in a temper. But I should have known if she'd done such a thing." Kay looked straight at Mr. Tuke. "Why do *you* want to know?"

A sort of explosion was heard on the divan. Sir Bruton was amused. But he had the grace to come to his *alter ego's* assistance.

"Tuke's like the bloke in Little Dorrit. He always wants to know, you know. I made up a poem about him:

> A legal assistant named Tuke
> Remarked to himself in rebuke,
>   'I thought I could show
>   How I know what I know,
> But I've just learnt a fact by a fluke.'"

This *jeu d'esprit* relieved the slight tension, and made Kay smile again. In her anxiety to show her ill-fated cousin in the best light, she even went into explanations.

"I never took Corinne seriously when she talked like that. She'd do or say anything in a temper—like running away, or bringing up this business of the money. Or talking of killing herself, even. . . . But underneath she was very kind-hearted and generous." Kay shook her dark head reflectively. "People are funny mixtures, aren't they?"

"You're telling *me* !" said Sir Bruton, with a rather sinister chuckle. Heaving himself up among his cushions, he retrieved the ball from Mr. Tuke. "Your cousin talked of doing away with herself, did she? You said so before."

"Oh, but I told you!" Kay cried. "It meant nothing! Just temper. 'One of these days I'll kill myself'—that sort of thing. When you talk like that, you don't do it, do you? That's why I can't believe it, even now."

"Did she talk that way to her husband the other night?"

"Clifford hasn't said anything about it. Of course, I don't suppose he remembers half she said. When you've had the same thing pretty often, you don't *listen*."

"She'd been in a bit of a doodah all the evening, Tuke seems to think."

"He exaggerates," Mr. Tuke said. "I thought Mrs. Reaveley must be a little on edge, because that reference to the ghost obviously irritated her extremely. And then she stamped pretty heavily on Mr. Coverdale."

A slightly wary look came into Kay's usually candid gaze. "I don't know anything about that. What they were sparring about, I mean." With the air of closing the subject, she added: "But Corinne *had* been nervy. I was partly responsible. I saw a police notice in the park the day before about that poor man being drowned, and I told her."

"Whichcord? And the news upset her?"

"She didn't say anything, but she stared at me as if she'd had a shock. After that she went about brooding, and she was definitely queer with Clifford. Though that," Kay said thoughtfully, "really began a week or two ago. When we heard about the ghost appearing again. It was all round the neighbourhood, and people asked silly questions, because we live in this house. Anyway, Corinne seemed to change after that. She kept looking at Clifford. Watching him . . ." Kay gave Mr. Tuke a shrewd glance. "I suppose you know all about the ghost by now? I saw you with Miss Plimsoll. . . ."

Mr. Tuke grinned. "Well, I wanted to know, you know. And it's all in the papers, isn't it? So you noticed a change in your cousin's attitude to her husband after the story of the ghost's reappearance got about?"

"Yes, she was queer," Kay repeated. "I don't know why it should have worried her. Her only connection with the original business, seven years ago, was having been engaged to Felix Demarest. And Clifford wasn't mixed up in it in any way. I don't know much about it myself. I wasn't even in

London then. I call it business," she added with a little smile, "because—well, what *is* one to call it?"

"Poppycock!" said Sir Bruton loudly.

"He doesn't know what to think," Mr. Tuke said. "Any more than you do. Or I."

Kay frowned in perplexity. "Do *you* believe in that sort of thing? Ghosts, I mean?"

"I believe in evidence. This is an unusually well-attested apparition."

"Oh, I know! Miss Plimsoll has told me about that night. And then there was this man Whichcord . . ." Kay's puzzled frown had deepened. She made a small gesture of exasperation. "But it's so incredible! What *is* one to think?"

Sir Bruton snorted. Mr. Tuke, with a slight shrug, returned from cause to effect.

"At any rate, you say the news of it seemed to worry your cousin. It made her behave queerly. And her recent behaviour is what we have to consider. I say 'we', because this is not pure nosiness on my part. Next Tuesday both of us may be asked some penetrating questions by the coroner."

"Oh, dear!" said Kay. "Yes, I suppose we shall."

"So perhaps you will regard me as a sort of ally, and tell me a little more."

"What do you want to know?"

"Anything more you can think of that will help to explain Mrs. Reaveley's behaviour. Especially on Wednesday evening. For instance, has she ever had a serious *crise de nerfs* of that kind before? Something more than a fit of temper? What you have called a brain storm?"

Kay shook her head decisively. "Never, that I know of. In fact, I've always thought that these tempers of hers were half put on—her method of getting her own way. They were soon over, as a rule. As soon as she got what she wanted. Then she'd be charming again. Like a child. She'd been spoiled. My Aunt Laura, her mother, always gave in to her."

"But she had gone to the length of running away before. From a sort of refrain in the story—'it wasn't the first time'—one gathers she made rather a practice of it."

"I shouldn't call it that." Kay's faint smile had a tinge of discomfort. "It had happened twice before."

"From this house?"

"Oh, yes."

"At night?"

"No, the first time it was in the morning. She and Clifford quarrelled about something at breakfast, and she went to stay with a woman she knew in Knightsbridge. Clifford fetched her back next day."

"And the second time?"

"Oh, does it matter? . . . Anyway, it was in the evening. I believe she came back in a few hours. She wasn't far away. I don't know much about it. I wasn't here, either time." Kay's tone implied that that was enough of that. She went on quickly: "'Running away' sounds so *drastic*, but it wasn't, really. Corinne meant to be fetched back, all the time. Or to come back."

"It was only pretty Fanny's way? A projection of her method, so to speak?"

"I've always thought so," Kay said. "So did Clifford, and he understood her. Gervase Coverdale says she ought to have been christened April."

"Very poetic of Mr. Coverdale," Mr. Tuke remarked. "He's an old friend of hers, I take it?"

"Oh, yes. An older friend of Clifford's, of course."

"I gathered somehow that he lives near here."

Kay raised her eyebrows. "Yes. In Craven Hill."

Again there was an air of withdrawal, a slightly wary look in her frank face. Mr. Tuke removed the ash from his cigar, and leaned back in his chair; and the other member of the team, who for some moments had appeared to be in a coma, woke up and inquired torpidly:

"By the way, where did Mr. Reaveley—whom I haven't the pleasure of knowing, though I like his taste in sofas—these are what I *call* springs—nearly been asleep on 'em—where did *he* come in, in the beginning? Through young Demarest, I suppose, being a cousin of a sort?"

Kay nodded. "They used to go rock climbing together.

That's how Clifford met Corinne—during one of Felix Demarest's leaves. Of course she didn't climb. She sat at the bottom and got bored." The girl pointed to a photograph on the wall. "There they are. Corinne took that."

But when Mr. Tuke got up to inspect the photograph it was impossible to distinguish one from another of the two small figures spreadeagled against the face of a precipice—one of them long since drowned, while the girl who sat at the foot of the mountain, and took photographs, and got bored, had now shared his fate. Water had proved an unlucky element for them both.

The electric clock chimed a quarter past five. Mr. Tuke looked round the oddly proportioned room.

"One appreciates the peculiar shape of this house better in daylight."

"It's a triangle with a bulge in front," Kay said. "The rooms are nearly all triangular, or worse. It's like living in a problem by Euclid. When you fit a carpet, you have to take the square of the hypotenuse. And it's full of dark little cubby-holes in the odd corners and places."

"Queer houses fascinate me," Mr. Tuke went on, judging that Miss Kittredge was indeed much recovered. "Before we prise my revered chief off that sofa, I wonder if you would show me a floor or two. I love cubby-holes."

"If you like," the girl said, with the air of accommodating a harmless whim. She glanced at the divan as she rose, but Sir Bruton had closed his eyes.

"No eight flights for me," he muttered. But he opened one eye to give Mr. Tuke an inquisitive look as the latter followed Kay into the hall.

"You've seen the dining-room," she said. Opening a door between that room and the study, she switched on a light. "Here are some of the cubby-holes. This is a store cupboard. That's the serving pantry, with a lift. There are the back stairs. Food used to be lugged up them, congealing on the way."

These cupboards, of all shapes and sizes, had never known daylight. Narrow breakneck stairs wound up and down in a species of dark chimney. Mr. Tuke, displaying a childlike interest, asked if they might climb the stairs.

"If you like," Kay said again. "They're frightful. Maids won't use them nowadays, and I don't wonder——" She stopped. "Oh. . . . Corinne came this way. I'd forgotten."

Mr. Tuke, who had not forgotten, offered to go up alone. But she lifted her chin and braced herself.

"I don't mind. There are no ghosts here."

And she led the way up the dusty, twisting stairs, turning on more lights as she went. If there were no ghosts in this black funnel, more like a vice in some mediaeval keep or church tower than a domestic feature of a supposedly enlightened era, it was surprising: Mr. Tuke could fancy his shoulders brushed the shades of wearied maidservants, stumbling up by candle-light with trays and hot-water cans and portmanteaux. And Kay Kittredge, he knew, in spite of her brave words, was seeing in her mind's eye another shadow, hastening downward to the faint diminuendo of talk and laughter in the drawing-room above, hurrying desperately down to the hall and the front door and the dim, gas-lit street, at the end of which, retransformed by the eerie spell of night into the dire and gloomy forest they once had been, the glades of Hyde Park stretched blackly to the distant leaden shimmer of water.

The pair came out among more cupboards on the first floor. A further door gave on to the landing by the drawing-room. Remarking that they had had enough of the back stairs, Mr. Tuke followed Kay to the landing. He turned to the drawing-room door. The large, irregularly shaped room looked cold and lifeless now, its rococo furnishings arid and meretricious. The Spanish sofa on which he had sat with Miss Plimsoll was shown up for the tawdry pretence it was. All this artificiality needed artificial light; daylight betrayed it. It was difficult, even, to recapture the atmosphere of less than forty-eight hours ago. He walked across to the bow. In addition to the three long windows there, a fourth looked over Gloucester Terrace, for the room extended over the hall. But he was chiefly interested in the window above that from which, in the dining-room below, Miss Plimsoll had watched Mrs. Demarest talking with the dim shape in the night time seven years before. Lancaster Terrace sloped beneath him to the corner, and Bayswater Road, and Kensington Gardens. Among the yellowing trees rose the gable of the Alcove and the pinnacles of the pumping house at the head of the Long Water. The traffic lights changed, and cars and omnibuses streamed between his coign of view and the pavement where he had stood with Sir Bruton and where the ghost of Felix Demarest had vanished from his mother's sight. It was all very normal and noisy, and the only wraiths were puffs of blue exhaust gases dissolving in a utilitarian reek of petrol.

When he rejoined the girl, who waited for him in the doorway, her words were an echo of his thoughts.

"I think this room's awful, don't you? The dining-room's better—the furniture suits the house, anyway. Because of the war, Corinne had to stop when she'd done this, and her bedroom, and Clifford's study."

In a room behind, over part of the built-out study, they were back with Edward VII and Victoria, among mahogany and yellow wallpaper and iron bedsteads with brass knobs. Before the cheval mirror the ladies had reviewed their make-up on Wednesday night. Mr. Tuke, whose interest in the house seemed to be puzzling Kay a little now, said he would like to see one more floor; and as they climbed the main stair the girl switched on the lights, for here it was almost as dark as in the grim shaft they had first mounted. On the second floor landing she threw open a door, and imprisoned daylight streamed out.

"Corinne's bedroom," she said.

This, immediately above the drawing-room, was all ormolu and apple green silk. At least it was bright and cheerful. In a party wall, cutting off the rectangular space over the hall, was a second door, that of Corinne's bathroom, Kay said; but as she remained on the threshold of the bedroom—she seemed rather to shrink from entering—Mr. Tuke continued his explorations alone. When he later remarked to Sir Bruton that he must have had a Leading, the Director readily thought of another word for it.

The bathroom, of which the *décor* was primrose, was nearly all bath. A half-sunken pool of yellow tiles, this had a step along its seven-foot length. On a chromium tray, before a battery of chromium taps and sprays, lay the sponge which had been thrown at Clifford Reaveley. Corinne had liked her things on the grand scale—her bottles of bath salts were magnums—and the sponge was the biggest Mr. Tuke had ever seen. Saturated with water, it would make a disconcerting missile. His lips twitched as he picked it up: weighing it in his hand, he rolled it about, squeezing it over the bath before he replaced it on the tray. As he brushed his hands together, his expression was faintly perplexed.

Kay's slender black figure was still poised impermanently in the bedroom doorway. She seemed glad to close the door behind them.

"That's Clifford's bedroom, and bathroom." She pointed down the landing. "Here are the usual cupboards."

The door she opened corresponded to those midway along the landings underneath. Another windowless little passage was lined by doors. At the end the servants' staircase still wound up towards the attics. Kay pulled at the double leaves of a large cupboard.

"This one's almost a room,' she said. "Clifford pretends it *was* one—that somebody's maid had to sleep here. It really isn't worse than some of the basement rooms."

In the shadows cast by the light she had turned on, the cupboard seemed indeed the size of a small room. Although it contained several trunks, a damaged chair, a parrot-cage and assorted cardboard boxes, to say nothing of golf-clubs, a pair of waders, alpenstocks, ice-picks, coils of rope and a number of old garments on hangers, it was far from crowded. It would have enchanted Mrs. Tuke, who held a poor view of such accommodation in modern flats.

Kay was closing the doors when she stooped to peer into a dark corner. Retrieving an object from the floor, she stared at it as it dangled in her hand.

"How on earth did this get here?" she said.

CHAPTER VI

MISS KITTREDGE IS SCARED

THE OBJECT was a bathing-cap of green oiled silk.

"When Corinne had just had her hair set," Kay explained, still with a puzzled frown, "she always wore a bathing-cap in the bath. But I don't know what it's doing in this cupboard. There's nothing here she would come for."

She stooped to peer again, touched the cupboard floor with her finger-tips, and abruptly stood erect and closed the doors sharply. The light above their heads cast a shadow on her face, but Mr. Tuke thought her perplexity had increased. Her swift closing of the doors had foiled his attempt to peer past her into the dark corner.

She shivered suddenly, and flung the bathing-cap on to a linen basket.

"I hate this place!" she said almost violently. "Let's go down."

Down they went, accordingly, in uneasy silence. It was this, no doubt, rather than any pricking of his thumbs or other omens, that conveyed to Mr. Tuke a strong sense of some new brooding cloud of trouble that went with them.

They had reached the final turn of the stairs above the hall when Kay stopped.

"Listen!" Then, as the sound of voices came up to them from the study, she looked at Mr. Tuke with something like dismay. "Clifford must be back," she said.

Mr. Tuke afterwards blamed himself because, at the moment, that fleeting expression merely puzzled him. Kay was a young woman of character and self-possession, whose role in this household plainly was a highly confidential one. Whatever the circumstances, to be found giving tea to some guests, or even abetting the inquisitiveness of one of them, scarcely seemed a situation likely to discompose her. Yet, as he realised later, for an instant she was more than discomposed. There was alarm, almost, in her wide eyes.

In a flash it was gone, and she was descending the stairs again. It was to that look, however, that Mr. Tuke reacted.

"I must apologise to him. It was bad taste to make you connive at my revolting curiosity. He will be rather surprised to find us here, anyway."

"Oh, Clifford won't worry," Kay said, lightly enough. She flashed Mr. Tuke another enigmatical look. "*I'm* very glad you came," she added.

It was plain to the ear, as they approached the study, that Sir Bruton had his part of the situation in hand. Nor was Mr. Tuke surprised to gather, from a species of peroration, that much of the onus of what was, after all, an intrusion, was being shuffled on to him. When the errant pair re-entered the room, it was to find that Clifford Reaveley had not come home alone. With him was the dark, florid Mr. Coverdale, contriving to look a trifle overdressed, with too much waist to his grey suit, and too much of his white cuffs showing.

"Ah, here you are, Tuke," said the Director, who was standing, waving his cigar in ample gestures. "I've been apologising for you. High time we went now."

"I can do my own apologising, thanks." Mr. Tuke smiled at Clifford Reaveley. "Insufferable of me, nosing about your house. My only excuse is, I like architectural oddities. I more or less compelled Miss Kittredge to show me a floor or two."

"That's all right," Reaveley said, and if with less than his usual bonhomie, this was not surprising. His blue eyes, staring from Mr. Tuke to Kay, betrayed nothing of his thoughts. He gave a short laugh. "Oddity's the word. I hate the place! I'm getting out as quickly as I can."

The sudden note of controlled violence was more revealing. With the tautness of his ugly, good-humoured face, and the rapid, jerky movements with which he took a cigarette from the glass box and snapped a lighter to it, it spoke of nerves still shocked and quivering. Yet there were odd contrasts. His colour was fresh, his curiously blank eyes were clear, his powerful shoulders stiff and erect under his black coat. Kay had said he blamed himself for the recent tragedy, but he scarcely carried himself like one burdened by self-reproach.

As dark as his friend was fair, and as tall, though slighter, Coverdale appeared outwardly the more shaken of the two. Mr. Tuke noted with interest that the touch of the Latin or the Jew in the man's florid good looks was accentuated. Even his predatory nose seemed longer. His brown eyes were restless, and so were his long-fingered hands. The air of swagger, of being too pleased with himself, was subdued. But he had his pleasant sympathetic smile for Kay as he said in his soft voice:

"I looked in on Clifford at the ministry, and came along with him."

"Anything I ought to see to, Kay?" Reaveley asked.

Kay seemed quite herself again, though she had looked a little startled by his outburst about the house. She smiled with tolerant understanding.

"Nothing I can't do. You're better out of the way."

Reaveley gave Mr. Tuke a shamefaced flicker of a grin.

"I'm afraid I've ratted. But, my God, I can't stand this house. I want her to go away too, but she won't . . . Why the hell," he burst out irritably again, "should we be at the beck and call of every blasted busybody, anyway? Reporters, damned silly women, the telephone going. . . ." His broad shoulders lifted in an exasperated shrug. "Sorry," he said. But it was evident he felt the need to exculpate himself, and his blue eyes sought Kay's dark ones again. "You're a trump, Kay, but look here——"

She flipped a small palm at him. "Oh, shut up, Clifford. I'm all right. If I find I can't stand it, I'll enlist Miss Plimsoll. But we're tougher than men, you know—and much more practical in a crisis."

"I sometimes wish *you* weren't," Reaveley said moodily.

Under his stare, Kay began to look faintly uncomfortable. Her colour rose. Mr. Tuke, watching Reaveley's face, the blue eyes in it no longer blank, but darkened and alive, reflected that perhaps the man had feelings, after all. He seemed oblivious of the others in the room.

In the brief silence Sir Bruton, who had been brooding over the scene with a shrewd if protuberant gaze, rolled his cigar rapidly from one side of his mouth to the other, and cleared his throat.

"Hrrrm. Well, we'll be going. Come along, Tuke. Shake a leg." He turned massively to Kay. "Anything we can do, ma'am—I've been saying the same to Mr. Reaveley—don't hesitate. Women may be tough—you ought to see my nieces—but remember we're in the telephone book, or Devonshire House will find us in the daytime."

"You're very kind," Kay said, including Mr. Tuke's saturnine visage in her warm, friendly look.

Coverdale uttered an exclamation. "Did you say your name was *Kames*, sir?"

"Probably, Mr. Coverdale. Because it is."

"I didn't realise. But Devonshire House. . . . Sir *Bruton* Kames? The Director of Public Prosecutions?"

"Professionally, Mr. Coverdale, professionally." The Director leered amiably. "But as a friend I drop into poetry, so to speak. Or to tea—eh, Miss Kittredge?"

And with a chuckle, which was now perhaps in the faintest degree sinister, he trundled towards the door. Reaveley was quick to accompany him, but when Kay followed with Mr. Tuke, Coverdale remained in the study, and, from Harvey's farewell glimpse of him, in a brown study of his own.

Kay's small pale face and slender black figure, beside the taller and heavier bulk of Clifford Reaveley in the doorway of No. 7a, was the last memory the visitors took away with them as they turned the corner. In Lancaster Terrace a disengaged taxi was slowing up for the traffic lights. As Mr. Tuke hailed it, he said:

"Will you come back with me?"

"I want some sherry. Is your wife at home?"

"No. But when she comes in I want her to do something."

"I was thinking the same," said Sir Bruton, and Mr. Tuke glanced at him curiously. Though the old boy would have snorted at the phrase, they seemed to be more than usually *en rapport* that afternoon.

"A bit pointed, weren't you?" he remarked, as the taxi turned into the park through Victoria Gate. "Why drag in Devonshire House?"

The Director's chuckle was definitely malignant. "Thought I'd shake 'em up a bit. General principles. Not only that. I saw the gal's face as she came in. What was she scared of?"

Mr. Tuke looked at his chief with as much respect as he ever permitted himself to show.

"You spotted it, did you? I couldn't see her face then. She looked at me on the stairs as though Reaveley's arrival had given her a jolt. But she said she was expecting him."

"Not till we'd gone, perhaps."

"No, I don't think it was that."

"Anything happen upstairs?"

"She found Mrs. Reaveley's bathing-cap in a cupboard where it should not have been. There was nothing else——" Mr. Tuke corrected himself. "Bar the sponge, of course. But she doesn't know about that."

"Whose sponge? And what about it?"

"I'll tell you when I've made an experiment with my own. How did Reaveley react to finding you on his divan?"

"I wouldn't know," said Sir Bruton. "Poker-faced feller, isn't he? A bit stiff, but polite enough."

"It would stiffen anybody. Did he know who you were?"

"Dunno. Told him my name." Scattering ash about the cab, the Director added sourly: "That ought to have been enough, dammit. I'm somebody, even if I don't get my name in the papers. And I suppose he knows all about *you*?"

"He may not have known, until now. I doubt if anyone at the dinner party, except Cartwright, knew or cared what I was. The others are rather outside our orbit. Cartwright evidently told Miss Kittredge, but she and Reaveley have had more urgent things to discuss. And who am I, or you, for that matter, to excite public interest?"

"People mix us up with the police," said Sir Bruton, with

another sinister chuckle. "I've been distinctly *persona non grata* at a dinner party before now. I won't say a skeleton at the feast—it don't go with my figure. But if that poker-faced feller didn't know who I was till his semitic looking pal asked me, he bore up well. Didn't bat an eyelid. Unlike Coverdale."

"Yes, I thought he became rather *distrait*," Mr. Tuke said. "But why should either of them bat eyelids?"

Sir Bruton settled his massive shoulders more comfortably in the angle of the seat.

"That," he said, "is what you're going to tell me."

The taxi swung round the curve south of the Magazine. They were passing the Serpentine again. The Cockpit and the isolated ash tree flashed by. Mr. Tuke thought once more of Wally Whichcord, sitting higher up the slope in the night-time and seeing the phantom walk down it to the ash and vanish.

"Snap out of it," said the Director. "I told you you might have tumbled into something. That's what comes of dining outside your ruddy orbit. You and that gal were up to some game. She wasn't the only one whose face gave her away. When you look like a Doré illustration to the *Inferno* you've got some dirty trick up your sleeve. You're gloating over it now. Cough it up."

Mr. Tuke's satanic features were indeed at that moment uncommonly grim. From Wally Whichcord, Sir Bruton's words sent his thoughts back to Lancaster Gate. He saw again Kay's scared look, and now suddenly the dim presage which, as in the old rhyme, had led him upstairs, downstairs, and in my lady's chamber, began to assume substance and meaning. Factors hitherto unrelated fell together, and the whole picture which resulted shocked and alarmed him.

"I'm not gloating," he said. "Far from it. I'm a bit scared myself. I'm thinking of that cupboard. It's a very large cupboard. It would hold several bodies."

PART THREE

SATURDAY, SUNDAY

"Furthermore, herein will be found mythology, necromancy, biography, topography, history, theology, phrenology, anatomy, legal ingenuity, affecting anecdotes, etc., etc."

The Mysterious Murder of Maria Martin.

CHAPTER I

MR. TUKE MEDDLES

HARVEY TUKE's routine appearances in court seldom made news; and a good many years had passed since certain extra-official activities got his name, and even his photograph, into the papers, thus providing Sir Bruton Kames with a perennial cautionary theme. On one or two later occasions, however, Mr. Tuke had gratuitously meddled (to quote the Director again) in conundrums which came his way out of office hours.[1] A taste for meddling was thus perhaps whetted. He himself liked to call it a *flair*. The Assistant Commissioner shared Sir Bruton's preference for the English word; but even Wray, if like the Tuscans he forbore to cheer, admitted grudgingly that these meddlings, more by luck than judgment, had proved helpful.

Had Wray himself been available on the morning, that of Saturday, after the tea party in Lancaster Terrace, Mr. Tuke would have sought him out. There were things he ought to know, as the Director now fully agreed. But Wray was out of town; and though the Central Office knows nothing of week-ends, matters still of so much conjecture, not to say guess-work, were better filed until his return on Monday. They did not seem to be urgent.

Mr. Tuke had plenty of other things to do that morning. The previous afternoon having been encroached on, work which should have been done then had to be got through now. There was so much of it that an appointment with Mr. Draycott, the Treasury Counsel, arranged for mid-day, had to be postponed until after lunch. This caused Mr. Draycott no particular vexation, for he was at home with a sprained ankle; but Mr. Tuke was less pleased. He liked his Saturday afternoons as well as the next man.

[1] "Death Wears a Mask." "Too Many Cousins."

And with all this, the things which the Assistant Commissioner ought to know about 7a Lancaster Terrace refused to be filed. They haunted Mr. Tuke's mind, amid sinister implications. He was far from happy about the present state of affairs in that house. He was mystified to the point of irritation by the whole business of the ghost. The brief press paragraphs on the previous day's inquest on Wally Whichcord's remains merely bore out Fenne's report; the ghost had not been raised (except in passing by *The Morning News*), nor anything else of interest. The speedy adjournment might mean that Mr. Akers, the coroner, had something up his sleeve, or hoped to have something next time; but this was small comfort at the moment, when Mr. Tuke, in spite of logical arguments to the contrary, had a nagging suspicion that matters might be urgent, after all. He could not say why, and this irritated his tidy mind still further. And even Sir Bruton was not there to be consulted: like Wray, he was out of town.

One thing, however, sometimes leads to another in an almost providential way; and the afternoon's appointment was to lure Mr. Tuke straight back into the tangled case of the Hyde Park Ghost. For remembering that Mr. Draycott's house was in Albert Road, St. John's Wood, it occurred to him that Albert Road led to Camden Town, where, according to Fenne, lived Wally Whichcord's sister. Here was a leading, if ever there was one. And this train of thought evoking further ideas, Mr. Tuke, smiling happily if fiendishly, decided to let his *flair* have its head. His chief clerk, Chaffinch, was set to work on the telephone. The Coroner's Officer at the court in Horseferry Road supplied Mrs. Boyle's address, and Fenne was run to earth in bed. The reporter was induced to part with the names of certain public houses in the Paddington area lately used by Wally Whichcord, and on the understanding that he would not be forgotten, even agreed to curb his professional interest in these inquiries.

In the triangular district of immense terraces, now mostly converted into flats, lodgings and hotels, which is bounded by Bayswater Road, Edgeware Road, and Praed Street, a few streets of shops cater for the inhabitants of these warrens.

Just after one o'clock Mr. Tuke was disgusting a fastidious palate with a glass of something called sherry in a public bar in Spring Street, near Paddington Station. He judged that Wally Whichcord's boon companions would not be found in the saloon. He could be a good mixer when he chose, and the talents which had induced Miss Plimsoll to reveal considerably more than she intended were not called upon with the easy-going regulars in the bar. Everyone there who had known Wally was ready to talk about him, for he had plainly been a popular character. One customer, for old lang syne, as he quaintly put it, had attended the previous day's inquest. For some time, however, nothing new emerged beyond a fuller picture of Wally himself.

He appeared as a companionable little man with a smattering of education, unorthodox habits, and an inveterate dislike of regular work, who had contrived a living by means not always too respectable, as can be done by the resourceful in a city like London. He admitted having been in the hands of the police for petty offences. His unorthodoxy came out in his liking for spending his nights in the open air when season and weather permitted. He boasted of gypsy blood, and said he had tramped all over England when younger. In middle life he had gravitated to London, and to that part of London where, besides less innocent attractions for those who live by their wits, one can still walk for miles over grass and beneath trees. And of all this green oasis in a desert of houses, Hyde Park drew Wally like a magnet. He came to know every yard of it, and to be known himself to every keeper and every policeman from the rural station by the Ring. Since his inquisitive eyes missed none of the many queer things that befell within their view, it was believed that selected services from time to time—Wally had his own code—had perhaps purged past misdemeanours.

From this preamble, gossip in the bar was led easily to the topic of the ghost. No one now present had been there in the eventful September of 1940, but the story of Wally's first encounter with the phantom was well known. He had always been ready to talk about it to newcomers. And the barman and two others were witnesses of his excited entry one morning, now nearly three weeks ago, with news that he had seen the ghost once more. The little man, they agreed, was somewhat shaken. Time, and the repetition of a popular tale, had dulled whatever misgivings he felt seven years earlier, after Mrs. Demarest's complement to his nocturnal adventure came to his ears. But it was one thing to hold forth airily on so old a theme, and another to see again that figure in naval uniform materialise in the dim light—this time the moon was in its last quarter, and there were no searchlights—walk noiselessly away, and vanish into air as before. Wally Whichcord was not happy about it, and jests on the subject raised only perfunctory smiles. He found money for two double whiskies, instead of his usual mild and bitter, and then departed moodily.

He was seen in the bar only once again. He came in one evening about a week before his death. Now his mood had changed; jokes were taken in better part, but absently. Unusually reserved and thoughtful, he was not to be drawn into talk. He took his pint to a corner, where he sat brooding and watching the door, eyeing each newcomer as though he were waiting for someone. But nobody joined him, and after half an hour he went out.

From this behaviour it followed that his story, as now reported, wanted the detail of his previous adventure in the supernatural. The small touches that gave verisimilitude, the moonlight on peaked cap and brass buttons, references to this tree and that, were lacking. It was clear only, as Fenne had said, that the general venue of this encounter was that same slope by the Cockpit where the ghost had loomed and vanished seven years before.

Judging he had gleaned all that he could here, Mr. Tuke soon took himself off, abandoning half his sherry. From Spring Street he turned down Craven Road, where the line of Praed Street falls to the dip of the Westbourne. He entered another public bar. Playing for safety, and ordering brandy, he applied the same technique, and a sympathetic allusion to Wally Whichcord evoked the same instant response. The little man had been well known here too. Here again, however, those now in the bar knew the old story of the ghost only from later repetitions, while none of them, except the barmaid, had been at hand when Wally described his second meeting with it. As in Spring Street, this had been on the day of the occurrence, but in the evening. From the barmaid's account, Wally had by then pulled himself together, though he was quieter than usual, and, she noted, had a whisky before his beer. But in telling the story to one or two cronies he was ready enough to bandy chaff about it. The barmaid, being busy, could not give it the attention she would have liked—an omission, in view of poor Wally's fate, she now regretted. "It must have been a warning," she said. "Makes you think, don't it? What with gunmen and ghosts, a girl's scared to be out alone of nights. You won't see *me* in the park again, after dark, I give you *my* word."

Again, therefore, the oft-told tale lacked precision. For though Wally was in the bar two or three times afterwards, his behaviour in Spring Street was here repeated—with an interesting development. A client in a cloth cap took up the narrative, and told how the little man had changed within a week. When next in the bar, he did not seem to want to talk about the ghost, or indeed about anything, which was most unlike him. When spoken to, he answered absently, his mind elsewhere; he often withdrew to a corner, to be alone; and his eye was always on the door, watching all who came in.

"It must have been the next time," the man in the cloth cap said to the barmaid, "that 'e began to ask after that there Joe."

"He didn't ask me," said the barmaid. "I know half a dozen Joes, anyway."

"A little chap, the size of Wally," said the man, "bandy-legged, and wears a blue cap and a blue scarf wiv white dogs on it. You'll know 'im, Miss."

"Oh, that one," said the barmaid. "I haven't seen him for a week or two."

Mr. Tuke asked idly: "Who is this particular Joe?"

"Dunno who 'e *is*," said the man in the cap. "'E's in 'ere now and then. Not regular, like. 'E's one of them quiet ones—keeps 'isself *to* 'isself. He come in wiv another chap oncet, and 'is mate called 'im Joe."

"He's Gas, Light and Coke," a second man put in.

"That he ain't," said a third. "Water Board, or something. Or maybe it's the railway."

"Finish your beer," Mr. Tuke said to the man in the cap, "and have one with me. Did Whichcord and this man Joe ever get together, do you know?"

"I don't mind if I do," said the man in the cap. "Aye, they got together, all right. Ten days ago it must be now. This Joe 'e come in, and Wally 'opped up and spoke to 'im, and stood 'im a pint, and they went off to that table in the corner, and 'ad reg'lar pow-wow. Last I saw of 'em, they had some bit of paper out, studying it, like."

"I was here," said one of the other men. "It was a map they was looking at, with streets and things on it. Taken from a book, I'd say."

"Well, I 'ad to go," said the man in the cap. "It was the last I seed of Wally, too."

"Same here," the second man added, shaking his head with a vague air of valediction. "Him and this Joe went off together, and I never set eyes on him again."

No more could be elicited from customers or barmaid. Wally, the latter thought, had been in the bar once again, but alone. Of the bandy-legged Joe all that emerged was a general impression that he was employed by some public utility concern. His surname, and everything else about him, remained a mystery.

This well being dredged dry for the moment, Mr. Tuke lingered only a few minutes longer. He played with the idea of visiting a third bar mentioned by Fenne; but there are limits of self-sacrifice in the best of causes. It was now a quarter to two, and he took his way to the Great Western Hotel for lunch.

CHAPTER II

MRS. BOYLE CALLS IT GAMMON

SOON AFTER four o'clock Mr. Tuke left the shabby old house where Mr. Draycott, a confirmed praiser of times past, lived amid their relics and memorials. To right and left Albert Road stretched its dreary arc alongside the Regent's Canal. Beyond that sunken waterway the peaks of the Mappin Terraces rose among the autumnal trees of Regent's Park against a sky within the last hour turned wild and menacing. Animal sounds from the Zoo added their melancholy note to the depressing scene.

Mr. Tuke was without his car because he had left home that morning unprepared for a journey to these high latitudes. Happily he secured a taxi which had just shed its fares at the Zoo, and having looked up his destination on the map was able to direct the driver, who had never heard of Garnett Street, N.W.5. Beyond the sordid road junction at Camden Town Station they entered a grisly region which wore a dreadful uniform of greyness. Grey bricks, grey stucco, grey tiles, grey faces at grey windows, merged in a camouflage of sullen dilapidation with the grey of a premature twilight. For the uncertain sun now disappeared for good, and a dark pall overhead indicated that the weather was at length about to catch up with the Air Ministry's forecast of three days ago.

Among railways and small factories they found Garnett Street. It was as drab as the rest; but No. 23, where Mrs. Boyle lived, though its London stock was sooty, its mortar perishing, and its stucco flaking, made a brave attempt to rise to higher things. Its front door was a crude but heartening green, the brass knocker was polished, and the window curtains were freshly washed. Mr. Tuke, eyeing the leaden cloud, ordered the taxi to wait; and two small boys, a small girl, a dog and several cats watched him ply the gleaming knocker. At the sound, more grey disembodied faces materialised like wraiths at neighbouring dingy windows.

From within the house came a patter of footsteps, almost at a run. The door opened about twelve inches, and a little dark woman with a sharp nose and an incipient beard on her equally sharp chin fixed a penetrating look on the caller's shoes and said curtly, without looking up:

"No, not to-day."

She had already begun to close the door when something in the appearance of the shoes provoked second thoughts. Her eyes travelled up Mr. Tuke's long form and paused at his face. Circumstances combining to render this peculiarly devilish, the little woman blinked, and stared again.

"Mrs. Boyle?" Mr. Tuke inquired.

"That's my name," she said aggressively.

"I want to ask you a few questions about your brother."

"Who are you?"

"My name is Tuke."

"Never heard of you."

"I don't suppose you have. May I come in?"

"Why?"

"To ask the questions I referred to."

"You can ask them here. *I've* nothing to be ashamed of." Mrs. Boyle snapped out her words like machine-gun bullets. Her shrewd eyes studied Mr. Tuke suspiciously, but now with a puzzled air. "Where are you from? If it's about one of his games, it's no good your coming to me."

"I'm from the Department of Public Prosecutions, but that is beside the point," Mr. Tuke said. "This is a private errand. I am merely curious. About ghosts."

"I thought your shoes didn't look like one of Wally's shady friends." Mrs. Boyle confirmed first impressions by another glance at them. "Bespoke—I can see that. My husband was a shoemaker. Public Prosecutions, eh? Something to do with divorce? No, that's the King's Proctor—I knew there was a P in it—*and* the Admiralty, if you can tell me why. Anyway, Wally was no lady-killer, whatever he was. Ghosts, did you say? Gammon, you mean." Her eyes fell on the interested audience of small children, about to be reinforced by a slatternly woman, and she added in her abrupt way: "Oh, well, come in. You look respectable. Quite a change for this street. That your cab?"

"Yes. It will wait. I shan't keep you long."

Mrs. Boyle shrugged bony shoulders. "It's your money, if you like to throw it away."

Closing the door smartly on the disappointed onlookers, she led the way at a smart trot through a dark little hall, where the linoleum shone and felt like glass.

"My own house," she snapped over her shoulder as she opened the door of the front sitting-room. "Or I wouldn't be living here. Would you? Of course you wouldn't. You needn't try to be polite. This neighbourhood's gone down something shocking. I keep to myself, and they don't like it. Pah! Let them do the other thing. There, sit down. I can't bear people standing about like mummies."

A first glance at the sitting-room explained how even Garnett Street could be made endurable. It was comfortable and scrupulously neat. What light there was filtered through the net curtains on to mahogany polished until it added a lustre of its own. Michaelmas daisies filled a vase on the table. Shelves of well-worn books, Goss china, photographs in plush or silver frames, a match-container resembling a pig and inscribed "Scratch Me", a clock suspended in a model of the Eiffel Tower, an overmantel with as many pinnacles as St. Pancras Station, oleographs and prints of "The Soul's Awakening" and "Dignity and Impudence"—this handful from a host of ornaments recalled to Mr. Tuke the house in Albert Road he had so recently left. They brought to mind, too, the rooms still unaltered at 7a Lancaster Terrace. Parks and the late Victorian era seemed to be his portion just now.

Mrs. Boyle had seated herself across the table from her visitor, with the air of preparing to conduct a business interview. She now, however, said unexpectedly:

"Smoke, if you want to."

Mr. Tuke explained that he only smoked cigars.

"Well, what's wrong with them? I like the smell. If I could afford it, I'd hire a man to walk in front of me smoking a good cigar." She gave a sudden short laugh, like a bark. "Wouldn't that knock 'em in the High Street?"

With the rapidity that marked all her movements she sprang up again and flew to the door. An immense tabby cat, its tail vertical, stalked in and glared malevolently at Mr. Tuke.

"Called after Joe Stalin," Mrs. Boyle explained. "Because he's got such large feet."

Among human weaknesses usually well concealed, Mr. Tuke liked cats, much preferring them to dogs, which animals he thought stupid, slavish and noisy; and Joe Stalin, approaching cannily to investigate, was tickled so voluptuously behind the ear that he jumped heavily on the caller's knees. Discovering immediately that these were neither adequate nor soft, he leapt down again and retired beneath a chair, his broad back to the company. Mrs. Boyle had re-seated herself, and while Mr. Tuke lighted a cigar her sharp eyes, set deeply in her sharp little face, were once more studying him.

"Well, what about these questions of yours?" she demanded. "You don't look the sort who'd know Wally."

"I never met him. I would like," Mr. Tuke added formally, "to express my sympathy."

"What's done, can't be mended." Mrs. Boyle shrugged again and waited.

Harvey drew on his cigar. "I believe you saw your brother from time to time?"

She uttered her little bark of a laugh. "From time to time," she repeated sarcastically. "Yes, when he wanted something."

"Had he been here lately?"

"He was here last week—a week yesterday, it was. Mind you," said Mrs. Boyle aggressively, "I don't have to pay rent, and my husband put a bit by, and I got a bit more from my Aunt Sarah at Market Deeping—I'm one of the idle rich, *I* am." She barked again. "That's another thing they don't like about me round here. If you've twopence to rub together, they call you a parasite. Pah! They wouldn't know the word if it wasn't for these silly meetings they go to. What I mean is, I didn't grudge Wally the money, in reason. He was my brother, say what you like." She looked defiantly at Mr. Tuke, who had said nothing. "I'd have liked him to come, just now and then, when he *didn't* want something. But he wouldn't think of that. Men are all alike. Lumps of selfishness. Look at Joe. He'd walk out to-morrow if I didn't fill his fat stomach."

Joe laid his ears back and turned his head to give his mistress a green and baleful glance. Mr. Tuke said:

"What interests me, as I mentioned, is this story of your brother's about a ghost. You appear to have heard it."

Mrs. Boyle made a contemptuous noise. "Oh, I've heard it, all right. Years ago, it began, when there was that piece in the paper about it. Pleased as Punch, Wally was, over that. Carried it about with him, and pulled it out to show everyone. Ghost, my foot, I said to him. Gammon, I said, if you ask *me*."

"You don't believe in ghosts?"

The little woman did not answer directly. "Don't tell me *you* do?" she said.

"I believe in evidence," Mr. Tuke replied once again. "Your brother saw something, and he was not the only one who saw it. Didn't he come to believe in it himself?"

Mrs. Boyle plucked at her bearded chin. Her sharp little face, which contrived to resemble both nut and nut-crackers, so wrinkled and brown and pointed was it, was screwed up in an expression mingled of disbelief and doubt.

"After the last time, he did," she said.

"After its second appearance to him, a fortnight or three weeks ago?"

She nodded in her quick way. "He came straight here, that very morning, before I'd even had breakfast. He hadn't condescended for a couple of months. Quite in a twitter he was—not like Wally. Whatever he saw, it gave him a turn. Of course he'd come for money—to buy himself a stiff whisky or two, he told me as bold as brass."

"Did he describe what he had seen?"

"Two or three times over," said Mrs. Boyle. "Seemed like he couldn't get it out of his mind."

When prompted, however, her version of Wally Whichcord's story was no more helpful than those Mr. Tuke had already heard that day in public bars. The figure in naval uniform had come and gone as mysteriously as it had come and gone seven years before. One moment it was there, walking across the grass in the night-time, the next, *non erat inventus*. Mrs. Boyle's knowledge of Hyde Park was too superficial for her to recognize the scene described, but, like other hearers, she gathered that the apparition had repeated its previous performance in every respect. This, indeed, was what shook Wally. He kept nagging at the question Mr. Tuke himself had put—why did the thing pick on *him*? Why, having lain low for seven years—for had it materialized in the interim he must have heard—why did it then choose, out of all the hundreds of acres in the park, the same one of his haunts (it seemed he had others) for its return? On the earlier occasion, said Mrs. Boyle, confirming the evidence of the public bars, Wally had soon forgotten his alarms. It was worth while meeting a ghost to get in the papers and become a popular raconteur. But this duplication was another pair of shoes. The theory of a Warning got hold of him.

"And he was seven years older," said his sister tolerantly. "That life of his didn't do him any good. Don't you tell *me*. A man of sixty-four sleeping out in damp grass like a cow. And a bedroom waiting here for him. Oh, he'd use it in the winter when he couldn't pay for a bed—but only when he couldn't. That was Wally. No decent family feeling, except to touch you for a bob or two. Why I put up with him, I don't know."

Her expression defied Mr. Tuke to probe into this.

"Your brother must have been pretty tough," he observed. "The gypsy strain, perhaps? Or isn't there one?"

Mrs. Boyle snorted. "Gypsy, indeed! I saw that in the paper. Gammon! Just one of Wally's silly lies. *I* told him off about it. Gypsy! There isn't a sounder stock in all Kesteven, where we come from."

Mr. Tuke was looking round for an ashtray, and she bounced indignantly from her chair to fetch a lustre dish round the rim of which were the words, "Use ME, not the Carpet." This she banged in front of him. "Gypsy!" she muttered, and Joe Stalin turned a green eye on her.

"How was your brother the next time you saw him?" Mr. Tuke asked.

"I didn't see him again, not till yesterday week. Oh, he was all right then, so far as I could see. He didn't give me much of his precious time. Just popped in, long enough to wheedle a ten bob note out of me. Full of one of his schemes, he was. Going to make a fortune, and repay all I'd given him with five per cent interest, and I don't know what. As if he ever kept an account! I have, though. I never expected it back," said Mrs. Boyle belligerently, "and I wouldn't want it back, but I've got a conscience, like anybody else. When I think I ought to have done this and that for Wally, I look up what he's had out of me. It's a comfort, in a way—now."

"I'm sure you have been extremely long-suffering," Mr. Tuke remarked. "What sort of scheme had your brother in mind, if one may ask?"

Mrs. Boyle tightened her lips. "The less said about that, the better," she said tartly—the more tartly, perhaps, because of her betrayal of feeling. "Not that I listened. I know Wally's games. A disgrace to the family, and so I've told him. He was up in the air about it, that's all I know. An annuity, was the word he used. And something about stubbing his toe on it. Easy Street for the rest of his life, he said. Then off he went, and I didn't see him again. Not till yesterday. . . ."

She sniffed suddenly and loudly, and then whisked out a handkerchief and dabbed rapidly at her eyes, immediately afterwards fixing Mr. Tuke with a fierce if slightly watery stare that dared him to take any notice. The room had been growing steadily darker, and now a diversion outside took Mrs. Boyle's thoughts from the mortuary in Paddington where Wally Whichcord's dream of Easy Street had come to an end.

"Here's the rain," she said.

The heavens had opened upon Garnett Street. Reminded of the waiting taxi, Mr. Tuke rose and collected his hat.

"Did your brother say anything more about the ghost?"

"Not a word." With a final sniff, Mrs. Boyle had risen with him. "Much too full of his precious annuity, whatever he meant by that."

"You weren't questioned about the ghost at the inquest, apparently."

"The coroner had too much sense," said Mrs. Boyle, quite herself again. "If he'd ever heard of it."

"Did you mention this annuity business?"

"Certainly not. I wasn't asked, and I held my tongue. Wouldn't you? It was something I'd be ashamed of, I'll be bound. I knew Wally. The coroner asked me how he made a living—very nice about it, he was—and I said beyond what he'd got out of me, I didn't know."

Pausing to tickle Joe Stalin, who had also got up, apparently with some idea of speeding the parting guest, Mr. Tuke made for the door. In the dark little hall, now so black that Mrs. Boyle switched on a light, she suddenly put a hand on his arm.

"Tell me this," she said. "How did Wally come to get drowned like that?"

Mr. Tuke looked down at her wrinkled, nut-like face. In the cold light of the electric bulb she was old and tired. He realised that Wally Whichcord must have been by some years the younger of the two.

"I don't know," he replied gently.

For a moment her eyes, as they held his, filled again. She dashed her worn hand angrily across them.

"Don't tell me it was suicide," she said. "I wouldn't believe it if the angel Gabriel came down and said so. He wouldn't know Wally like I do. And if it wasn't suicide, what was it? Fell into the water? Gammon!"

"I don't know," Mr. Tuke said again, watching her.

She blinked rapidly. "I shall take a lodger," she announced inconsequently. "There's no reason why Wally's room should stand idle any longer. *He* won't want it. A lodger'll be company. A man, of course. I won't have women. Joe will like another man about the house. Well, it's nice to have seen you, even if you did only want to ask questions." She opened the front door upon the pouring rain. "I'd like to ask a few," she said. She looked up into Mr. Tuke's dark face, now unusually sympathetic. "Public Prosecutions, you said, didn't you? That's something to do with the police. Ask 'em how Wally got into that water. Annuity? Gammon! I know Wally. Good-bye."

The green door slammed behind Mr. Tuke as he ran for the taxi.

CHAPTER III

SYMPOSIUM ON THE HISTORIC PRESENT

THE RAIN continued into the night, causing a further fall in a temperature already low for that ideal September which exists only in the graphs of meteorologists; and when, shortly after noon on Sunday, Mrs. Tuke left the *Institut Français* in Queensberry Place and emerged into Cromwell Road, under a blue sky a cool wind was ruffling the trees before the Natural History Museum and blowing leaves along the pavement, and she was thankful for her furs. By one of those conjunctions in time and space which impress one with a sense of causal connection, at the moment when she looked about her for a taxi, Gordon Cartwright was crossing the road towards her. They met with appropriate expressions of surprise, and the novelist explained that after paying a call at 7a Lancaster Terrace he had walked back across Kensington Gardens. This of course brought up the tragedy which had occurred since their last meeting. Kay Kittredge, said Cartwright presently, was now entertaining a distant and tiresome Demarest relation who had come to condole and stayed to lunch. A certain relish in his tone as he added that Clifford Reaveley had been haled from his club to do his share of the work suggested that Miss Kittredge was becoming less willing to be imposed upon.

Cartwright seemed rather careworn himself, and Yvette, in the informal way she had learnt among the English, asked him to tea that afternoon. On her way home it occurred to her that Kay, to whom at a hint from Mr. Tuke a general offer of help and hospitality had already been extended, might be invited too. The call to Lancaster Terrace had been put through when her husband, who was present, interposed.

"Ask her for Miss Plimsoll's telephone number."

This being supplied, after Kay had gratefully accepted the invitation, Yvette raised her eyebrows.

"Am I to ask Miss Plimsoll too? Must my tea parties be turned into Roman holidays? Or do I mean busmen's?"

"We may as well have a symposium while we are about it. If Miss P. is willing, I'll call for her with the car."

Mrs. Tuke, being in a classical mood, murmured something about Greek gifts as she dialled the number of the boarding house near Queen's Road which was now Miss Plimsoll's home. That lady was there, and after polite skirmishing said she would be delighted to come. She declined transport. She always walked in the Gardens in the afternoon, and train or omnibus would bring her to Westminster.

Cartwright was the first of what Yvette called the unconscious victims to enter her charming drawing-room, where the furniture was a happy association of Hepplewhite and Louis Quatorze, and the wallpaper a copy, in a pastel shade of pink, of a Toile de Jouy print of the Four Seasons. Mr. Tuke emerged from his study, and conversation at first turned inevitably on Corinne Reaveley's tragic end. But Mr. Tuke, his eye on the time, soon diverted it by a sympathetic reference to Kay Kittredge.

"Yes, I'm worried about Kay," Cartwright said, his intelligent face, with its somehow incongruous toothbrush moustache, drawn into lines of irritable anxiety. "I want to get her out of that house. I've even tried the selfish tack—pointed out that all this is interfering with my work. She's worried too, you know, though I can't get her to say why. I've a feeling that something's happened in the last day or two." He looked curiously at Mr. Tuke, who, however, was not to be drawn, since Miss Kittredge herself saw fit to withhold explanations. "She admits now that she hates the place," Cartwright went on. "And she's making Reaveley toe the line, instead of letting him hide in his club and inventing excuses for him. I can't stand the fellow! I haven't seen him since the dinner, but Kay says he was good enough to look in on Friday, when you were there. How was he taking it all? What did you make of him?"

To this sudden burst of candour Mr. Tuke replied cautiously that Clifford Reaveley knew how to conceal his feelings, and, the visitor being in this mood, went on to pump him tactfully for information about the young engineer. But not much came out, since Cartwright only met Corinne and her husband after Kay Kittredge went to run their house for them. His dislike of Reaveley was obviously a recent growth, and simply explained. Its roots, however, went a little deeper.

"You know how it is," he said, with a smile at Yvette, for their meeting that morning underlined his theme. "I'd barely met Reaveley when we clashed again somewhere. Then he took to coming to the Savage with Crookes, the actor, and I was always finding him there. Then one day I ran across a fellow in the same ministry, and heard a few things. Oh, I didn't fish for them"—Cartwright's tone implied distaste for the whole subject,—"but I happened to mention Reaveley. All it came to was that he always has some girl in tow. I knew from Kay that he and his wife went their own ways, so it was no business of mine, until at that dinner. . . ."

He hesitated, and Mrs. Tuke finished for him.

"One must admit that Mr. Reaveley kept looking at Miss Kittredge with a certain *empressement*."

Cartwright smiled wryly. "As obvious as that, was it? Well, having seen him putting on the same act with another girl at the Cordova only a week ago, I thought it a bit thick. It explained a lot, too. Kay tries to see the best in everyone, and she was always saying how kind the Reaveleys were, but I'd begun to realise that she wasn't too happy there. I put it down to Corinne—*de mortuis* notwithstanding, she was completely selfish—but on Wednesday evening I tumbled to the real trouble."

"The Cordova is not cheap," Mr. Tuke remarked.

"My publisher took me," Cartwright said with a smile.

"I am wondering how Mrs. Reaveley liked paying for the entertainment of other women. Reaveley can hardly do much of it on his salary as a civil servant. He must be quite junior. Of course he came into some money seven years ago, I'm told."

The novelist shrugged. "Corinne had the virtues of her defects, Kay says. Her philosophy was live and let live, and she was free with her money. And there was a marriage settlement, I believe. But I fancy Reaveley has got through that, and anything else he had. The man I spoke of hinted pretty broadly——" Cartwright checked himself with a little grimace. "I might be in a ministry myself. Scandal-mongering holes. . . ."

"Well, let us batten on some other reputation," Mr. Tuke suggested. "Mr. Coverdale's, for instance."

But Cartwright knew even less about Gervase Coverdale. The latter was unmarried, and had been a friend, or acquaintance, of Clifford Reaveley's since pre-war days.

"And of Mrs. Reaveley's too?" Mr. Tuke said.

"Well, I suppose he would be."

"That was an odd little scene between them at dinner."

The writer nodded, but before this subject could be pursued Miss Plimsoll was announced. With an exact appreciation of the right dress for every contingency, Miss Plimsoll wore a sort of half mourning of black with touches of grey, expressing her position in, but not of, the family. Salutations were exchanged in an extremely genteel atmosphere; and, immediately after, tea and Kay Kittredge followed. Kay looked white and fatigued, but her small face lighted with pleasure as well as surprise when she saw Gordon Cartwright. Her arrival, while it made the tea party appear more than ever like a plot, plainly delighted the novelist. Whatever small rift had grown between the pair was as plainly healed.

"Dear me, Gordon," said Kay, "I seem to be always falling over you. How nice to see you too, Miss Plimsoll."

"A most agreeable surprise for us all," Miss Plimsoll said. "So thoughtful of Mrs. Tuke. And so good for you, Kay dear, to get away from that dreadful house."

Kay looked at her searchingly. "Do you mean that it isn't only now that it's dreadful?"

"The tone of the house has altered completely, and for the worse, of late years," Miss Plimsoll replied. "I am sensitive to atmosphere, and it positively oppresses me. I will say no more. Clifford will be well advised, however, to get rid of it. He should not have left you alone there, and I intend to tell him so when I see him. You should let me stay with you, Kay."

For a moment, Mr. Tuke thought, the girl wavered. He was to wonder afterwards how the course of events would have been influenced by Miss Plimsoll's presence at No. 7a during the next few days and nights. But if Kay hesitated, some stubborn core in her prevailed. Her small chin was lifted, and she shook her head.

"It's sweet of you, Miss Plimsoll, but I can cope. And I'm not alone. Parker is there. The maid," she explained, turning to Mrs. Tuke. "What a charming room this is! It's got the right sort of atmosphere."

Nothing more, by common consent, was said for the time being about Kay's troubles and all that lay behind them. While she relaxed in a deep chair, Mrs. Tuke served tea, and conversation became general and innocuous. Mr. Tuke alone did not seem to be doing his share. But when he judged the girl to be somewhat rested and refreshed, a casual remark to his wife, who had recently visited her parents in Dijon, led her to describe the difficulties of travel in France, and the miracles already accomplished there in restoring railways and bridges; and before anybody (except his involuntary accomplice, who made a small face at him) quite realised how it had come about, talk had returned, by way of engineering in general, to certain engineers known to them all, and Miss Plimsoll was innocently replying to a direct question about Gervase Coverdale.

"My acquaintance with him is very slight, Mr. Tuke. I have met him a few times at Lancaster Terrace. Clifford and Corinne have been most kind in inviting me there since it ceased to be my home. Mr. Coverdale is an old friend of Clifford's, of course. They were together before the war, doing some kind of engineering, as you say. Clifford calls it plumbing, but it is on a very large scale, naturally," Miss Plimsoll explained, to remove misapprehensions raised by so sordid a word. "Something to do with our public buildings, no doubt." She cocked her neat head at Kay Kittredge. "What *was* that story, Kay, about an adventure of Mr. Coverdale's in connection with his work? Squadron Leader Garroway referred to it on Wednesday evening."

Kay looked blank. "I didn't hear anybody talk about it then, but I know what you mean. I can't remember it, though. My head's so full of other things."

"I thought Coverdale was rather under the weather when we saw him on Friday," Mr. Tuke remarked. "Natural enough, of course, in an old friend—of Mrs. Reaveley's, too."

"He was upset, of course," Kay said, with a slight air of reserve. She seemed to have awakened to the trend the conversation was taking. She frowned a little as she added in her candid way: "Now you talk of it, he did behave rather queerly after you and Sir Bruton Kames had gone. He wanted to know why you had come, and what we had talked about. He harped on it, rather."

"Meaning, had we talked about *him*?"

"Perhaps. . . . Anyway, Clifford made a silly joke about his past, and a guilty conscience—Corinne brought that up, you know, whatever it meant—and he didn't like it."

"Any knowledge of Mr. Coverdale's past, Miss Plimsoll?" Mr. Tuke inquired of that lady.

"Dear me, no." Miss Plimsoll was just a trifle distant. "I explained that I hardly know him."

Mr. Tuke's grin had that engaging touch he could impart when he wished to its sardonic norm.

"However, you are a mine of information about other things. You are our link with the historic present. For example, you must have known Mr. Reaveley for a long time."

"Certainly," Miss Plimsoll said. "Since he was a boy. Though he only came to the house occasionally. He and Felix were much the same age. When they grew up they used to go mountaineering together."

"I suppose in those days Mr. Reaveley's circumstances were rather different from Felix Demarest's?"

"Clifford's parents were none too well off," said Miss Plimsoll, withdrawing a little again. "He had to earn his living, while Felix went into the Navy."

The distinction, if somewhat confused, was clear. Gordon Cartwright smiled as he observed:

"They must have been very much alike in looks."

Miss Plimsoll was surprised. "I should not have said so, Mr. Cartwright. No, indeed. Except for the eyes, perhaps. Both had blue eyes, like Mr. Hugo Demarest. But Clifford is so very blond, and Felix had dark hair and complexion."

"I was thinking of that photo you showed me, Kay," Cartwright said to the girl. "In the family album, where they're sitting on some mountain."

"They look alike in that," Kay agreed. "Some effect of sunlight, I suppose, made Clifford's hair appear dark."

"They might have been twins," said Cartwright. "Interesting how the bony structure persists in families, while pigmentation plays all sorts of tricks."

Mr. Tuke seemed to find it interesting. A gesture from his wife reminded him that the visitors were ready to smoke. When he had fetched cigarettes, he turned again to the mine of information, who had declined one. But it was to resurrect a different topic from the historic present.

"Dip into your memories again, Miss Plimsoll. I am still curious about the family ghost."

"But I have told you all about that, Mr. Tuke."

"Not quite all, I think. There were reservations the other evening." Mr. Tuke still wore what his wife called his party smile, but his fingertips were coming together in his forensic attitude. He leaned forward. "Will you take my word for it that I have good reasons for asking these questions? Since we met last, something very shocking has happened. The case is altered, as Plowden said. And however Mrs. Reaveley came by her death, I suspect that the root of the matter may go a long way back. And about that past you know more than anybody."

Though holding a proper opinion of herself, Miss Plimsoll had diagnosed an ulterior motive behind this invitation, at short notice, from comparative strangers. And by now a fellow guest at her boarding house had thrown some light on Mr. Tuke, though an imperfect light, so that she fancied him to be a superior sort of policeman. She expected, however, nothing more than a cosy discussion of the recent tragedy, in which he and his wife would have a special interest. The presence of Kay Kittredge and Cartwright was indeed suggestive; but only now did she fully grasp the fact that a social function was becoming an investigation. She looked a little disturbed.

"I assure you, Mr. Tuke," she said, "there can be *no* connection. . . ." She hesitated, for in fact poor dear Corinne's tragic end had disinterred some unhappy misgivings about the past. She fell back on another line of defence. "And, anyway, it is all being dealt with. There will be this horrible inquest on Tuesday. Though I hope," said Miss Plimsoll, fervently and injudiciously, "there will be no raking up *there*. . . ."

"So there *is* something to rake up?"

Though the party smile had not quite faded, Miss Plimsoll underwent some of the trapped sensations of the cross-examined; and Yvette Tuke interposed firmly.

"Harvey, you are not in court." She smiled and shrugged apologetically to her guest. "You must forgive him, Miss Plimsoll. He does not know how fiendish he looks at times. But if he says he has good reasons for behaving like a bear, at least he probably has them."

"I am sure of that," said Miss Plimsoll, rallying. She composed herself, her neatly shod feet crossed, her slender veined hands on her black silk lap. "And of course, as you say, Mr. Tuke, the case is sadly altered. It is all very painful, but when I used the words 'raking up', I did not mean that there is anything to *hide*. What is it you want to know?"

CHAPTER IV

CONTINUATION OF THE SAME

MR. TUKE, since his wife's warning, had relaxed, leaning back and swinging one long leg over the other. His expression was only normally satanic. Kay Kittredge, in the depths of her chair, was listening wide-eyed. She, too, was beginning to realise that this tea party had a purpose. Cartwright, absorbed though he was, kept watching her.

"I want the ghost story again, please," Mr. Tuke said. "Including the items you left out before. Let us start at the beginning, which seems to be the crystal-gazing Madame Varché. I am not clear as to how she first came into it. Was Mrs. Demarest addicted to that sort of thing?"

"Oh, no!" said Miss Plimsoll. "She had been sceptical about it. It was only after the death of Felix that she took it up. Madame Varché was the first and only medium she went to. It was really due to Corinne——"

Kay sat up with a startled look. "Corinne?" she exclaimed. "Why, she never even hinted to me that she had anything to do with it."

"I am expressing myself badly again," said Miss Plimsoll. "Corinne herself was not at all interested in spiritualism. But her mother was."

Again Kay showed surprise. "Aunt Laura? I never knew that either. She wasn't in the old days."

"I think it only began just before the war, Kay dear, when you and your mother were living in Bournemouth."

"Aunt Laura was no letter-writer," Kay agreed. "She was always too busy about nothing to write to people. But it *is* queer that Corinne never mentioned all this. She did say once, when I asked her about the ghost, that Mrs. Demarest had been to a medium, but that was all. Of course, she never seemed to want to talk about that time."

"It was an unhappy time for us all," said Miss Plimsoll. "At any rate, your Aunt Laura *did* take up spiritualism about then. And to cut a long story short, soon after that the war began, and then, later on, when Felix's ship was lost, and the Admiralty letter came, and poor Mrs. Demarest was in a distracted state of mind, Corinne happened one day to speak of this Madame Varché, who was her mother's latest discovery. *Most* unfortunately, as I still think, but dear Corinne was sadly distressed herself, and I dare say less flippant than she had been about such things. Anyhow, the idea was planted in Mrs. Demarest's mind. She went to see your aunt, and eventually was induced to make an appointment with Madame Varché. I did my best to dissuade her," said Miss Plimsoll, turning to Mr. Tuke again. "In spite of my own remarkable experience, I still do not believe that *true* comfort can be gained by such means. But Mrs. Demarest had made up her mind."

"The séances, I suppose, were the usual sort of show?" Mr. Tuke queried. "Dark room, trances, controls, and so on?"

"The room was unlighted, Mrs. Demarest told me, except for a small red lamp. Like a photographer's dark room," said Miss Plimsoll drily. "Madame Varché went off into what she called a trance, and snored, and then spoke in different voices. It all sounded most dubious to me."

"And was one of the voices Felix Demarest's?"

"Not the first time. But an uncle of Mrs. Demarest's spoke to her. About a dictionary. He had compiled one."

Miss Plimsoll's tone was even drier. Mr. Tuke grinned.

"I gather you thought the uncle dubious too?"

"He was a famous scholar," Miss Plimsoll said, "and it did occur to me that Corinne, who of course knew about him and his dictionary, might have repeated what she heard to her mother. Kay will forgive me if I say that Mrs. Shefford, her Aunt Laura, was a sad gossip. Then, Mrs. Demarest's first séance could not be arranged for a fortnight. If Madame Varché saw Mrs. Shefford in the interval, she could perhaps have *wormed* out of her, if I may use the term, such scraps of information about the new client she was recommending."

"You may certainly use the term," said Mr. Tuke warmly. "You describe the method of these impostors with perfect accuracy. No doubt similar scraps of family history were subsequently dredged from the spirit world?"

Miss Plimsoll nodded unhappily. "That is so. I never spoke to Corinne about it. If she was the agency through which this tittle-tattle passed, it would have been unkind. But I did put my line of reasoning to Mrs. Demarest. As I think I told you, Mr. Tuke, she was at first by no means wholly convinced by Madame Varché. She was an intelligent woman, and my suggestion impressed her."

"But did not deter her?"

"There is another colloquialism for her state of mind—wishful thinking. She was clutching at straws," said Miss Plimsoll, abandoning herself recklessly to clichés. "Once this hope of somehow getting into touch with Felix had been raised, she could not forego it."

"And, somehow, she did get in touch?"

"Yes, I told you." A slight gesture on the black silk lap implied distressed bewilderment. "It was at the third séance she attended. She returned home in a state of most unhealthy excitement—you must remember she was an invalid—and said that Felix had spoken to her."

"Yes, you told me," Mr. Tuke agreed. "But when I asked you what he talked about, you evaded a reply."

He was leaning forward, his fingertips together. Miss Plimsoll continued to look ill at ease as she replied:

"He asked her to promise to look after Corinne."

"Oh, he did, did he?" Mr. Tuke's black brows went up. He caught a glance from his wife, and perhaps repressed further comment. "Well, well," was all he said. "And after this," he went on, "was Mrs. Demarest converted?"

"She would believe, and then she would doubt, Mr. Tuke."

"So she went again?"

"As she said, how could she *not* go again? There were three more séances. At two of them Felix spoke to her."

"To the same effect?"

"He spoke of other things, but each time he asked her to

make this promise about Corinne. He told her he could not rest for thinking and worrying. Something like that."

"It sounds as though his mother was not quite converted."

"Oh, she had *promised*, Mr. Tuke, from the very first—she had meant to do something for Corinne, in any case—but at these rather tawdry meetings, with other people, strangers, sitting there, she really couldn't, as she put it, discuss *business*. And it seemed a little *sordid*. . . ."

"Quite like a money-lender's office," Mr. Tuke commented. "However, it is satisfactory to know that in the next world one will retain one's practical instincts."

Yvette frowned, but Miss Plimsoll looked at him shrewdly.

"And after all, why not?" she said. "Oh, I know what you think. I had some very uncharitable ideas myself at first. You will forgive me again, Kay dear. . . . But then in the light of what happened afterwards—oh no, Mr. Tuke. Corinne's mother *may* have foolishly allowed this woman to wheedle things out of her—and that is only supposition—but anything worse. . . . Oh no! Because Felix not only spoke at these séances. That *might* have been fraud, I suppose. But he came back. I saw him."

There was a quiet finality about this. While Mr. Tuke took out his cigar-case—in his interest in Miss Plimsoll's story he had for once forgotten to smoke—he looked meditatively at this prim elderly witness of the supernatural. Kay Kittredge and the novelist sat equally spellbound, for much of what they were hearing was new to them. From Mrs. Tuke's placid air it was impossible to divine what French logic made of it all.

The cigar was lighted with Mr. Tuke's customary care.

"Now," he said through the smoke, "we come to the crux of the matter. Something more evidential than a voice in a dark room."

"Mrs. Demarest *knew* the voice," Miss Plimsoll put in. "And it used little turns of phrase Felix had used."

"I think you have in mind," Mr. Tuke said, "that according to reliable authorities, apparently genuine phenomena can be mingled with hocus-pocus." As Miss Plimsoll nodded, he went on: "Well, now for the crux—that night in September, 1940——"

"It was the thirteenth," Miss Plimsoll said. "I thought of that at the time. Seven years ago next Tuesday."

"Indeed? The Ides of September. And the inquest is on Tuesday. How tidy coincidences are sometimes."

Miss Plimsoll looked startled. Mr. Tuke seemed to ponder this particular coincidence before he continued.

"May we run over the events of that evening once more? I think you said that Mrs. Demarest had not even hinted to you that she was expecting something to happen?"

"She had not *said* a word," Miss Plimsoll replied. "But she had been to a séance that afternoon, and came back in a sadly excited state. It had been a special séance for her. No one else was there. As a rule, she told me all that had gone on. But when I asked her, she only said that Felix had spoken to her again. Then she changed the subject. It was not like her. She used to talk too much about these séances—to all her friends, and before the maid. That is how it all got about. I was disturbed by her reticence, and by her nervous condition."

"So much so, that when, during the night, you heard the front door close, and found she was gone from her room, you guessed she had left the house?"

"I suppose so. I don't remember thinking it out."

"Your reaction, anyhow, was to run upstairs to the dining-room and look out of the window?"

"It all happened very quickly. I suppose I thought that if she *had* left the house, she might still be in sight. I was not," Miss Plimsoll added with a faint smile, "exactly dressed for the street myself."

"And from the window you saw her at the corner, by the traffic lights? These were not functioning at that hour, and the street lamps were permanently out, but there was a bright moon, and diffused illumination from searchlights. Mrs. Demarest was not thirty yards away, and you saw her clearly, and also the figure of a man, dressed apparently in naval uniform—the sort worn in rough weather?"

Miss Plimsoll nodded. "I could see his cap, and beard. His coat made him look padded out—quite broad-shouldered for Felix, who was tall and thin."

"How near was he to Mrs. Demarest?"

"About as near as I am to you now, Mr. Tuke."

"A yard or two away? And they were talking together?"

"All I saw was Mrs. Demarest stretching out her hands. Then the figure turned away, and began to cross the road."

"It went straight across to the park railings?"

"Yes. I was surprised because I heard no footsteps. The windows were open, in case of blast, and the gunfire had ceased just then. You know how noises used to carry when there was no traffic. But the figure did not make a sound, though it walked fast." Miss Plimsoll paused, to add in her precise way: "It did not walk *straight* across the road. It crossed diagonally, towards the first small gate into Hyde Park, though not so far as that, of course."

A line etched itself between Mr. Tuke's black eyebrows.

"A new point," he remarked, "and a curious one. The small gate was closed, of course, like the others?"

"They were all closed. I am not likely to be mistaken," Miss Plimsoll added, "because Mrs. Demarest followed in the same direction. When *I* went out, I found her by the park railings, almost opposite the Tube station."

Mr. Tuke was still ruminating rather ferociously. He was recalling a remark made by Wray about Barrie and Kensington Gardens, and his own retort that the Assistant Commissioner sometimes talked sense without meaning to.

"Quite a diagonal," was all he said. "We need a street map, but the Tube station must be forty or fifty yards east of Lancaster Terrace. Well, now about the actual vanishing, Miss Plimsoll. You did not see the figure reach the other side of Bayswater Road?"

"I could not see whether it reached the pavement. That side of the road was in deep shadow, from the trees in the park. Mrs. Demarest said the same. She was nearer, but her sight was not as good as mine. We both lost sight of the—the figure while it was crossing."

"Mrs. Demarest was then still where you first saw her?"

"Yes, at the corner of the Terrace."

"By the time you ran out, she, too, had crossed the road. How long, do you think, had all this taken?"

"It is so many years ago," Miss Plimsoll said. "Two or three minutes altogether, I suppose, from the time I looked out of the window. I had to get my coat from the hall cupboard. Perhaps it was less. I don't know. . . ." She suddenly faltered, and put a hand to her eyes. "How it all comes back!" she said. Her voice trembled. "The empty street, and my poor friend stretching her hands through the railings, and calling, 'Felix, Felix!' . . ."

Kay moved uneasily, and Mrs. Tuke murmured:

"Poor, poor woman! Harvey, can't you stop now? This is distressing Miss Plimsoll."

"We are nearly done," Mr. Tuke said. Miss Plimsoll lowered her hand, and gave him a little nod, and he went on: "After you had induced Mrs. Demarest to return——"

"I *dragged* her back to the house, Mr. Tuke. The guns had begun to fire again."

"You seem to have acted throughout with courage and presence of mind. Well, then she told you why she had gone out, and what took place at the corner. At that afternoon's séance an appointment was made. I think that was your term. But you did not explain it. You shied off again."

"It seemed to me," said Miss Plimsoll, "the most suitable word. At the séance, the voice, speaking through Madame Varché, reproached Mrs. Demarest for still having doubts. She was greatly distressed by this—perhaps because it was true. Then Felix's voice said that if she would come out that night, after midnight, into the street, where there could be no possibility of deception, she should be convinced. Or at least he would try to appear to her. She must come alone, and tell no one beforehand. If a third person were present, or even *knew*, the conditions would be unfavourable. I am summarising what Mrs. Demarest said," Miss Plimsoll added. "She was rather incoherent. But that was the gist of it."

"And what were your reactions to this explanation?"

"What could I think? It all sounded most improbable. But there was the evidence of my own eyes."

"The eyes of the third person, who should have rendered conditions unfavourable. After the story got about, did you hear of anybody else who saw what you saw? From a neighbouring window, for example?"

Miss Plimsoll shook her head. "Most of our neighbours had left London. Those still at home were in their basements. Besides, no one else *would* see anything. . . . You see," she said earnestly, "I *could* explain my own experience. I had lived for twenty-five years with Mrs. Demarest, as a friend as well as a companion. I had known Felix since he was a baby, and I felt his loss only less deeply than she did. I had shared her thoughts, and suffered with her, and I saw with *her* eyes. That is how I thought it out. . . ."

Mr. Tuke's tone was sympathetic as he replied.

"Though plausible, your theory does not explain the case of the late Mr. Whichcord. However, before we come to him, let us finish with what happened at the corner. When Mrs. Demarest reached it, was the figure waiting for her there, or did it come from across the road, or somewhere?"

Miss Plimsoll had again shaken her head, with an air of deep perplexity, at the mention of Wally Whichcord. She passed a fragile hand once more across her eyes. She was looking tired, and Mrs. Tuke watched her solicitously.

"I never thought of asking," she said. "Mrs. Demarest, I think, used the words, 'there he was'."

"And what had he to say to her?"

"He asked her if she was now convinced. Then he made her promise once more, solemnly, always to care for Corinne. He said something about being at peace now, and then he left her. She made some movement, I suppose, because he warned her not to come any nearer, and not to follow him. It was all over, she said, in a few seconds. They must have just come together when I looked out of the window."

"However, she did follow?"

"Yes—but only after he vanished in the dark."

"She saw nothing more, and heard nothing?"

"Nothing whatever, Mr. Tuke."

There was a little pause. Mr. Tuke relaxed his intent attitude and reached for an ashtray. Miss Plimsoll seemed to be looking into the past, and she started slightly when Yvette said to her, in her pretty English:

"It was a terrible ordeal for both of you."

"It killed Mrs. Demarest," Miss Plimsoll said. "Oh, she would not have lived long, but the doctors had given her another year or two, if she took things very quietly. She refused to leave London when the bombing started, and *that* was rather wearing, of course, and then came these wretched séances to excite her, and put a further strain on her heart. And after that night she had a serious attack. She was terribly agitated. From that time she seldom left her bed." Miss Plimsoll turned to Mr. Tuke. "And as if that was not enough, there was this man Whichcord. . . ."

"Ah, yes, Whichcord. Mrs. Demarest knew about him?"

"I tried to keep the story from her. I warned the maid, and I was quite *rude* to that reporter who came pestering us. But of course she heard about it before long. Friends came to see her. Some of them had read the article in the *Morning News*. It agitated her again dreadfully. She begged me to find the man, but a park keeper, who knew him, said he had not seen him for some days. I pretended to Mrs. Demarest that I was still trying to get news of him, but I was glad to let the matter drop. She was soon too ill to bother about anything. A week or two later she died."

"And what did you make of Whichcord's experience?"

The hands on the black silk lap expressed bewilderment.

"I did not know *what* to make of it. It confirmed my own, but why should *he* see Felix?"

"Why, indeed?"

"Of course, I knew nothing about him," Miss Plimsoll went on. "It appeared, however, that he was quite a local character. I have often thought about it all, and wondered." She gave Mr. Tuke an apologetic little smile. "It even occurred to me that perhaps it was a *warning*. It sounds melodramatic, I know, but one has heard of such things.

However, it all more or less passed from my mind, until a fortnight ago a maid at my boarding house told me of this new story of his having seen Felix *again*. After seven years! . . . And the next thing was, I saw the police notice saying that he had been found in the Serpentine."

She looked curiously at Mr. Tuke. But he made no comment on this belated vindication of the theory of a warning. He had had his own warning, from his wife's eye, and there was a brisk air of finality in his tone as he said:

"Just one or two more questions, Miss Plimsoll, and you may stand down from the box with the thanks of the court. I take it that it was very soon after this famous 13th of September that Mrs. Demarest drew up a new will?"

This plainly was not the sort of question Miss Plimsoll expected, or much cared for. But she met his look squarely.

"Yes, it was three days after—as soon as she was well enough to see her lawyer."

"How did Miss Shefford, as she then was, take the news of her good fortune? Or didn't she know until later?"

"Oh, Corinne knew," Miss Plimsoll said. "Mrs. Demarest told her. I thought she was quite sensible and nice about it. She admitted the money would mean a lot to her. And there were no near relatives, as she knew. She was particularly nice about the very generous annuity my kind friend bequeathed to me. Of course, I don't think Corinne ever really believed in what had happened that night. Mrs. Demarest told her all about it, but she obviously thought that we had both imagined the whole thing—or that Mrs. Demarest had, and I had just seen somebody in the street."

"Did you hear Mr. Clifford Reaveley's views on the will at this time?" Mr. Tuke asked.

Miss Plimsoll's eyebrows rose a shade. "The will was of no interest to Clifford *then*, Mr. Tuke—except that, like all the relatives, he received a larger legacy than he would have done had Felix lived. And with Felix at sea, we had seen very little of him. He had not been to the house for months. Corinne may have met him, but they did not become engaged until the new year."

"One other person must have been gratified by the turn of events. Or did Madame Varché blush, like the Roman augurs, when she heard the news?"

"I do not know about that," Miss Plimsoll replied drily. "I understand that Mrs. Shefford advertised the story widely, and no doubt Madame Varché benefited. I heard that she retired a year or two later."

"On her ill-gotten gains? Or if it was in 1942, a number of these practitioners went out of business then. The Witchcraft Act of 1734 was revived that year."

Though doubts of Madame Varché might linger, even after she had, so to speak, delivered the goods, her official rating as a witch caused Miss Plimsoll's eyebrows to rise again. But Mr. Tuke was now glancing at Kay Kittredge.

"My last," he announced. "On a different theme. Harking back to that allusion, on Wednesday evening, to some story of Mr. Coverdale's, it arose from a remark by Mrs. Reaveley about rain. Afterwards she rather pointedly asked her husband if he was getting jumpy about the weather again. Do either of you ladies know what she meant?"

"I don't," Kay said; and Miss Plimsoll shook her head.

"Some old argument about climbing, perhaps?" she suggested. "Good weather must be very important to mountaineers."

Mr. Tuke looked dissatisfied, but his wife, reminding him that this was his last question, firmly assumed control of the proceedings. While he lay back in his chair, wreathing his dark face in cigar smoke, Kay and Gordon Cartwright, who had so long been listeners, were led into talk on topics far removed from the tragical and macabre. Miss Plimsoll, no doubt gladly, took up their late rôle, contributing no more than politeness required. Only towards the end did conversation again trench remotely on recent themes. The link was topographical. Cartwright had been speaking of the neighbourhood in which he lived, and of Regency streets and even rustic corners surviving in South Kensington.

"Wake up, Harvey," said Yvette. "Recite *your* discoveries. He was so enchanted, Miss Kittredge, by the view from the back of your house that he made researches in his old books. But perhaps you know all about it?"

Kay disclaiming any knowledge of the history of Lancaster Gate, and Miss Plimsoll confessing to equal ignorance, Mr. Tuke communicated the result of his researches. In the days when the Westbourne flowed through the dip behind Lancaster Terrace to the Serpentine, a rural lane had run beside it to Bayswater Road, then carried over the stream by a bridge. Most of this lane had since merged its identity in Craven Terrace, but its old name was perpetuated in Elms Mews, into which one looked from the rear windows of No. 7a.

"That's where our garage is," Kay put in at this point. "At the back of the houses there's a little alley running to what used to be Lancaster Street. Since it was blitzed they haven't bothered to put the name up again. Our fire escape—those iron stairs you saw from the study, Mr. Tuke—leads down to the alley. You can get to Marlborough Stables and Elms Mews that way. Clifford uses it when he's in a hurry. Otherwise you have to go round to Bayswater Road or Lancaster Street, and down some steps."

At the end of the 18th century, Mr. Tuke said, resuming his lecture, all this ground was a botanical garden, the property of the herbalist, Sir John Hill. On his death it was transformed into New Baggnigge Wells, a pleasure resort more on the lines of Vauxhall and Ranelagh than of the original Baggnigge Wells, where people went to drink the waters.

"The Westbourne fed artificial lakes in the gardens. The whole area seems to have bubbled with springs—one of the oldest conduits in London must be buried under those flats opposite your door in Gloucester Terrace, and when Craven Road was first built over it was Conduit Street. Spring Street marks another," Mr. Tuke added, but did not mention how recently he had been there, and in Craven Road. "The Wells went out of fashion in the early 1800's, and the place was turned into a cheaper sort of floral tea garden. That seems to have existed till the 1860's, when they began to build those shocking houses, of which your No. 7a is one. The bridge over the Westbourne was removed, and the road raised. Hence, no doubt, the steps you speak of, Miss Kittredge. I must explore one day."

Kay's brow was wrinkled in thought. "Ranelagh . . ." she said suddenly to Miss Plimsoll.

"What about it, Kay dear?"

"Curse, I've lost it again," said Kay. "That story of Gervase Coverdale's. It had something to do with Ranelagh. It was on the tip of my tongue, but it's gone now."

"Ranelagh means nothing to me in that connection," Miss Plimsoll said.

Conversation became discursive again, until, very shortly after, Miss Plimsoll said she must be leaving. As Kay was going in the same direction, the party thereupon broke up. In the hall of the flat Mr. Tuke drew the girl aside for a moment.

"Did you solve the little puzzle of the bathing cap?"

A shadow of old anxieties, always near the surface, again clouded Kay's charming face.

"No," she said.

"Your maids can offer no explanation? Or Reaveley?"

"I haven't asked the maids. And I haven't—anyway, I shouldn't bother *him* about it," Kay said.

PART FOUR

Monday, Tuesday

"Here's a corpse in the case with a sad swell'd face,
And a Medical Crowner's a queer sort of thing."

Rev. R. H. Barham
(A Lay of St. Gengulphus).

CHAPTER I

MR. TUKE DOES HIS DUTY

"I CAN GIVE you ten minutes," Wray had said. "I've got a conference at eleven-thirty."

This was on the telephone, on Monday morning. Soon after eleven Mr. Tuke was in the Assistant Commissioner's room in Norman Shaw's lofty Later Renaissance building on the Embankment. At eleven-fifteen, Wray's sandy eyebrows, which had shot up almost as soon as his caller began to speak, were still raised in incredulity.

"Really, Tuke . . ." he said.

He reached for a Turkish cigarette from the silver box on his table, lit it, blew a cloud of aromatic smoke, laced his fingers, and cracked them loudly.

"Your case," he said, "if I've got it right——"

"Hypothesis," Mr. Tuke amended. "One of them."

"Call it what you like. It comes to this. At the dinner party last Wednesday, after your hostess had bolted upstairs in a pet, her husband followed her. When, by his own account, he was trying to make her see reason, he was actually drowning her in her bath. He then wrapped her in a bath towel, popped her in a cupboard, strolled downstairs again, and told you all she'd be down herself to apologise. All this, by the way, in five minutes or so. A little later, as she didn't appear, he left the drawing-room once more, ostensibly to see what she was doing. Instead, he ran down to the hall and slammed the front door. He returned to his guests to explain that his wife had gone to bed after all, but told Miss Kittredge that she had left the house. Your evidence for this fantastic theory is a bathing-cap in a cupboard, a sponge which seemed to you drier than it should be, the woman's running off without money or luggage, and in the underclothes she'd been wearing with evening dress, plus the expression on a girl's face."

Wray shrugged his slim, well-tailored shoulders in patient wonderment. "Come, come, Tuke, you can do better than that. You haven't told me yet how the body was later conveyed all the way to the Serpentine."

"No," Mr. Tuke agreed equably. "That is the snag."

"Glad you see it. The husband couldn't use a car—the park gates are still closed at midnight. He'd have to cross Bayswater Road first. It's well lighted, and takes a lot of traffic at night—lorries going out, stuff coming in from the market gardens. Then he'd got to carry his corpse half a mile across Hyde Park. This is far from deserted at night, now there are no railings. The most direct route from Lancaster Terrace to where the body was dredged up must pass very near the park police station——"

"Yes, yes," Mr. Tuke said. "I told you this was a hypothesis, a basis for reasoning, nothing more. But it strikes a chord, don't you think?"

"I must be deaf."

"It smacks of our old friend, the ghost."

Wray threw up his hands. "Oh, lord, the ghost again!"

"Whatever happened, the ghost is at the back of it all."

"Your ten minutes are up anyway . . ."

"Not quite," Mr. Tuke took out his chronometer. "And you still have twelve before your conference meets. Just about what Reaveley had, to rebut your question-begging objection on that score. Not 'five minutes or so' . . . In the classic case, George Joseph Smith was playing 'Nearer, my God, to Thee' on the organ a very few minutes after running upstairs to hold Miss Mundy's head under water. And don't you remember Superintendent Neil's reconstruction of the murder? He got an expert woman swimmer to lie in the bath. He jerked up her ankles, and she went under at once, and only recovered consciousness after half an hour's artificial respiration. It gave Neil the fright of his life. There was a slamming door in that case, too . . . Reaveley had time to drown his wife a dozen times. All he had to do after was to carry her to the cupboard on the landing outside. By the way, I think Miss Kittredge saw something else there, besides the bathing-cap. She shut the doors too quickly for me to see what it was. But she stooped to touch the floor. A still damp patch, do you think? . . . To return to Reaveley, no doubt he also left in the cupboard the raincoat he'd slipped on."

"He had a raincoat, had he?"

"He'd need something, to protect his dress shirt. If this *was* a crime, it was premeditated. Some garment would be at hand for whenever opportunity should occur. And what an opportunity, with a house full of people! . . . However, his shoes and the bottoms of his trousers got wet, and, of course, his hands. He was wiping them when he rejoined us. Hence the story of the sponge."

"That seems to me one of your flimsiest efforts."

"I'm rather pleased with it myself," Mr. Tuke said. "Whatever did happen in the bathroom, it means that Reaveley told a lie. My own sponge went under the tap on Friday evening, and it still held water this morning. Mrs. Reaveley's, a much bigger one, was bone dry less than forty-eight hours after it is said to have been thrown while wet."

"I thought she was always having baths."

"For her nerves. No doubt she generally lay about and soaked. Her sponge certainly hadn't been used for days."

"And the bathing-cap came off while she was being inserted in, or removed from, the cupboard?"

"Perhaps the towel loosened it. Reaveley forgot it, and didn't see it. It was in a dark corner. He must have been in a hurry when he got her out, and though he's a cool customer, I should say—mountaineering needs nerve—even you or I would be a bit rattled in the circumstances. When he came down to us the first time he obviously wanted the couple of neat whiskies he put down. And having just seen his wife in a tantrum, we were all so sympathetic."

"And why not?" Wray said with his foxy grin. "This is only a basis for reasoning. What about the hypothetical risk he was running, by the way, with a house full of people?"

"There was virtually no risk. The ladies powdered their noses on the first floor, behind the drawing-room. The one maid sleeping in had gone to bed in the attics. Nobody would go up to the second floor except Miss Kittredge, and with host and hostess absent she couldn't leave the guests. *Afterwards*, of course, she could scout about as much as she liked. Reaveley would want her to. She had already got it fixed in her mind that her cousin had left the house. She wouldn't look in cupboards. This one has a key, anyway."

Wray glanced at his watch, and pushed back his chair. Mr. Tuke, without moving, went on talking.

"When we'd all gone, Reaveley did his telephoning act, pretended to run out to the garage, and eventually persuaded Miss Kittredge to go to bed, having given her a nightcap which he dosed. I'll bet his wife had all sorts of opiates. The girl was ashamed because she slept so well."

"You have an explanation for everything—up to a point," Wray said, collecting a file from a tray.

"Well, to conclude, as far as the hypothesis goes," Mr. Tuke continued, "Reaveley seems to have made a second mistake when he dressed the body in a coat and skirt, but without the appropriate underclothes. Perhaps he was in a hurry again, or he may have had some idea of supporting the suicide theory. But according to Yvette——"

"Have you been discussing this with your wife?"

"Calm yourself, Wray. I have not. But I mentioned this matter of underclothes to her, and she pounced on it at once. Any woman, she says, bothering to fish out a coat and skirt, would automatically get the right stockings and things first—even if she *was* going to commit suicide. It would be second nature. Yvette was so struck by this inconsistency that I fancy she's uneasy in her mind without any prompting. She didn't like the house, you know."

Wray was tapping the table irritably. Once more he looked at his watch, but he remained in his chair. His next words even conceded a point.

"I presume even you wouldn't be taking up my time if you didn't think there might be something in this precious hypothesis of yours. But, really, Tuke, even if you could explain how the woman got to the Serpentine, otherwise than on her own legs, it would all still be extremely thin.

And what has your wife's dislike of the house got to do with it? I hope you're not going to drag in another ghost, and suggest it's haunted?"

"I should say it is," Mr. Tuke replied. "Though not in the way you probably mean."

Wray tittered. "Are you being intuitive now?"

"Intuition is really no more than cumulative observation. Miss Kittredge, for instance, has come to dislike this house so intensely that she makes excuses to get out of it. What has happened is that her mind has been collecting unconsidered trifles for months—actions, moods, and so on—until one day it subconsciously added up a number of hitherto unrelated ones and found the result disturbing. She has not yet realised why—or I hope she hasn't. I'm rather afraid that when she found that bathing cap the data began to form a picture. Take Reaveley, again. He says he hates the house, and I think he means it."

"He's got some reason to, on your hypothesis."

"I doubt if he's the type to boggle at bathrooms, so to speak, whatever happened in his wife's. Not enough imagination. But the affair brought to a head an antipathy to the house based on something that has been going on there lately—thoughts and schemes of his own, perhaps. Anyway, he has run away from the place. There's a stronger motive there than a regard for the conventions—and, I repeat, he's not an imaginative man."

"These distinctions are too fine for me," Wray said. "What about the wife, anyhow? She ought to have felt your atmospherics, if anyone did."

"Perhaps she did feel them. She has talked of moving, And she had run away. Twice——"

"Twice . . .?"

"Yes. And she had been behaving queerly since the ghost, and then Whichcord, came into the news again."

"Whichcord now!" Wray groaned. "Still trying to connect the two cases?"

"Oh, my dear Wray, use your head. They *are* connected. And the link is the ghost."

Wray shrugged. "Have you tried this stuff on Kames?"

"Oh, yes. Having seen Miss Kittredge and the bereaved husband, not to mention another dark horse, in both senses—Mr. Coverdale—Kames fully agrees with me now."

Having witnessed the Director's overt reactions to the first news of the affair, Wray was plainly impressed. The imminent conference apparently forgotten, he beat another irritable tattoo on the table.

"Where is all this getting us, anyway?" he asked impatiently. "Why bring it to me now, in this state? Do you expect me to act on intuition and the subconscious?"

"My dear Wray," Mr. Tuke said again, "what would you have said afterwards if I had *not* come to you? I'm not only a witness, I'm an officer of the court, working in with your department. As a mere citizen, you'd have read me a lecture about duty. Besides, I thought you said on Friday that you were going to look into the case?"

"I believe I said I might—from the money angle. But I shall wait to see how the inquest shapes."

"You ought to have taken up politics," Mr. Tuke said acidly. "Well, have a word with Akers, anyway."

"Akers knows his business, as I know mine, thanks."

Mr. Tuke smiled diabolically. "Better. That's why I suggest it. I'll do you an *aide mémoire* to pass on to him. Apropos, he seems to have adjourned Friday's inquest, on Whichcord, in short order. Anything in that?"

"Not that I know of." Wray sounded huffed. "Insufficient evidence to show how the man got into the water. Akers is always thorough. But we've had no query. The locals will be working on it." The Assistant Commissioner suddenly recalled the flight of time, looked at his watch, and jumped to his feet. "Damn it, you've made me late . . .!"

"Go to your conference," Mr. Tuke said. "I'll jot down my notes here."

"Please yourself," Wray snapped as he went out.

Mr. Tuke grinned again at the closed door. He rose and

walked to the large window, where he stood for a moment looking across the river at the unhappily proportioned vastness of County Hall. Fancy pictured Mr. Gervase Coverdale looking out of *his* window at New Scotland Yard. Mr. Tuke walked thoughtfully back to the Assistant Commissioner's table. He took out his fountain pen.

CHAPTER II

AIDE MÉMOIRE

"*Notes on events arising from the presumed death at sea of Lieut. F. Demarest, R.N., in the spring of 1940.*

"For the consideration of the Assistant Commissioner (C).

(*A*) *The Ghost.*

"1. The following notes and queries are based on the assumption that this bogey is bogus. Conversely—but, as you observed, thaumaturgy is not your pidgin.

"2. The persistent theme at Mme Varché's séances that Mrs. Demarest should do something for Miss Shefford, a theme reiterated at the street corner meeting, suggests collusion from the first with Miss Shefford and/or Clifford Reaveley.

"3. It is most unlikely that anyone not a member of the family could have carried out the physical deception.

"4. Felix Demarest was dark. Reaveley is very fair. But both were tall, with blue eyes, and there was a family resemblance between them so close that in a snap photograph they could be described as looking like twins. A dark beard would aid the illusion. Voice and tricks of speech could be imitated. The lighting conditions on the night of the 13th/14th September 1940 were a misleading mixture of moon and searchlights. The ghost (as we will continue to call it) warned Mrs. Demarest not to come too close. She was in an excited and receptive state, having been more than half persuaded beforehand that she had spoken to her son at the séances.

"5. The vanishing trick. When the ghost warned Mrs. D. not to follow, was it in the belief that she would, and so somehow confirm the illusion? Is there anything in the odd fact that on leaving her it did not cross Bayswater Road in a straight line, but took a diagonal towards Hyde Park? Were the railings lower there?

"6. Reaveley is a mountaineer. Could he have got over the railings, perhaps with the aid of a rope, in a few seconds and without making a sound? The whole business had no doubt been rehearsed.

"7. The ghost undoubtedly got into Hyde Park, where Whichcord saw it near the Serpentine. The half hour interval is conjectural, but the ghost seems to have taken its time in covering half a mile. I have been shown the spot where it repeated its vanishing trick, and without going into it all here, this is as big a puzzle (if Whichcord is to be believed) as the original disappearance *via* the railings.

"8. However it was done, the trick worked. Mrs. Demarest drew up a will directly benefiting Miss Shefford, and indirectly Reaveley, whom Miss S. subsequently married.

"9. Can any connection between either of the pair and Mme Varché now be traced? Mme V. was known to Mrs. Shefford. What has become of Mme V? She is said to have retired from business a year or two later.

"(*B*) *Mrs. Reaveley.*

"1. If she was not implicated in the original fraud, she must soon have suspected it. She seems to have been unwilling to discuss the affair with Miss Kittredge.

"2. Giving her the benefit of the doubt, did she later get the truth out of her husband? If she did, with her fits of temper and habit of saying the first thing that came into her head, she would be a danger to him, however difficult it might be, as time passed, to pin anything to him. During the last few years they had been drifting apart, as novelists say. Suspicion by itself would account for Mrs. Reaveley's behaviour, described by Miss Kittredge, after Whichcord's latest story got about. She would wonder what her husband was up to, masquerading as the ghost again after seven years. Did she tax him with it? The news of Whichcord's death seems to have made her definitely uneasy. She kept watching her husband. In view of all this, it is no wonder she found the silly hoax on Wednesday evening too much for her nerves. Her exclamation to Reaveley, as she rushed out of the room, 'You devil!', may have sprung from something more than temper.

"3. There is no evidence for the theory that she took her own life. Tantrums and vague talk mean nothing with a woman of her type. Considering where her body was found, in a few inches of water, accidental death is even more unlikely. If there were external injuries, possibly from a fall, but sufficient to stun, you would have heard by now.

"4. I have reminded you of the Mundy case. Mrs. Reaveley's bath is a very big one, and tiled, with nothing to grip.

"5. What did Miss Kittredge see in the cupboard, besides the bathing-cap? I still like the idea of a damp patch. Anyway, after being first merely puzzled, she became definitely scared (see my lecture on the sub-conscious), so much so that Kames noticed it and was moved to put her publicly under the protection of the Department. I also got my wife to offer ours. Miss Kittredge may want to run away too.

"6. Reaveley, on this occasison, seemed perfectly at ease, but he never gives much away. On the other hand, Kames' pointed behaviours hook R.'s friend Coverdale. (See (D) below).

"7. Finally, how was the body conveyed to the Serpentine? Even I can't think of an answer to this at present, except the unlikely one that Reaveley took the terrific risk of carrying it across the park. He is a powerful man, and she was a small woman, or at any rate a very thin one.

"8. Until (7) is answered, we have no case.

"(*C*) *Whichcord*.

"1. Why did the ghost turn up again, after seven years, on the same spot in Hyde Park? Echo answers, Why?

"2. You did not give me time to tell you, but I have been making a few inquiries on my own. Chaffinch is carrying on with these. Preserve absolute tranquillity.

"3. It looks as though Whichcord tumbled to something soon after he saw the ghost for the second time three weeks ago. He talked about an annuity. Blackmail?

"4. Did W., having meddled, like me, pay for it? And don't you wish I would?

"(*D*) *Coverdale.*

"1. From what Miss Kittredge said, or did not say, I fancy that when her cousin ran away from home the second time she went to Coverdale. It was in the evening, and she came back in a few hours. Did Coverdale persuade her nicely, or throw her out?

"2. The pair were old friends, and had been so intimate that Mrs. Reaveley knew something about Coverdale's past apparently unknown to her husband, though he and Coverdale were even older acquaintances, having worked together before the war. A threat about this past threw Coverdale into a rage. Query, fear of exposure, and to whom?

"3. The above suggests another hypothesis, as follows. On the night of Wednesday/Thursday did Mrs. Reaveley in fact leave the house? Did she go to Coverdale's place, as she had done before? As he lives in Craven Hill, just along Gloucester Terrace, she would not need money or a hat. She may have had a key. Coverdale was in her drawing-room when we heard the door slam, but he left soon after with the rest of us.

"4. On Friday he seemed more shaken than Reaveley. He is the type to show natural feeling more readily, but when he found out who Kames was, he was obviously taken aback. On the general principles, because nobody loves the D.P.P? Or because of his past? Or does he know something about Mrs. Reaveley's death?

"5. This theory leaves much unexplained: the bathing-cap, the sponge, the underclothes, not to mention the ghost.

But it does away with the major snag in Hypothesis 1. Mrs. Reaveley was not carried to the Serpentine—she walked there, with Coverdale. A stroll across Hyde Park in the small hours is at least no more improbable than a ghost. She may have intended to stay with Coverdale (as before?), and then flung out again because he wasn't forthcoming, and decided instead to go to some friend in Knightsbridge. She ran to one there the first time she bolted. Coverdale follows, perhaps as an escort. They quarrel again en route, and she goes into the water.

"6. This does not invalidate the theory of the original fraud. As for the ghost, Reaveley may still have been up to his tricks again. Was his second impersonation perhaps on Whichcord's account? Or did his wife's death forestall some other scheme?

"7. If Hyde Park is as crowded after dark as you say, surely somebody saw something of what went on there that night?

"*Mes compliments.* I'll try to think up something else for you.

12.9.47 "HARVEY TUKE."

CHAPTER III

NOTHING BUT THE TRUTH: THE OFFICIALS

THE CORONER'S COURT at the back of Paddington Green having been destroyed by a bomb, which however left the mortuary intact, the King's Coroner for West London was holding his inquiries into the causes of violent or unnatural deaths occurring in the Paddington area at his court in Horseferry Road, Westminster, where he sat on Tuesdays and Fridays. On that Tuesday, the 13th of September, when the inquest on the body of Corinne Reaveley was to be opened, Mr. Tuke had been warned to present himself at the court before half-past eleven. It was twenty minutes past the hour when he parked the Delage in front of the compact red brick building, dated and dwarfed by adjacent towering office premises and chequer-board council flats. Inquests formed no part of his routine, but he knew the coroner, Mr. Geoffrey Akers, quite well. They were fellow members of the Senior Universities.

When he let himself quietly through the double doors of the court-room on the first floor, where another inquiry was in progress, the coroner's officer led him on tip-toe to the seats allotted to witnesses. The room was crowded. Half a dozen reporters, Mr. Fenne among them, sat at the press table immediately beneath the wide raised desk of the coroner, and at Mr. Tuke's entry, Fenne turned to stare. There were two solicitors at the table reserved for counsel; quite a cloud of witnesses almost filled the benches on the far side of the room, and the *Morning News*, through Fenne himself, having reminded its readers in that day's issue that the latest development in the mystery of the Hyde Park Ghost was due for open hearing, there was no space left at all on the public seats, usually vacant. In front of these sat four large police officers. Two professional witnesses were readily identified as doctors, and Mr. Tuke, in passing, glanced with some interest at the woman in severe black in the witness stand, reading from a foolscap report, for the terms of this revealed her to be the pathologist, Dr. New, whom he had not met. The bench behind the witness stand was vacant, for the coroner was sitting without a jury, in accordance with wartime regulations still in force.

Mr. Tuke squeezed his long form beside Miss Plimsoll on one of the rear benches. That lady's presence there somewhat surprised him: she had said nothing on Sunday about being summoned. Kay Kittredge sat next to her, Clifford Reaveley on the other side of Kay. On the bench in front were Coverdale and Peter Warrener, together with two strangers—an elderly man in a blue uniform, like a commissionaire's, and a disreputable little creature with a greasy collar turned up to his ears, an almost bald head, and something furtive in the stoop of his sloping shoulders.

The benches in front and behind were filled by witnesses in the case now proceeding, or in those to come. For the coroner was having a fairly busy morning, though by no means an abnormal one. Daily, in the vast area of London, a score or so of human beings come to unnatural ends, and the inquiry into the death of Corinne Reaveley, if of peculiar interest to Mr. Fenne's public, was to Mr. Akers merely one of five which he hoped to dispose of before lunch time. In his unhurried but expeditious way he had soon polished off the first in order, and the second was nearing its end as Dr. New, in pleasant conversational tones, recited the results of her *post mortem* examination. She handed her report to the coroner's officer, Mr. Akers murmured, "Thank you, doctor," and before she had withdrawn to her seat he was briefly summarizing the case. His glasses flashed in the light of the green-shaded lamp on his desk as he took up his pen and recorded a verdict of death from accidental causes.

"Witnesses in the last case may now leave the court," his officer announced loudly, adding in the same breath: "Mr. Benton."

The persons indicated rose, among them being one of the

doctors, a solicitor, and two police officers. The man in the blue uniform in front of Mr. Tuke rose also, and the third inquest had begun.

Amid the shuffle of departing feet the new witness took his place on the stand, revealing a weatherbeaten face and two rows of ribbons on his blue tunic. He was handed a Bible and prompted in the words of the oath.

"I swear by Almighty God that I will speak the truth, the whole truth, and nothing but the truth."

Mr. Akers looked benevolently across at him.

"Your name is Robert Albert Benton, and you live at 93 Poland Street, Pimlico. You are an official—in fact, the chief boatman—at the Royal Humane Society's receiving house in Hyde Park?"

"Yes, sir," said Mr. Benton.

"On the morning of Thursday, the 8th of September, you were outside your boathouse. At what time was this?"

"About a quarter past six, sir. I'd come along early, like I sometimes do——"

"Yes. And what did you see?"

"I saw a swan, sir, picking at something in the water. I went along, and there was the body of a woman, just awash, about a hundred yards west of the public boathouse."

"What did you do, Mr. Benton?"

"I pulled the body out of the water, sir."

"Did you apply artificial respiration?"

"I did, sir. But I knew it was no good. The woman was dead. I've seen 'em before," Mr. Benton added knowingly.

"How was the woman clothed?"

"She was fully dressed, sir, in a coat and skirt."

"Was she wearing a hat?"

"No, sir. And no gloves, neether. She had a diamond ring on, and one of them wedding rings of platinum."

It was easy to hear Mr. Benton, but heads were craning to catch the sense of the coroner's soft modulations. Beside Mr. Tuke two pairs of black-gloved hands were folded on two black laps. Kay's fingers twisted nervously. Beyond her,

Reaveley's fresh-coloured face and blue eyes were expressionless. The backs of Coverdale and Peter Warrener by contrast plainly registered discomfort. Coverdale's reddish neck and sleek dark head moved uneasily, and the younger man was never still. The sorry creature beside him hunched his bald head still lower into his collar.

"Had you seen the deceased before, Mr. Benton?" the coroner was inquiring.

"Not to my knowledge, sir."

"You describe the body as being awash. Do you mean it was only partly below the surface?"

"The hair was floating, sir, but the body was just under water. There's a sloping cement lip round the Serpentine. The body was lying on the slope."

Mr. Akers was making a note. Still writing, he said:

"No doubt you are an authority on the Serpentine, Mr. Benton. What is its greatest depth?"

"Twenty feet, sir."

"Whereabouts is that?"

"Between the boathouses and the Dell, sir."

"At the east end. Does the shore shelve gradually from this cement lip?"

"Once you're past the lip, sir, you can wade out quite a way."

"Is there any current?"

Mr. Benton shook his head. "No, sir. Things what float drift to the edge. It's all according to the wind, sir. There's what we call London Soot—that drifts into the corners by the Dell when the wind's westerly, and t'other way about with an east wind."

Mr. Akers made another note. "Having satisfied yourself that the deceased was already dead, Mr. Benton, what did you do next?"

"I ran up to the police station, sir."

"The Hyde Park police station?"

"Yes, sir. It's not three hundred yards away. I reported to Sergeant Cowley——"

"Thank you, Mr. Benton. I think that will be all."

As the coroner's officer beckoned the witness from the stand, he was calling:

"Sergeant Cowley!"

One of the police officers rose, passed the Humane Society's official as he walked heavily to the stand, took the Bible in an off-hand manner, and recited the oath in one breath.

"You are Harold William Cowley," murmured Mr. Akers, "a sergeant in 'A' Division of the Metropolitan Police, and you are attached to Hyde Park police station?"

"Yessir."

"The previous witness has told us that on the 8th of this month he reported to you his discovery of the deceased. At what time was this?"

Sergeant Cowley's large blunt fingers were turning the pages of a notebook.

"Six twenty-three a.m., sir."

"What action did you take?"

"I instructed one of the constables on duty to fetch a stretcher, and we accompanied the witness to the spot."

"The body was then lying on the path?"

"It was, sir."

"Did you recognize the deceased?"

"I did, sir," said the sergeant, with a sort of gloomy satisfaction. "I recognized her as Mrs. Corinne Reaveley, of 7a Lancaster Terrace." He licked a finger and turned the pages of his notebook. "On the 3rd of June last, Mrs. Reaveley called at the station to report the loss of a diamond clip. She thought it might have become unfastened while she was sitting with a friend near the Cockpit. I was on duty at the time, and took down the details——"

"Yes, I see. Having conveyed the body to the Receiving House, did you take any further steps?"

"I 'phoned the divisional surgeon, sir, and reported the matter to Inspector Meeking on his arrival at 8 a.m."

"I think that will be all, sergeant, thank you."

"Dr. Mears," called the coroner's officer.

Dr. Mears, a tall, shaggy man, exchanged places with Sergeant Cowley and took the oath in a rapid mutter.

"Your name is Randolph Etherege Mears," queried Mr. Akers, almost inaudibly, as though his thoughts were elsewhere, which was by no means the case, "and you live at 25 Tattenham Place, W.1. You are a registered medical practitioner. Did you, on the 8th of this month, examine the body of the deceased at the Humane Society's receiving house in Hyde Park?"

"Yes, yes," muttered Dr. Mears impatiently.

"At what time?"

"Eight forty-five."

"Did you form an opinion as to the cause of death?"

"The superficial symptoms were those of asphyxiation by drowning."

"How long before you saw the body would you say death had taken place?"

"From six to ten hours before."

"Were there any external injuries? Any bruises, or signs of violence?"

"None whatever."

"Was the face much swollen?"

"Scarcely at all. . . ."

A slight disturbance at the double doors heralded some whispering and the entry of a belated witness, who was led to the back of the room. The coroner was enjoying a brief professional colloquy with Dr. Mears—coroners in the London area have to be medical men as well as barristers—and Mr. Tuke, his attention wandering, found himself speculating on the choice of his fellow witnesses. Why was Miss Plimsoll there? And why Coverdale, rather than one of the other guests at the dinner party? Coverdale, of course, was an old friend, and there was that odd little scene. . . . Mr. Tuke's eyes, wandering like his thoughts, fell at this moment upon a familiar face among the general public across the aisle. The owner of the face met his glance, and looked away again; and Miss Plimsoll, out of the corner of her eye, saw her neighbour's black brows rise. For the man across the aisle was a detective-sergeant of the C.I.D., whom Mr. Tuke had last seen in the witness box at the Old Bailey. That talk with Wray, and the *aide mémoire*, seemed to have borne fruit.

"I am obliged to you, doctor," Mr. Akers was saying in his soft voice. "If you have other engagements, you need not wait."

As Dr. Mears hurried from the stand and from the court, the next witness was being called.

"Mr. Clifford Reaveley. . . ."

CHAPTER IV

NOTHING BUT THE TRUTH: THE HUSBAND

REAVELEY rose abruptly, shooting up to his considerable height as though his previous immobility had been that of a coiled spring. He looked very tall, and his squared shoulders very broad, as he edged his way past the knees of his companions on the bench, strode to the witness stand, and took the oath with an air of getting to grips with a distasteful ordeal.

"Your name is Clifford Eric Reaveley?"

Mr. Akers, in his gentle voice, ran through his customary gambit. His well-brushed silvery hair gleamed in the light from his green-shaded lamp, the only living point of colour in the court room, which was a monochrome in mahogany. Panelling, benches, desks, tables, witness stand, the sort of palisading behind which Mr. Akers himself sat loftily entrenched—one and all were of that hue, if not of that wood; and though one and all were highly polished, the effect was of pervasive if appropriate solemnity. On the mahogany mantelshelf, above a repellent fireplace in tiles of sulphur and blue, a glittering water carafe, a tumbler inverted on its neck, competed gamely with a large square mahogany clock and a larger round mahogany calendar. Above the panelling a cream ceiling curved to a flat glass-sided superstructure, the purpose of which, that of admitting light, had been undone by the later erection outside of the towering offices and flats, while the vault thus created perhaps accounted for the poor acoustics of the room. The windows at either end were of ground glass, having little more than token value on a normal English day. The day being thoroughly normal, the sky hung with cloud and more rain threatening, this subdued illumination, half absorbed by a forest of mahogany, combined with the universal black of the ranked witnesses, the dark blue of policemen, and the subfusc block of spectators, to make up a scene not merely solemn but gloomy; and the coroner's officer was now happily moved to take action. He pressed a switch, and half a dozen pendant lights flashed into being. In an instant the court room became a cheerful and homely place. Faces leapt from the shadows, the liver-coloured woodwork shone, and on the rounded window above Mr. Akers' silver head the royal arms, hitherto a leaden silhouette on the grey glass, suddenly sparkled in gold.

"You identify the deceased, Mr. Reaveley, as your wife?" Mr. Akers was asking.

"Yes," said Clifford Reaveley, a faint contraction passing across his fresh, impassive face.

"I wish to spare you all the distress I can," Mr. Akers murmured. "But I have to ask you if you know of anything that will account for this tragedy. Has your wife been unusually worried or depressed lately?"

"She has had no worries that I know of." Reaveley's voice, though low, carried well. His blunt features were set in a slight frown of concentration, his blue eyes met the coroner's look with candour. "She has had fits of depression, but that was not unusual. She was always either in high spirits, or—or feeling fed up with things."

"Has she been ill recently?"

"Oh, no."

"Her general health was good?"

"I always thought so. She talked a lot about her nerves, and she took stuff to make her sleep, but I put it down to too many late nights, and parties, and all that. . . ."

The broad black shoulders had shrugged slightly, and in reply to a further question the witness explained that his wife was out late three or four nights a week, and played a good deal of bridge during the day. He himself was very busy at the ministry, and was often away from London. To a considerable extent his wife had to find her own amusements. He agreed, with the merest shade of his infectious, companionable smile, that she had a quick temper. She was inclined to go off the deep end over trifles.

"But usually it didn't last," he said.

Mr. Akers bent over his notes before he inquired:

"During these temperamental moods, did your wife ever run away, or threaten to run away?"

Reaveley braced his square shoulders, as though for the first time conscious of the attentive audience. His eyes flickered to the reporters, busy scribbling at their table beneath the witness stand.

"She ran away from the house—twice," he said, clamping his lips tight on the word.

"Was she away for long?"

"The first time I fetched her home the next morning. The second time she returned within a few hours."

"When was this last occasion, Mr. Reaveley?"

"About a year ago."

"And after these—er, escapades, did the situation in your household return to normal?"

"Oh, yes." Reaveley spoke more easily. "They didn't really mean anything. I mean, they might have happened anywhere. If my wife was—well, in a temper, she was quite likely to fling out, wherever she was. In the middle of a party, for instance. That is why, the other night——"

"Yes, we will come to that in a moment." The coroner passed a hand over his smooth silver head as he looked up at the tall black figure on the stand. "Has Mrs. Reaveley ever threatened to take her life?"

Again a spasm contracted the witness's face, and his strong fingers gripped the rail before him as he agreed that once or twice his wife had talked wildly—when she had been over-doing things, or was in a rage. When she was in that state of mind she said a great deal more than she meant. He never took it seriously. The low voice, which had been rigidly controlled, rose a tone as Reaveley added: "I can't now. After all, we don't *know*! It may have been an accident. It *must* have been——"

"That is what we are here to find out," Mr. Akers reminded him gently. "I am anxious to be quite clear in my mind about these moods, and their cause. For instance, besides being temperamental, and overdoing things, did your wife perhaps sometimes drink more than was good for her?"

Reaveley lifted his hands in a little gesture. "It depends on what you mean. I used to tell her so, because I thought it got her down. But all her crowd do, you know."

He glanced again, with an expression of disgust, at the newspapermen below. Mr. Akers nodded, and made a note.

"On the whole, though," he asked, "would you say she had every reason to enjoy life? She was well-to-do, she had a comfortable home, many friends, and so on?"

"Yes, yes," Reaveley replied eagerly. "That's what I mean. She *did* enjoy life. Anyone will tell you——"

"And—I have to ask this—there was no recent cause, no serious cause, that is, of trouble between you?"

"Good Lord, no!" The ejaculation seemed spontaneous, with just the right note of aggrieved surprise. "We had our little squabbles, you know, but nothing like that. We have always jogged along. . . ."

At Mr. Tuke's side Miss Plimsoll held her neat black figure very erect on the hard bench. She belonged to the generation which did not loll. Kay Kittredge's hands were now still; she watched and listened; only once her eyes left Clifford Reaveley, on the witness stand, to rest on the back of Coverdale's dark head, and then a small worried frown contracted her forehead before she recalled herself to the dialogue between coroner and witness. Coverdale, too, had ceased to fidget, but Peter Warrener was as unhappily restless as ever.

Mr. Tuke's mind, while he missed no word or inflection of that dialogue, was able from long practice to rove afield on other matters, such as the significance of a detective officer's presence, its relation, if any, to the choice of witnesses, and the business of the lawyer who remained sittting by himself at the table reserved for his kind. He might, of course, be waiting for another case to open; but solicitors are busy men, and though he showed no special interest in the examination of Clifford Reaveley, he had the air of holding a watching brief. Having seen none of the persons concerned since Sunday, Mr. Tuke was left to wonder whether, his *aide mémoire* apart, there had been developments after his interview with Wray the previous morning.

Mr. Akers had begun to take his witness through the events of the now famous dinner party, and he was dealing with them very summarily. Having brought out the fact that Corinne Reaveley had been on the edge of one of her 'moods', or at least in a state of nervous irritation, during dinner itself, he appeared satisfied. He asked no questions about the ghost, or about Wally Whichcord (into whose death he himself had begun an inquiry only four days before), or about Corinne's flare-up with Gervase Coverdale. He went straight to the climax of the evening.

"Now, Mr. Reaveley, was there later an unfortunate occurrence which seriously upset your wife?"

"Yes." As Mr. Akers merely nodded, the witness went on: "My friend Warrener played a silly practical joke."

"What sort of joke?"

"He went out of the room, switched off the lights, and pretended to be a ghost."

Mr. Akers looked mildly interested. "There is some story of a ghost connected with your family?"

"Oh, yes, but it wasn't that. Warrener pretended to be a man called Whichcord. You know all about him——"

"We will ignore anything I may know outside this inquiry. However, the upshot was that your wife was much incensed and upset, and rushed out of the room. This, I understand, was about half-past eleven?"

"I didn't notice the time," Reaveley said.

"Well, what did you do?"

The witness described his visit to his wife's room a little later. He had then noted the time: it was about ten to twelve. His wife was in her bath. She said she was going to bed. At first she seemed quite frantic, but it was, as he put it, a general hate, and not specially directed against himself. He repeated that when she was really worked up she was scarcely accountable for what she said. Altogether, this account of the strange scene in that bathroom of yellow tiles and chromium added little to that which Mr. Tuke had already heard at second hand.

"All this time your wife remained lying in the bath?" the coroner queried. The witness nodded without speaking, and Mr. Akers went on in his quiet conversational way: "Did she throw anything at you?"

Reaveley's blunt features showed a flicker of some feeling that might have been irritation, or merely disgust at this airing of mortifying details. As he stood stiffly in the mahogany box, the hanging lights gilded his fair hair and heightened his fresh colour. He threw a quick frown at the press table as he replied:

"She threw her sponge at me."

"The sponge was full of water?"

"It was."

"Did it hit you?"

"It hit my legs."

The witness's tone was curt, and his frown more marked. Mr. Akers, unperturbed, went on blandly to inquire if Mrs. Reaveley took many hot baths, and was told, still rather curtly, that she did. She thought they soothed her nerves, and she always flew to her bath when upset.

"As she had been," Mr. Akers commented. "Hot baths, in moderation," he murmured at large, "are an excellent thing, but many women overdo them."

Clifford Reaveley was then led on to describe how after Corinne had run on, in his own phrase, for a minute or two, she quieted down, and at length agreed grudgingly to dress and return to her guests. When he left her, she was out of the bath. He thought the whole argument had lasted five minutes or so.

"But in fact," said the coroner, "Mrs. Reaveley did not come down to the drawing-room again?"

"No."

"So you went up to her room once more? How soon after you first left her was this?"

Reaveley showed a touch of impatience. "I can't remember all these times." He smiled suddenly, showing his white teeth. "I'm sorry. I had a lot on my mind. I was thinking of my guests. I waited ten minutes or so, I suppose."

He told how he had found the bedroom empty, the green frock on the bed, the bathroom vacant too. But he thought he had realized by then that his wife had left the house.

"I remembered hearing what sounded like the front door slam as I got to the landing. My wife could have used the back stairs. And—well, she had done it before, you see."

"Did you think of following her?" Mr. Akers asked.

"Oh, of course. . . ." Reaveley lifted his broad shoulders. "But by that time—well, she could have been out of sight, whichever way she'd gone. Our house is on a corner where three roads meet. It was hopeless. . . . And I hadn't really begun to be *worried*, and I had to think what to do about our guests. I decided to tell them my wife had changed her mind. As soon as they left, I could get busy."

Mr. Akers made a note. Until he looked up again, the witness stood watching him, studiously ignoring the pressmen below. Then the coroner, in his detached, softly modulated voice, began to deal with the later events of that calamitous night. He wasted no time over them. Reaveley's account again bore out that given by Kay Kittredge to Sir Bruton and Mr. Tuke. At the end, when he had told how he had made Kay go to bed, a few more questions terminated his ordeal. The final one, however, was to spring a surprise.

"You have told us, Mr. Reaveley," the coroner said, "that when you found your wife had left the house you were not at first seriously worried. Later, however, when you could get no news of her, and realized that she had taken no luggage, and apparently no money, you must have begun to feel perturbed. Did you think of applying to the police?"

"Of course I felt perturbed," Reaveley said sharply. "And I thought of the police. I talked it all over with Miss Kittredge. But it still did not occur to me that anything could have happened to my wife. I thought she had bluffed me all along—that she only pretended to be coming down to get rid of me. If she had made up her mind to run off, she would be in a hurry to get away before I came up again. In that state of mind she might not think about money, even—especially if she was going to some friend near by. She had several living near us, but I don't know the names of half of them. There must be some I don't know at all. My wife was always making new friends, and they were always perfectly marvellous to start with. Anyway, that is how I thought it out at the time."

He ended a little defiantly. Mr. Akers nodded.

"I see. Yes. It was a difficult situation for you. By the way, you did not even know whether your wife was wearing a hat?"

Reaveley's hands tightened on the rail of the stand.

"I didn't know then. She had so many hats. Even Miss Kittredge could not be sure. I know now that——"

"We will come to that presently," Mr. Akers put in. "Just tell me if you recognize this cap."

His officer, who stood beside the witness stand, was producing from somewhere, with the air of a conjuror, a dark green beret. He handed this to the witness, who stood crumpling it in his strong fingers, staring at it.

"It's like one she used to wear sometimes," he said in a low voice. "I can't swear to it."

"Very well, Mr. Reaveley." The coroner nodded in a friendly way. "That will be all. Thank you."

Reaveley lingered, still gripping the beret, until the officer retrieved it, at the same time calling out:

"Miss Kittredge!"

Kay rose with a little nervous start. Clifford Reaveley was leaving the stand, and as the pair passed in the gangway a perfunctory smile touched his lips, but the blue eyes in the fresh-coloured face were icy as they stared past the girl to the witnesses' benches.

CHAPTER V

NOTHING BUT THE TRUTH: WHOSE BERET?

"YOUR NAME is Katherine Lacy Kittredge, and you live at 7a, Lancaster Terrace? What is your position there, Miss Kittredge?"

Mr. Akers looked benevolently at Kay, a slender figure in black, standing very straight in the mahogany pen, and Kay looked gravely at Mr. Akers.

"I'm the housekeeper. Mrs. Reaveley was my cousin, and when I came out of the Wrens, and took up domestic science, she asked me to run her house for her, to help her and get my hand in."

"You have heard the last witness. This beret, I believe, was brought to you yesterday. Do you recognize it?"

As Kay took the green beret from the coroner's officer she turned it to examine the lining.

"It's exactly like one Corinne—one Mrs. Reaveley had. I was with her when she bought it. Here's the name of the shop—Sully's, in Bond Street. Of course," Kay added, "they stock others like it."

"Since this was returned to you, have you looked through your cousin's things for a similar beret?"

"Yes. I can't find hers."

"Take your mind back to last Wednesday night, or rather Thursday morning, Miss Kittredge. After Mrs. Reaveley disappeared, you and Mr. Reaveley examined her wardrobe. Did it occur to you then that a beret was missing?"

"No," Kay said. "I'd forgotten about it. She hadn't had it long, and she didn't often wear it in London."

"Were all her other hats there?"

Kay smiled faintly. "I thought so. But she had dozens. She was always buying hats. No coupons, you know."

Mr. Akers glanced at his notes. "How long have you been living in your cousin's house?"

"Six months."

"Had you seen much of Mrs. Reaveley before that?"

"Very little, since we were children."

"Mr. Reaveley has told us that his wife once or twice spoke of taking her own life. Did she ever talk in that strain to you?"

The girl nodded slowly. "Once. And I heard her say it to Mr. Reaveley. But he told you, too, that he didn't take it seriously. Neither did I. My cousin constantly used—well, extravagant expressions, that meant just nothing at all. She enjoyed life very much."

"She still had every reason to, would you say?"

Kay lifted her shoulders in a little shrug. "So far as I know. She had almost everything she wanted."

"She seems, however, to have been rather easily thrown off her balance. As on the night of this dinner party."

"I have seen her almost as much upset. And you must remember," said Kay, smiling in her friendly, confidential way at Mr. Akers, "that it *was* a dinner party. I mean, a lot of mixed drinks had been going round."

Mr. Akers smiled back. "And your cousin would be tempted to take rather more than her share, if she was already rather wrought up, as has been suggested?"

"Yes," said Kay, more doubtfully.

"You must have seen more of her than anyone else lately. Can you throw any light on her state of nerves? Has anything occurred recently, that you know of, to upset her?"

Kay hesitated, her attractive face troubled.

"Only this business of the ghost," she said.

"No ghost," murmured Mr. Akers, "has yet been put in evidence. I have heard some story of a family apparition, which is said to have reappeared recently."

"When my cousin heard about it," Kay said, "she seemed rather upset. Well, thoughtful, anyway. . . ."

"Did she discuss it with you?"

"No."

"You think it may have been on her mind last Wednesday?"

"Yes, I think it was," said Kay. "You see, it was all mixed up with this man Whichcord, and only the day before I'd told her about his being drowned. She seemed to brood over that. But she didn't talk about it—to me, at any rate. And I knew very little about the old story then."

"Your cousin was still reluctant to discuss the matter at dinner next day?"

"Yes."

Kay bit her lip, watching the coroner somewhat warily now. She seemed to brace herself against further questioning. The reporters at the table below, pencils poised, looked up at her charming face with frank approval. Once more, however, Mr. Akers appeared prematurely satisfied.

"I don't think I need ask you anything more, Miss Kittredge," he said blandly. "Thank you. . . ."

"Mrs. McWhirter!" his officer called.

If Mr. Tuke, among others, wondered who Mrs. McWhirter might be, the name was plainly no surprise to Kay Kittredge, who seemed to stiffen before she left the stand. Clifford Reaveley stirred in his seat, and something in the set of Coverdale's back, a tall-tale jerk of his dark head, suggested that the name was known to him too. And the solicitor at the counsel's table sat up, and became alert.

Mrs. McWhirter proved to be the tardy witness who had arrived while Dr. Mears was giving evidence. A tall, big-boned woman, her iron-grey hair drawn tightly back into a bun, she wore rusty black silk that crackled as she walked, and a black hat no doubt fashionable in the Hebrides in the time of King Edward VII. Her dour, long-lipped face suggested her native granite, for she was as Scottish as her married name. She took the oath disdainfully, rolling her *r's* and referring to the Deity as 'Gud'.

"Your name is Isabella McWhirter?" Mr. Akers began.

"*I*-sabella," Mrs. McWhirter corrected.

"I beg your pardon. You are employed as housekeeper at 105, Craven Hill?"

"Aha."

"The house is divided into flats, I believe?"

"Aha."

"On the second floor, for instance, there are two flats. Will you tell me who lives in them?"

"A body ca'd Mrs. Forrd bides in Number Thrree, and Mr. Coverdale has Number Fourrr."

"Is there a landing between the flats, with a sofa, so that callers who have to wait can sit down?"

"Aha."

"Will you tell me when you clean these landings?"

"Monday forenoons. A' the week-ends there are folk in and oot, so I dae the landings Mondays. Ither days I juist redd them, and gie them a bit dusting."

"So you cleaned the second floor landing yesterday?"

"Aha. But no in the forenoon. Miss Biddle, o' Number Six, is ganging awa', and lending her flat tae anither leddy. I was helping her sort her gear, and tak' some of it doon tae the dunnkens——"

"The dunnkens . . . ?" Mr. Akers queried.

"The cellars, ye ken. So I didna get roond tae the landings till I'd ta'en my bit dinner."

"At what time was this?"

"After I'd redded up. It wud be twa, mebbe."

"Now," said Mr. Akers, "when you were doing the second floor landing, did you find something?"

"Och aye," said Mrs. McWhirter. "I foond a leddy's green bonnet, the like they ca' a berett."

A sort of rustle went through the court room. Gervase Coverdale jerked his shoulders. The solicitor leaned forward, his eyes on the witness.

"Where did you find this beret?" the coroner asked in his quiet tones.

"On the sofy, thrrust doon ahint a cusshion."

"Is this the beret?"

The coroner's officer repeated his conjuring trick. Mrs. McWhirter took the green beret in her muscular hands.

"Aye," she said. "This is the wee bonnet."

"Had you ever seen it before yesterday?"

"I thocht I kenned it. There was a leddy cam' tae veesit Mr. Coverdale twa-thrree times whiles I was aboot. No sae lately, ye ken—the last time was a month or twa syne, mebbe. And then she wore a bonnet like this yin. But I'll no swear tae it," the witness added, fixing Mr. Akers with a stern look.

"Do you know the lady's name?"

"Och aye, the puir body. She tell't me hersel'. Mistress Rreaveley—her whit was drooned."

Again there was a faint stirr among the intent audience.

"Do you think," Mr. Akers inquired, "that this beret could have been hidden behind the cushion since the night of last Wednesday?"

"Mebbe," said Mrs. McWhirter cannily. "I wudna say. Whiles I plump the cusshions when I'm aboot my bit dusting, and whiles I dinna. I've a muckle deal o' worrk, ye ken, and I canna ca' it tae mind."

At the table for counsel the solicitor half rose from his chair, and the coroner looked at him.

"With your permission, sir," the solicitor said, "I would like this point cleared up, if possible. I am sure the witness, being a Scot, is very thorough in her house work. I would like a more definite opinion from her as to the likelihood of this beret remaining on the sofa for several days without her discovering it."

"You hear the question, Mrs. McWhirter," said the coroner. "What *is* your opinion?"

"Weel," said Mrs. McWhirter judicially, "I wudna ha' thocht it. But I'll no swear tae it," she added quickly.

The solicitor glanced again at Mr. Akers who nodded.

"I believe you live in the basement of the house, Mrs. McWhirter," the former said. "Where—where the dunnkens are?"

"Aha."

"When you are down there, I take it that visitors to the flats above can come and go without your knowledge?"

"Aha. Whiles."

Having digested this, the solicitor bowed to Mr. Akers.

"Thank you, Mr. Coroner," he said, and sat down.

The coroner resumed his interrogation.

"Having found this beret yesterday afternoon, Mrs. McWhirter, what did you do with it?"

"When I'd redded the landings, I had tae gang oot for some messages, sae I took the berett tae Mistress Rreaveley's hoose forbye. I kenned where it waur frae a' the carfuffle in the papers."

"The reports of her death? Yes, I see. You did not wait to tell Mr. Coverdale when he came home?"

"For why? It was no his wee bonnet."

Subdued snickers were heard, hastily stifled as Mrs. McWhirter looked sternly at the offenders. Mr. Akers, unmoved, continued.

"Whom did you see at 7a, Lancaster Terrace?"

"The yoong leddy yon." The witness nodded towards the seats from which she had come. "I gi'ed her the bonnet."

"You mean Miss Kittredge . . .? Well, later in the day, did you speak of all this to your husband?"

"Och, aye. When McWhirter cam' hame tae his tea—he worrks for the borrough, ye ken—I tell't him aboot the bonnet, and he said I shud ha' ta'en it tae the poliss. As if," said Mrs. McWhirter scornfully, "I didna ken that fine. But I'm no sic a fule as tae pit my neb in a poliss station. It's a', 'coom awa' ben', and 'wull ye set yon', and 'wull ye bide a wee for the inspectorr body' . . . Wasting a beesy wumman's time! Na, na, I ken better."

"However," said Mr. Akers with a fleeting smile, "your husband himself reported your discovery to the police?"

"Aye," said the witness tolerantly. "He kens the constable on the beat, and he was ganging oot, onyways, for his dram."

The coroner nodded. "Thank you, Mrs. McWhirter . . ."

He bent to his notes, and as Mrs. McWhirter left the stand in a stately manner, Gervase Coverdale was being called. He almost sprang up, giving the same impression as Clifford Reaveley of controlled impatience set free. With his rather swaggering walk, swinging his arms, showing his cuffs, he strode up the gangway, glanced at the lawyer, mounted the witness stand almost at a run, and rattled off the oath without waiting to be prompted.

Mr. Akers looked at him mildly, and took his time over the preliminaries. Having verified the witness's name and address, he went on:

"You are employed in the chief engineer's office at County Hall, Mr. Coverdale?"

"That is so," Coverdale agreed easily.

"When you returned from your work yesterday, did the housekeeper report finding a woman's beret, which has been produced, on the landing outside your flat?"

"She did." The pleasant voice was rather curt, and Coverdale's florid hooknosed features darkened with a flush of anger as he added: "She also told me that her husband had taken it on himself to go to the police about it."

The solicitor caught his client's eye, and shook his head slightly.

"Do you recognize the beret?" Mr. Akers queried.

Coverdale in turn handled the green cap. "It is like one I have seen Mrs. Reaveley wearing. I can't say more than that."

"In the circumstances, would you not have taken it to the police yourself?"

"No," Coverdale said flatly. "I've been thinking about it, of course. Well, anybody might have left the thing there—a caller waiting for my neighbour across the landing, for instance. As Miss Kittredge said, there must be plenty about. And it might have been—it still may have been—left in the last day or two. The housekeeper plainly doesn't think she can have overlooked it for the best part of a week. No," the witness said again, with a faint smile. "If *I* had found the beret only yesterday, I don't think I should have associated it with Mrs. Reaveley. I should have given it to the housekeeper, to make inquiries."

Mr. Akers glanced, or affected to glance, at his notes.

"The housekeeper's words," he murmured, "were, she wouldn't have thought it. True. On the other hand, she may be unconsciously reluctant to believe she had overlooked it. And one has to consider whether a caller, in a normal frame of mind, who came wearing a hat, would be likely to go away without it. However, the point about your neighbour can no doubt be cleared up." He made a note. "Now, Mr. Coverdale," he went on, "last Wednesday evening, at the time when Mrs. Reaveley appears to have left her house, you were still there, with the other guests?"

"That is so."

"Did you hear the front door slam?"

"I heard *a* door slam."

"How soon after did you leave?"

"About ten minutes later. We all left together."

"Did you go straight back to your flat?"

"Yes."

"Did you see Mrs. Reaveley again?"

"I did not."

"There was nothing to suggest, shall we say, that she had gone to Craven Hill, waited for you for a few minutes, perhaps, and then changed her mind and left again?"

"Nothing that I could see," Coverdale said. "Such an idea never entered my mind. Why should she?"

"You were old friends, I suppose?"

"Certainly. Since the time of her marriage."

"Her husband being a still older friend?"

"I have known him longer," Coverdale said.

"You have heard him say that his wife has twice before run out of the house. Did she ever come to your flat?"

Though Coverdale glanced at his lawyer, and then at the pressmen, he replied as though prepared for the question.

"Yes. Rather less than a year ago she turned up one night. I had gone to bed. She was in a very excited state. I couldn't get much out of her, except that there had been some sort of a quarrel, and she had run out in a temper."

"Why should she come to you, Mr. Coverdale?"

The witness spread out his hands in a rather Latin gesture. His full red lips curled again in a slight smile.

"It was literally a case of any port in a storm. She had rushed out without thinking where she was going. It was a filthy night, raining hard, and if she had thought of going to an hotel she must have realized that she might try a dozen without getting a room at that hour. So she took the line of least resistance. I live quite near, and she came to me. The conventions," said Coverdale, with another deprecatory smile, "and, if I may say so, other people's convenience, meant nothing to Mrs. Reaveley when she was in one of these moods. She simply did what she felt like doing at the moment. She had done the same thing before."

This refrain was a sort of epitaph on Corinne Reaveley. She had done it before. Only now she would not do it again.

While pencils were busy at the press table, Mr. Akers looked thoughtfully at the witness. With the rays of the green-shaded lamp shining on his silver hair and on the pale coloured framework of his spectacles, he was a study in pink and white, in strong contrast to Coverdale's sombre figure, and glossy black hair, and small dark eyes in a sanguine, hook-nosed face. Coverdale stood patiently, with a sort of dignity, the aquiline nose a little in the air, the dark intelligent eyes fixed on the coroner.

"How did you handle this situation, Mr. Coverdale?" the latter queried gently.

"Naturally," said Coverdale, "I tried to persuade her to go home. I made her some coffee, and talked to her—well, pretty straight. After all, I knew her very well."

"Had she no plans?"

"None whatever." Again the full red lips curved in a smile that invited comprehension. "You had to know Mrs. Reaveley to understand this sort of thing. She acted first, and thought afterwards. It was—one of her attractions, in a way."

"Did you persuade her in the end?"

"Yes. I got her to see sense at last. I put on some clothes, and walked to Lancaster Terrace with her."

"At what time was this?"

"About two in the morning."

"Did you see anybody at her house?"

"I didn't try to. I watched her let herself in, and went back to bed."

"Are you on the telephone, Mr. Coverdale?"

Coverdale's smile, as he nodded, acknowledged the point.

"You are wondering why I didn't telephone to her husband. I thought it better not to, in her presence. It might have set her off again. Once I had talked her round, it didn't seem worth while. Also, I didn't know what story she was going to tell."

Mr. Akers appeared to ponder, his eyes on his notes. He looked up at the witness.

"That will be all, Mr. Coverdale. Thank you."

CHAPTER VI

NOTHING BUT THE TRUTH: PHANTASMAL

PETER WARRENER had been called; but Mr. Tuke's eyes were on the last witness, now passing the younger man in the aisle. The ordeal was over, control was momentarily relaxed, and the florid face showed some strong emotion. A rush of blood suffused it; the full lips were compressed into an ugly line, and the small dark eyes stared at Clifford Reaveley, sitting with his stiff square back, looking up at his old acquaintance. Suspicion, enmity—what that stare conveyed remained a puzzle as Coverdale swung into his seat and turned his back.

The coroner having got through his preamble, his questions to young Warrener, who looked deeply dejected and very nervous, took an unexpected course.

"I don't propose," said Mr. Akers, "to dwell on the unhappy practical joke you perpetrated, Mr. Warrener. The outcome will have been a terrible lesson to you. All I want you to tell me is how much you knew beforehand about the man Whichcord, whom, so to speak, you impersonated."

"But I knew nothing about him," Warrener muttered, so low as to be barely audible in the back benches. He stammered a little. "I—I never heard of him before th-that evening."

"How did you come to hear of him then?"

"One of the guests—Miss Plimsoll—mentioned his name during dinner."

"Speak up a little, please. How did the topic arise?"

"Miss Plimsoll asked Cor—asked Mrs. Reaveley if she had heard that Whichcord had seen the ghost again."

There was a stir at the press table, repeatedly disappointed by the few and cursory references to the Hyde Park Ghost. It was to be disappointed again, for Mr. Akers bypassed the phantom once more.

"We have been told that Mrs. Reaveley did not wish to discuss the matter. You learnt, however, that this man Whichcord was dead?"

"Not then," Peter Warrener explained. "Afterwards I asked Mr. Coverdale what it was all about, but he didn't seem to know much, except that it was some old story about a ghost, and this fellow Whichcord seeing it. Then we went up to the drawing-room, and I tackled Miss Kittredge, but she said she didn't know much either, and it wasn't worth repeating, anyway. I'm afraid," said the witness, looking more unhappy than ever, "I'd had a few drinks, and I was rather persistent, and Miss Kittredge choked me off. She said, 'The man's dead, you idiot. He's been drowned. Do drop it,' or something like that."

Someone sniggered, and the shamefaced witness flushed.

"This gave you the idea for a practical joke?" Mr. Akers inquired.

Warrener nodded miserably. "I—I suppose I was feeling annoyed. I thought I'd get my own back. I wish to God——"

But Mr. Akers had again established all he wished to establish. He was not interested in what constituted News, and to the disgust of the press table, alert for an account of the practical joke and its dramatic outcome, he interrupted the witness.

"Yes, thank you, Mr. Warrener. That will do."

His officer was calling Harvey Tuke as the young man left the stand with more alacrity than he had entered it. He looked bewildered at having been let off so lightly.

Mr. Tuke took his place. The embodiment of the Devil in dark grey suiting, he looked sardonically at Mr. Akers, and Mr. Akers, slightly plump and pink, looked blandly at his saturnine witness, as though they had never met before, or drunk the Senior Universities' sherry together.

"Your name is Harvey Mervyn Tuke, and you live at 28 St. Luke's Court, Westminster? You are senior legal assistant to the Director of Public Prosecutions?"

Mr. Tuke confirmed these assumptions.

"Were you a guest, Mr. Tuke, at the dinner party given by Mr. and Mrs. Reaveley last Wednesday?"

"My wife and I were both there."

"Had you known your host and hostess beforehand?"

"I had never met either of them before. Mrs. Reaveley was an acquaintance of my wife's."

"However, you no doubt formed some impression of Mrs. Reaveley's state of mind that evening? Was there anything about it that struck you as strained or abnormal?"

"During dinner," said Mr. Tuke carefully, "Mrs. Reaveley showed signs of nervous irritation. She seemed to throw this off, however. So far as I could judge, that is. All the rest of the evening she was playing bridge, while I sat out. I do not play cards."

Mr. Akers, a keen bridge player himself, was well aware of this. If he smiled to himself, no one in the court suspected any by-play between coroner and witness, who might have been total strangers; nor by the faintest inflection did his next question betray familiarity with another of Mr. Tuke's little fads.

"I am hoping you can help me, Mr. Tuke, in this matter of times. Mr. Reaveley has told us that his wife left the drawing-room at about eleven-thirty."

"That is substantially correct. It was a minute or two after the half hour. The clock in the drawing-room, by the way, was three minutes fast."

"The witness then said that he went upstairs himself, the first time, at about ten to twelve."

"It was rather earlier. At seventeen or eighteen minutes to the hour."

"He then told us that his argument with his wife, in her bathroom, went on for five minutes or so."

"He was actually away for twelve or thirteen minutes."

"You seem to have observed these times very precisely yourself," Mr. Akers murmured innocently, as he made a note.

"I was looking at my watch a good deal just then. It was getting late."

"You can rely upon your watch?"

"I can always rely upon my watches."

The coroner permitted himself to smile openly. "An enviable state of things. Can you tell me when Mr. Reaveley went upstairs the second time?"

"He returned from his first absence at five to twelve. It must have been five minutes later when he went up again. The clock had struck midnight a minute or two before. No doubt the interval of waiting seemed longer to him."

"Did you hear a door slam soon after?"

"Yes. Half a minute later, I should say."

"Thank you, Mr. Tuke. I am obliged to you."

As the witness turned to leave the stand, he caught Fenne's surprised glance. Mr. Tuke was a little surprised himself, but still more interested, by the brevity of his examination. The coroner's treatment of the whole inquiry was provocative of thought, less on account of what he brought out than of what he omitted to bring out. As Fenne himself put it, Mr. Akers was a downy bird. He also had his methods, and the present inquest was an instructive example of his arid and expeditious style when unhampered by a jury. To Mr. Tuke certain things were already clear. In the twenty-four hours since his own call at New Scotland Yard, and in part perhaps because of it, higher potencies and powers than the local police had been at work. The current proceedings, again, would not be concluded that day. And Mr. Akers might still have a surprise or two up his sleeve.

He had indeed. His officer had called Miss Plimsoll, who smiled at Harvey as they passed one another. She took the oath in her composed manner and agreed that her names were Euphemia Sybil.

"You were companion to the late Mrs. Hugo Demarest for a good many years, I believe?" the coroner began.

"For twenty-five years," Miss Plimsoll replied.

"During which time you lived at 7a Lancaster Terrace?"

"Yes."

"I want you to carry your mind back, Miss Plimsoll, to a night in September, 1940. The 13th, to be exact."

Now there was a stir among the pressmen, who had scarcely hoped for this. Neither had Mr. Tuke expected the ghost to be resurrected at this stage. The other witnesses seemed startled, the little baldheaded man, sitting by the trim blue figure of Mr. Benton, wriggled in his shameful coat, and Miss Plimsoll herself raised her eyebrows before she replied:

"I can remember that night very clearly."

"I understand you have reason to," said Mr. Akers. "To put it briefly, did you discover about midnight that Mrs. Demarest had left the house, although a raid was taking place, and did you, from a window, see her standing at the street corner, beside the figure of a man?"

"Yes," said Miss Plimsoll, taking her cue.

"How was this man dressed?"

"He wore a peaked cap, a thick short coat—like what I believe is called a reefer—and long boots, with light coloured stockings turned over them."

"Had he a beard?"

"Yes," said Miss Plimsoll again.

Mr. Akers smiled at her. "Thank you very much," he said in his most winning way.

Like Peter Warrener, Miss Plimsoll appeared perplexed by this summary ending of her testimony, but none the less relieved. Had decorum permitted, the whole press table would no doubt have groaned: and almost everyone else in the room was momentarily disillusioned and disgusted. But only momentarily: even Mr. Akers could not exclude News when it was evidence; and the sensation of the morning was launched when the next witness was called.

"Albert Jones."

The shabby baldheaded man rose with a jerk and shuffled to the witness stand, his head well down in his coat collar. Miss Plimsoll gave him a wide berth as they met. A grimy hand grasped the Bible, and he repeated the oath in a hoarse whisper which caused the coroner's officer to adjure him to speak up. Mr. Jones might have been anything between forty and sixty; he had watery eyes, and a red nose, and several days' stubble darkened his chin.

"Your name," said Mr. Akers, with no indication of belief or otherwise, "is Albert Jones?"

"Yus, sir," said Mr. Jones hoarsely.

"You have no permanent address or occupation?"

"That's right, sir. Well, it's like this 'ere, see——"

"Never mind, Mr. Jones. That is all I wish to know. Now are you in the habit of sleeping out of doors on warm nights? In Hyde Park, for instance?"

"That's right," said Mr. Jones again.

"Were you in Hyde Park on the night of Wednesday last, the 7th of this month?"

"Yus, sir."

"And did you yesterday make a statement to the police?"

"Yus, sir." Mr. Jones sniffed, and drew a ragged cuff across his nose. "It's like this 'ere. I bin finking over what I'd see'd. I knowed abaht pore old Wally——"

"One moment," said Mr. Akers. "You mean a man named Whichcord?"

"That's right. All the park knowed abaht *'im*—and what 'appened to 'im. So what I see'd fair put the breeze up me, strewth it did, and I bin giving the park a clear miss, see? Then I 'eard as 'ow this lydy'd bin found in the water, too, jest like Wally. Blimy," said Mr. Jones, "you could 'ave knocked me dahn wiv a fevver. No more 'yde Park for me, not never, I ses. It ain't 'ealthy. But then I ses to meself, you've got a dooty, ghosts or no ghosts. And there may be a bit in it, I finks. . . ."

The witness looked hopefully at the coroner, who merely nodded and recalled him to the point.

"So yesterday you went to one of the park keepers with your story, and he took you to the police station to make a statement there. Now, Mr. Jones, what *did* you see on Wednesday night? Or on Thursday morning, to be exact. It was in the early hours of the morning, wasn't it?"

"That's right, sir. I ain't got no ticker, but I 'eard Big Ben strike 'ar-past free. You can 'ear wunnerful at night."

"What were you doing at that time?"

"'Aving a stretcher, sir. It weren't too perishing warm, dossing dahn, so I took a trot."

"You were walking. Whereabouts exactly?"

"Along by the water, sir, between the boat'ouses and the bridge. I 'ad me peepers open, and I was keeping on the grass, so as not to wake nobody. Cops and keepers, see . . . ?"

Mr. Jones leered at the coroner. With the whole court room hanging on his words, and the pressmen scribbling furiously, the sorry creature had gained confidence. He stood more erect, and stuck his bristly chin out of his collar.

Mr. Akers prompted him. "Yes, go on, please."

"It was a luvverly night," said Mr. Jones, prolonging the suspense. "A bit of a moon, see, and the water shining like a picsher. I 'ad some fag-ends in me pocket, and I was jest finking as I'd 'ave a drag, when I see'd 'er."

"Whom did you see?"

"The lydy, sir."

"You saw a lady," Mr. Akers repeated, amid a tense silence. "What was she doing?"

"Setting on a chair by the water, sir."

"By the Serpentine. Was she near the edge?"

"Yus, sir. On the parff."

"Was she alone?"

"Yus, sir. At least, I *fought* so," Mr. Jones added meaningly.

"Well, what did you do?"

"I went a bit closer, sir, to 'ave a dekko. I fought p'raps she was one of the reg'lars. Summun I knows, see?"

"But she was no one you knew?"

"Lor' lumme, no," said Mr. Jones fervently. "Not in them trahsers." He coughed, and grinned sheepishly, with a show of intermittent blackened teeth. "What I mean, sir, I could twig she 'ad posh clo'es on."

"What sort of clothes? A coat and skirt of the same material, for instance?"

"That's right. Tweed, they was. And silk stockings—I seed 'em shine. And a sparkler on 'er 'and."

"Where were her hands?" Mr. Akers asked. "And how

was she sitting? Leaning forward, or against the back of the chair?"

"She was leaning back, sir, wiv 'er 'ands on 'er lap. She kep' 'er 'ead dahn, and 'er 'air was all over 'er face, but I twigged she was only a gal, like. A young-un, anyways."

"Was she wearing a hat?"

"No, sir, she 'adn't no 'at."

"You were close enough to see all these details?"

"Yus, sir. I crep' up pretty close. I fought p'raps she'd bin took ill, see?"

"Did she look round, or move at all?"

"No, sir. I s'pose she didn't 'ear me. I was on the parff then, but I was keeping quiet."

"So you didn't actually see her face?"

"That's right. 'Cause of 'er 'air being over it."

"Well, what did you do next?"

"I coughed, like." Mr. Jones coughed again, in illustration. "And jest then it 'appened," he said.

"What happened?" asked Mr. Akers.

"Something made me look rahnd." At the recollection the witness seemed to lose some of his newly-found poise. He hunched his head in his collar, almost as though ducking before a blow. "And there it was," he said hoarsely.

"There was what?"

"The man. Or whatever it was. Not ten yards away from me."

"You saw the figure of a man," Mr. Akers said quietly, while every head in the court room craned to hear. "Where was it standing?"

"On the grass be'ind me, sir."

"On the grass beyond the path? Did some sound make you look round?"

"No, sir, I didn't 'ear nuffin."

The witness still had an oddly shrunken air. If ever there was a man scared by a memory, it was Mr. Jones. The coroner looked at him thoughtfully before he inquired:

"How was this figure dressed, Mr. Jones?"

The witness's hoarse voice grated in the hushed room.

"It 'ad 'igh boots on, sir, and whitish sort of stockings turned over the tops, and a short dark coat. And it 'ad a cap wiv a peak, and a gold badge on it. I seed it shine."

In the tense instant before Mr. Akers put his next question, somebody dropped something—possibly a pin. It sounded like a bar of iron. Several people afterwards averred that the court room turned colder, an illusion perhaps created by the curiously shrivelled appearance of the deplorable little man in the mahogany box.

"Did this—er, apparition speak to you?" Mr. Akers asked. "Or did you say anything?"

Mr. Jones wagged his bald head. "It never said a word, sir. Jest stood there, staring at me. I couldn't 'ave spoke, not if you'd paid me."

"Well, then, what happened next?"

"It begun to come at me."

"*At* you?"

"Towards me, sir."

"And what did you do then?"

"I did a bloody bunk," said Mr. Jones simply.

Someone smothered a laugh which sounded more hysterical than mirthful. But for this the silence was still profound. Only at the press table the pencils were flying like things possessed.

"You ran away," Mr. Akers translated. "How far?"

"I didn't stop, sir, till I got to them trees by the Sooperintendent's 'ouse."

"Did you look behind you?"

With a nervous snigger at the very idea, the witness replied in the style of *The Ancient Mariner*.

"Look be'ind? Not me. I fought it was coming arter me."

"When you did stop, did you look back then?"

"Yus, I took a quick dekko, sir."

"The figure had not followed you?"

"No, sir."

"Could you still see it?"

"I couldn't see a fing any more. I'd run a good bit—couple

of 'undred yards, I dare say, and it was pretty dark, see, and then the trees was in the way."

"So you don't know what happened either to the figure in the peaked cap, or to the lady on the chair?"

"That's right, sir. Not a fing. I didn't 'ang abaht, believe *me.* I started finking of pore ole Wally, and when I got me bref I beat it again. Clean out of the park," said Mr. Jones. "I fought to meself, s'pose it's a Warning, same as Wally 'ad? I ain't bin near the place till yesterday, when I fought p'raps it was me dooty, like I says. But you don't catch me dossing dahn there again, not me. Not near the perishing Serpentine, anyways——"

"Yes," said Mr. Akers smoothly. "Thank you."

He bent over his notes. His officer beckoned, and upon this picture of a tattered, breathless figure fleeing from the dark glades of Hyde Park as though devils, or ghosts, were pursuing it, Mr. Albert Jones left the stand, the first witness, his tremors notwithstanding, to do so reluctantly. There was a gleam in his watery eyes as he looked at the press table. There was going to be a bit in it after all, or he was much mistaken. He shuffled to his seat, and the officer, who throughout his remarkable testimony had stood beside him with a perfectly wooden face, was calling again.

"Dr. New."

The graceful black figure of the pathologist, the antithesis, in every respect, of her predecessor, moved unhurriedly to the stand.

"You have already been sworn, doctor," Mr. Akers murmured. "We need not go into your qualifications again. Will you give me your results of your post mortem examination of the deceased?"

As Dr. New began to read quietly from another foolscap form, Mr. Tuke's thoughts were once more roving. They had a bagful to bite on now—such strange developments, and, again, such significant omissions. It was as gratifying as it was (to be honest) surprising that Section (D) of the *Aide Mémoire* should be so soon supported, if scarcely yet confirmed, to say nothing of the general official activities implied by the presence of the detective-sergeant across the aisle. Then there was the dramatic re-entry of the ghost, as unforeseen as it was inexplicable. . . .

The pathologist's quiet voice ran on. " . . . no organic disease . . . water in the lungs . . . the left ventrical of the heart . . . alcohol in the stomach . . . no external injuries . . . cause of death, asphyxiation by drowning."

"Thank you, doctor," said Mr. Akers, and immediately, as Dr. New handed over her report and returned to her seat, began to commune with himself, paying no apparent attention whatever to his audience.

"This is an inquiry into the death of Corinne Laura Reaveley, whose body was recovered from the Serpentine in the early morning of Thursday, September the 8th. As insufficient evidence has been forthcoming to show how deceased came to be in the water, I shall adjourn this inquest for a fortnight, until the 27th."

"Witnesses in the last case may leave the court," the coroner's officer announced.

Another name was called: another inquest had begun.

EXORCISM

Tuesday, Wednesday

"*Our Sovereign Lord the King, like a virtuous and most gracious Prince, nothing earthly so highly weighing as the advancing of the common Profit, Wealth and Commodity, of this his Realm, considering the daily great Damages and Losses which have happened . . . by occasion of Land-Waters and other outrageous springs, in and upon Meadows, Pastures, and other low Grounds, adjoining to Rivers, Floods and other Water-Courses: And, over that, by and thro' Mills, Mill-Dams, Wears, Fishgarths, Kedels, Gores, Gotes, Flood-gates, Locks and other Impediments, in and upon the same Rivers and other Water-courses . . . Hath therefore by deliberate Advice and Assent of his Lords, Spiritual and Temporal, and also his loving Commons, in this present Parliament assembled, ordained, established and enacted. . . .*"

23 Henry VIII., A.D. 1531.
(Cap. V.)

CHAPTER I

NO ONE ANSWERS THE BELL

GORDON CARTWRIGHT pressed the button again, keeping his thumb on it for several seconds. He could hear the bell, buzzing faintly somewhere below like an imprisoned insect. The rumble of traffic in Bayswater Road, horns hooting and exhausts banging, came to him with the loudness that precedes rain; but when he leaned against the door, listening for other sounds, hatless and breathing a little fast from haste and something like anxiety, not a whisper reached him from the tall house which had been Corinne Reaveley's.

A third time he jabbed the bell, and kept it ringing. When he released it abruptly it was to run back on to the pavement and look up at the house. The fanlight was dark, and there was no glimmer from the basement. From where his car stood at the kerb Gloucester Terrace stretched away into the night, half a mile of it, a long straight perspective of dwindling luminous dots from the feeble incandescent filaments of Paddington's gas-lamps. It was just after ten o'clock. The street seemed empty of human life. Across the road, bright windows shone here and there in the lofty façade of the flats; but the shattered houses of the terrace beyond 7a soared like a wall of black velvet, fading into grey nothingness at the razed corner of Lancaster Street. The sky was pitchy black, underhung with clouds that all day had been drifting from the west, though the rainfall they foreboded still held off. The air was no longer cool, but still and oppressive.

He hurried round the bow of the area railings into Lancaster Terrace. In the more numerous windows there no light showed. Or did one? For an instant Cartwright thought a fugitive gleam flickered and went behind one of the long windows of the dining-room, the curtains of which were not fully drawn. It could have come through the doorway, from the hall beyond; and Kay, if she were still waiting for him, might be in the study at the rear of the hall. But why had she not answered the bell? Or his telephone call? And had Parker, the maid, already gone to bed . . .?

At the foot of the short street the traffic lights blazed brightly and cheerfully, changing from green to orange and red. The tall standard lamps in Bayswater Road were brilliant. Gay scarlet omnibuses went by, and cars with golden headlamps. People were crossing the end of the Terrace, and on the opposite corner the Crown public house still glowed like a fair. After the sinister desert of Gloucester Terrace, here was the crowded, living world again. Cartwright shook off his fancies: Kay must have given him up, and gone out. Parker *had* gone to bed, on the fifth floor, where she would hear nothing.

But the fancies returned. There had been that urgent message. . . . He put his hand on the gate at the head of the area steps, with some idea of trying the basement door to the kitchen quarters. And it was then that the busy world seemed suddenly to surge towards him. Quite a procession was advancing up Lancaster Terrace from the main road. It filled the pavement. A voice hailed him.

"Good evening, Cartwright!"

The novelist blinked at the tall figure silhouetted against the traffic lights. Even before he identified it, he recognized something familiar in the rotund form trundling beside Harvey Tuke. Behind came two more men, carrying bulky objects like kit-bags.

"Hullo!" Cartwright said, staring in astonishment. "Are you coming here too? Kay ought to be in, but I can't make anyone hear the bell."

"Miss Kittredge was expecting you?"

There was a sharpness in Mr. Tuke's query. Sir Bruton Kames, in a haze of cheroot smoke, had come to a halt leaning on his cane. He tilted his ancient hat off his eyes to peer at the novelist. The other two men, with their bundles, which now appeared to be sacks, stood behind.

"Kay telephoned me," Cartwright said. "I was out. The

message sounded urgent—would I come round the moment I got back. I saw her here for a few minutes this afternoon. She seemed all right—a bit wrought up, of course, after the inquest. She told me about it. I'd have been there, but I've had a day of family business. Everything comes at once. This evening I had to go out again——"

"What time was this telephone message?"

"Just before seven. I only got home twenty minutes ago. I rang up, but no one answered. Then I drove round. I've been ringing and knocking. . . . There are no lights, though I thought I saw a flicker once, through this window."

As he pointed, Sir Bruton said soothingly, for with this recital formless fears had magnified, and Cartwright's voice betrayed them:

"Gal's probably gone out. Or dropped off to sleep. She's had enough to tire her out."

"What about the maid?" Mr. Tuke asked.

"I suppose she's gone to bed. Or she's out."

"You say Miss Kittredge seemed to want you urgently?"

"It sounded like that. She has never asked me round in a hurry before. But the woman at my place is rather a fool. She couldn't remember Kay's exact words."

The little crowd—for such it seemed in the emptiness of that backwater of Bayswater Road's bright and populous stream—had begun to move round the corner to where Cartwright's car stood before the door of 7a, which still towered lightless. The novelist ran up the steps of the porch, and for the fourth time rang the bell.

Mr. Tuke murmured to Sir Bruton, who shrugged his heavy shoulders and wagged his head. All could hear the bell's remote buzzing, but the tall house remained mute and dark. As Cartwright, his finger still on the button, turned with an expressive gesture of his other hand, Mr. Tuke spoke to one of the two strange men, who immediately walked back round the corner into Lancaster Terrace. Mr. Tuke himself joined the novelist under the portico.

"Is there any way in at the back?"

"Only a fire escape thing." Cartwright was still ringing

with savage persistence. "The tradesmen's door is below here, in the area. I was thinking of trying it as you came along." He dropped his hand, and the bell was silent. His anxious face close to Mr. Tuke's, he burst out: "Why? What are you afraid of? What has happened. What are you all doing here?"

Mr. Tuke did not at once reply to this. "Chaffinch has gone to the area door," he said. "He's my chief clerk."

"But why are you all here?" Cartwright cried again.

"We're doing a little exploring. We were not calling at the house."

The man who had gone round the corner ran up to join them in the porch.

"Locked," he said. "And the windows are barred."

Only now did Mr. Tuke reply to the questions he had appeared to ignore.

"Nothing has happened that I know of." He seemed to reflect. "But I'm not altogether happy about this, Cartwright," he added. "I don't like the date." And then, with a rather grim smile which in the darkness Cartwright could not see: "I think we are justified in breaking and entering. Sir Bruton and I will take the responsibility."

"Smash a window, eh?" The Director had joined them, and there was definite relish in his voice. "Up those steps at the back, and in at the study? Nice and quiet there. This bloke Joe'll have a spanner or something."

"He's not in this," Mr. Tuke said. "If any of us are going to be locked up, it will be you and I."

"Attaboy!" said Sir Bruton. He began to gobble and chuckle. "If we're copped, I'd give ten years of your life to see Wray's face. Think he'll bail us out?"

"Wray has put in some quick work since he got my *aide mémoire* yesterday morning, anyway. Of course," Mr. Tuke added, "we may see a light at the back."

"Then why hasn't Kay answered?" Cartwright cried, his worst imaginings confirmed by this startling bit of dialogue. "What *has* happened? I've felt for days that something was wrong here. . . ."

Mr. Tuke took his arm. "We're going to find out."

They all trooped down from the porch to join the man called Joe, who was waiting by the car. He was a small, elderly man with bandy legs, wearing a cloth cap. A dark scarf, knotted about his neck, was ornamented with figures of animals in white. Two bulky sacks were at his feet, and a pair of squat electric lamps dangled from his hand. The second stranger, Chaffinch, who carried a third lamp, appeared by dress and demeanour to be the pattern of a respectable lawyer's clerk. The poor light failed to reveal a sort of boyishness, a controlled reflection of Sir Bruton's more obvious zest for the unorthodox.

Mr. Tuke looked up the long shadowy vista of Gloucester Terrace, no longer quite empty, for a couple was approaching on the other side. He said to the Director:

"We'd better go this way. Round by Lancaster Street. Bayswater Road and the mews will be too public."

"Don't want a mob with us," Sir Bruton agreed with another chuckle. "Not to mention a bobby. We look like a gang of cracksmen, off home with the swag, as it is."

The party of five began to walk up Gloucester Terrace, Sir Bruton, Mr. Tuke and Cartwright leading, Chaffinch and the man Joe, with their mysterious sacks and lamps, following behind. The couple across the road passed by. On the near side, the damaged houses, their windows boarded, soon became mere blackened shells, gaping at the night, waiting for demolition. Where these ended, a new wall of salvaged bricks continued the line of the terrace to what had been Lancaster Street. Opposite this, beyond the flats, a pale whitish mass, amorphous in the dim radiance of a street lamp, was the west end of the parish church of St. James, its shortened spire spectral in the gloom.

Only a few steps had been taken when from behind the low wall ahead a figure appeared out of Lancaster Street. As it halted at the corner, Mr. Tuke halted too, putting a hand on Cartwright's arm. A clear coast was among the desiderata of breaking and entering.

While the little group stood still, the figure ahead seemed

to stare towards them. It was that of a man, but he was merely a dark shadow in the glimmer of the lamp by the church across the street. Though a hundred yards away, no doubt he could see them too, and the car drawn up before No 7a. Cartwright, if now he had all his wits about him, was confused and alarmed, and more than ever prone to sinister fancies; and it seemed to him that the distant unknown, poised there at the corner, had the impermanent air of one calculating, measuring, weighing chances one against another. Could they be encountering a fellow burglar, some sneak-thief escaping from a back window . . . ? But for this man, and themselves, the long street stretched empty again.

And then Cartwright felt a sudden stiffening of Mr. Tuke's fingers, still on his arm. Not half a minute had gone by; and what ensued seemed to happen with the speed of the nightmare it resembled. The figure at the corner ducked back behind the wall; Mr. Tuke started forward; and then that dark shape had leaped out again, and was running over the road. Some large burden hung over one shoulder—was everyone carrying sacks that night?—but the man ran fast, swaying a little, straight for the lamp-post before the church. Mr. Tuke was running too, and Cartwright with him, though why they ran he knew not, except that a sudden dreadful sense of urgency possessed him. He was aware that Chaffinch was beside him.

The man ahead, with his burden, had reached the opposite pavement. Now he was stooping, doubled up, under the lamp, the dark thing he had been shouldering dropped on the flags beside him. The three pursuers were running diagonally across the street; Mr. Tuke was calling out, and Cartwright found himself shouting also. They were half-way to the bent figure by the church. And then the man seemed to lift and heave; for an instant, amid confused movements, he stood half-erect; and then he appeared to shorten, and dwindle, and vanish. A clash and clang of metal reverberated down Gloucester Terrace.

Cartwright, now leading by a yard, leaped the kerb and stood panting by the lamp-post, staring incredulously about him at empty space.

CHAPTER II

L.C.C., M.D.

Mr. Tuke did not pause to stare about him. Panting for breath—he was forty-nine, and in no training for hundred-yard sprints—he stooped over the pavement. Chaffinch, also rather winded, bent beside him. Their actions, and that metallic clash, the echoes of which had barely died, jerked Cartwright's wits; and even before he distinguished the iron manhole-cover among the flags by the low kerb that once upheld the church railings, he was beginning to understand how a man could vanish under his very eyes.

As he, too, stooped over the iron lid, the man Joe was running up, minus his sacks, crying breathlessly in anger:

"Who is he? What's his game, going down there?"

"Which manhole is this?" Mr. Tuke asked sharply.

"The one we call the Subway, sir. What I was taking you down. That's the Ranelagh, along there——"

"Open it! We must get after him at once."

Glancing where the man pointed, though he could see nothing in the shadows beyond the lamp-light, Cartwright felt his shoe touch something that clinked. It was a simple key—a steel shank with a cross-piece. He reached for it, but Joe, whose hand had gone to his pocket, was before him.

"This'll do. The bastard forgot it, and it shook out."

"Be quick!" Mr. Tuke said.

The key was inserted by the rim of the manhole-cover. The iron slab rose almost silently, as though oiled. Beneath was a stout grating. Pushing the lid back until it stopped at an angle just beyond the vertical, Joe began to lift the grating. Chaffinch had switched on his electric lamp, and its beam fell upon the head of a narrow iron ladder descending the rectangular shaft.

The fifth member of the party was now lumbering up, dragging both the sacks, his cheroot clamped in his teeth. Puffing and panting, a sort of unholy glee mingled in Sir Bruton's crimsoned face with a more sober concern. He rolled a prominent eye at Mr. Tuke, who shrugged. Joe was already sitting on the edge of the shaft, his bandy legs dangling. Suddenly he cocked his head, and listened.

"Hear that?"

A distant sound reached them, a rumble as of drums.

"I told you," Joe said. "That's up Hampstead way."

"Get on, man!" Mr. Tuke barked.

"If he bolts below, sir——"

"We may have to go there too. Hurry, hurry . . .!"

"Well, he'll be for it. *And* us!" With a shrug, Joe added to the Director: "Best drop them sacks after us, sir."

He began to descend the iron ladder. In the pool of gas-light his waist, his shoulders, his head, disappeared jerkily below the pavement. Chaffinch's lamp, directed down the shaft, shone briefly on the cloth cap and dark scarf, now seen to be dotted with white greyhounds. Mr. Tuke, swinging the third lamp, was handing his felt hat to Sir Bruton, who, breathing heavily, leaned on his cane, the sacks at his feet. As the cloth cap dropped from sight, a longer ruffle of thunder jarred the ominously still air.

Until now, Cartwright had lived and moved as in a dream. The sudden action, the swift chase, this startling climax, left no time for conscious thought. Little more than a minute had passed since they started their pursuit. But the nightmarish element never left him; and, his wits working once more, his mind's eye seeing again that limp burden hurried across the street, flung upon the flags, and then, with the fugitive unknown himself, evanished beneath their feet, his resurgent fears were crystallized by Mr. Tuke's reiterated demand for speed. His heart contracted, and he cried out, although with sickening certainty he now knew the answer:

"Kay! Where's Kay . . .?"

No one replied. Mr. Tuke was lowering his long legs into the shaft. Down he went, more rapidly, because more recklessly, than the stolid and experienced Joe. His satanic face bobbed in the pool of light, and then, as he missed his foothold, no stage devil, such as he so closely resembled, ever fell faster from view. The direst misgivings failed to repress the Director's mirth. Sir Bruton's own figure seeming to relegate him to a surface role, Chaffinch, with formal courtesy, was now standing aside. In a frenzy of haste and dread, Cartwright slid his feet into the manhole, gripped the ladder, felt for a rung, and began his descent.

The manhole measured two feet by two and a half; the ladder was narrow and vertical. Knees bumped iron rungs, elbows scraped brickwork, as he lowered himself with awkward speed. But the shaft was only some eight feet deep, and Mr. Tuke was shining his lamp on the bottom rungs.

"Mind your head!" he cried, as Cartwright dropped.

Turning in the confined space, the novelist followed, crouching, into a low narrow tunnel, lit by the lamp. Scraping sounds behind indicated that Chaffinch was now coming down. A steady rushing as of water sounded ahead. Mr. Tuke's bent silhouette, in an aureole of light, filled the tunnel. But this ended almost immediately. The pair emerged into what seemed a spacious vault. The rushing water was louder, and plainly flowed underfoot.

Joe stood in the vault, flashing his lamp. Being short, as well as bow-legged, he scarcely stooped. Cartwright, incautiously straightening, cracked his head against the roof. The vault smelt musty, but seemed dry. The brick floor was almost flat, dipping a little to the middle, and the low brickwork of the roof made a wide, flattish arch. Slender stalactites hung from it, silvery threads in the light of the lamps. Above it was the roadway of Gloucester Terrace, and this vault seemed almost the breadth of the street. It might be no bigger than a large cellar, or it might stretch for miles; for the lamps being designed for endurance rather than for brilliance, and their beams blurred and diffused by a slight haze, one could see clearly only for a few yards.

His back to the way they had come, Joe was listening. Cartwright and Mr. Tuke stared into the haze, which caught and held the light as a sponge holds water. Through the rushing underfoot came confused sounds from the tunnel behind them.

"He'll have gone that way, anyhow," Joe said. His voice, raised above the ceaseless noise below, boomed with a muffled quality in the shallow vault. "The Subway's bricked up at Lancaster Terrace—*What's that?*"

Cartwright could hear nothing but the hidden stream. The man's ears were better attuned to subterranean sounds, and he started forward. The other two followed, stooping, just as Chaffinch, issuing bent double from the tunnel, dragging the sacks Sir Bruton had cast down after him, unbent too far, banged his head, and swore loudly.

There was a little water in a runnel along the middle of the brick floor, which was much worn and uneven. The arched roof had its own traps for the unwary; Cartwright's head scraped some projection, and he stooped yet lower. A silver stalactite snapped as he brushed by it. The musty air was heavy, the unending muted torrent underfoot, a utilitarian Alph running through its own measureless caverns to the sea, confused him. The blurred glow of the lamps, moving forward in a sort of bubble around the bent figures, baffled and bewildered. The nightmare was now complete in every circumstance, to the authentic pitch of horror, for somewhere in these dark catacombs Kay must be, helpless, perhaps injured, senseless. . . . That limp burden had seemed neither to stir nor cry as it was rapt from sight. He was still beyond wondering what these devilries meant, or whom, besides Kay, they were pursuing. Anguish for her racked him. If only they could *see!* If only they could hurry faster . . . !

Yet they were hurrying. Joe's bandy legs trotted in the forefront of the fan of light. Cartwright and Mr. Tuke were close behind him. Their shadows wavered over the uneven floor, footsteps echoed to the refrain of rushing water. And since they opened the manhole, only another minute or two had gone by.

A sudden outcry beat about the vault.

"I can see him!" Joe cried. "*Hi, you there . . . !*"

Cartwright could at first see nothing beyond their own moving halo. And then, somewhere ahead, another light flashed. A point of brightness, whether fifty yards away or thrice as far he could not tell, it pierced the luminous bubble, blazing at them; then it dimmed, and swept sideways. He thought now that it was very near. Joe was running; they were all running, breathless, stooping, lamps swinging, shadows leaping wildly, shoes clattering on the bricks. The refrain of the torrent beneath seemed louder.

The light in front went out, just as Joe checked so abruptly that Cartwright reeled against him.

"Gawd a'mighty!" he cried, and leaped forward again.

In the middle of the brick floor loomed dimly an object like the parapet of a well. It was perhaps two feet high. Draped over this little wall was something dark. A piece of old sacking? A strip of cloth . . . ?

It was neither. As they ran up, the light of the lamps focused on a girl's legs, bent from the knees, in grey silk stockings. No more of her was visible.

That instant's horror was to haunt Cartwright for weeks. In full daylight, the sound of rushing water, even the filling of a bath, was to sicken him with fear. Yet in the instant the worst was over. Kay lay doubled up, as though asleep, in a sort of cup, her legs dangling over the rim. At first sight the thing resembled a font, for within the brick parapet cement sides sloped inward. The rush of waters was loud beneath her; but only when Cartwright, with shaking hands, helped Joe to lift her out, was the cause of the man's outcry, and the fate she had by seconds survived, apparent to them all. The sloping cup became a funnel, and the lamps shining down it played on a swift brown stream, swirling and bubbling six or eight feet below. Those few seconds more, and she would have been forced, unconscious, down the funnel. But it was no more than an air shaft, and less than two feet square, and with the pursuers at his heels, the murderer had left his crime half done, to make his own escape.

They laid Kay gently on the brick floor. By the lamplight Cartwright touched her face; it was warm. He listened to her breathing. Chaffinch, who had not forgotten his First Aid, found her pulse, and raised an eyelid, and passed his fingers delicately through the tangle of her dark hair.

"She'll do. She's breathing easily." His own breath was coming fast. "She must be drugged. I can't feel any head injuries. She's been atrociously handled, poor child. . . ."

She had been, indeed. Her black frock was crumpled and stained and torn, stockings were laddered, smears of dirt streaked her pale cheeks. From a graze on her forehead blood trickled. Cartwright's violent revulsion of relief, as he knelt beside her, gripping a small limp hand, was swept away by a gust of suffocating rage. For the first time, the essential question seemed to explode in his mind.

"Who did this? *Reaveley?* Where is he?"

"I don't know who did it," Mr. Tuke said.

Like an answer, there came a yell from Joe. He had turned back to shine his lamp down the ventilating shaft.

"*I see you, you bastard . . . !*"

Mr. Tuke ran to him. "Where . . .?"

"He's gone!"

"In that water? Did you know him?"

"Only got a blink of his face in my lamp, as he looked up, the dirty swine!"

Cartwright had leaped to join them, and all three craned over the coping of the shaft, staring down at the brown flood. Under the lamp's rays only bubbles and eddies swept by.

"Is that the Ranelagh Sewer?" Mr. Tuke cried. "How the devil did he get there?"

Joe flashed his lamp behind them. Across from that sinister vent, in the wall of the vault, showed what appeared to be the mouth of another low tunnel. But when they ran to it, crouching to the curve of the roof, it was no tunnel, but a window. The lamp played through it upon a flight of steps, descending from the far end of what plainly was a second manhole, and passing out of sight beneath their feet.

"That's the Ranelagh manhole," Joe said. "What I showed you up above. He let himself down and dropped on them steps. It's only a matter of six foot or so. The Ranelagh's sixteen foot below ground, and we're a good eight under here."

Pressing between them, Cartwright looked over the sill. The lower steps, as they vanished below, shone with slime, but if one did not slip in landing, it was an easy drop.

"We can do the same," he cried. His voice was hoarse, and he still panted for breath. "Which way did he go?"

"He's making for the Middle Level." The jerk of the man's head indicated the way they had come. "He can nip over into the Storm Relief. There's no water in it—yet."

This was gibberish to Cartwright, who quite missed the significance of that 'yet'. He had forgotten the thunder. His thoughts racing, he glanced back at Kay, now but dimly seen stretched on the brick floor, a shadowy Chaffinch still standing guard over her. Chaffinch must have put out the lamp he had certainly been carrying in the street above. Kay, at any rate, was safe. She would do. Until she recovered consciousness, they could scarcely get her above ground. And what he wanted now, above all else, was to put his hands on the devil who had brought her to this. And the minutes were flying. . . .

In fact, not many had fled. Nightmares move fast; and that gallop up the vault, which seemed in retrospect half a mile, was no more than twenty or thirty yards. But another gust of fury possessed Cartwright, and he was past reason. He pushed between his companions at the window.

"I'm going after him!"

Joe gripped his arm. "Now, look——" he began.

But at that instant an uproar broke out down the vault. A light appeared, swaying wildly, and an enraged voice boomed under the low roof. Mr. Tuke cried aloud.

"Good God! He's come down!"

For there was no mistaking that voice, even though it sounded oddly choked. Sir Bruton, his figure notwithstanding, had refused to be relegated to a surface role.

He was bellowing again. "Tuke! *Oi!* Where are you? I've damn' near split my skull. I'm lugging these infernal sacks, and I suppose you're standing there laughing, curse you! What's up? What are you all doing?"

"Not laughing, anyway," Mr. Tuke called back, though his voice shook a little. "What are *you* doing down here?"

"Thought you'd have all the fun, didn't you? Poor old fatty, stuck up there on top of a hole in the ground, while you enjoy yourselves! Bah! I told Chaffinch to leave his lamp—— Oh, hell and damnation! Knocking my teeth out, now! Here, take these bloody sacks, somebody!"

Into the radius of the lamps lurched a singular figure, carrying its own aureole of light—by its teeth. This made the Director seem to grin like an ogre. Either hand dragged a sack; one clutched his malacca cane as well. Hatless, his face purple, his clothes smeared with dust—for the manhole had been a tight fit—he peered about him with an expression of extreme malevolence. Dropping the sacks, he took the lamp from his teeth. He was swiping irritably at a stalactite as his protuberant eyes fell on Kay's limp form by the ventilating shaft.

"Hullo! Hullo! Gal hurt?"

"Only drugged, apparently," Mr. Tuke said.

Puffing and blowing, stooping gingerly, Sir Bruton lumbered up to turn his lamp on the face of the unconscious girl. Her head now on Chaffinch's jacket, Kay still breathed easily. There even seemed to be more colour in her cheeks. The Director's air of exasperation had become one of formidable anger. He stood peering, pop-eyed, like a ferocious old fish. Mr. Tuke had joined him. Chaffinch was fetching the sacks. Cartwright stayed by the aperture in the wall, fuming at these delays, Joe's hand still on his arm. The rays of the three lamps mingled mistily, and in the great sewer below the water rushed incessantly by.

"You were right, eh?" Sir Bruton said gustily to Mr. Tuke. "What's this place? Smells like a morgue. And that water . . . ? And where's the hound who did this?"

Cartwright heard him. "Getting away!" he cried. "And we stand gabbling here!"

"Now, look," Joe said, resuming his interrupted speech.

He glanced round at the others, and raised his voice. "He's down there, in eighteen inches or two foot of water. Not more, at this time o' day, but enough to slow him up. He can't get out till he's in the Storm Relief. There's a manhole across from the Tube Station. But he's lost his key. You can open these manholes from below without a key, but it takes time. Some are harder than others—the catches are different. A mate of mine was near drowned, trying to work a catch. My guess is the bastard won't come up in the middle of a street, anyway. He's got no boots on—I could see that, the way he ran. A nice mess he'll be in. So he'll carry on, you bet, and try the park. Or go right on to Pimlico. He knows his way about, all right." The man glanced from one to another of the group. They had all come up, even Chaffinch, hauling the mysterious sacks. "I'd give something to know who the bleeder is," Joe said.

Sir Bruton looked at Mr. Tuke. "You don't know?"

"Joe got a glimpse of him, but no more." Mr. Tuke turned to the sewerman. "Do you know a Mr. Reaveley?"

"There was a Mr. Reaveley worked in the department before the war. He went into the army, I heard."

"And Mr. Coverdale?"

"Oh, I know Mr. Coverdale, all right."

"Could the man you saw be either of them?"

Joe's eyes popped open, their whites gleaming in the lamp-light.

"Gawd's truth!" he cried. "No, I couldn't say."

"Mr. Reaveley has fair hair. Coverdale's very dark."

"He wore a cap," Joe said. "I couldn't tell. And his face was all screwed up. Proper devil he looked, that's all I can say. He was gone in a flash." A sudden movement by Cartwright made him turn quickly to grasp the other's arm again. "Here, half a mo', sir. . . . ! Hold it! *Hold* it!" For Cartwright was still backing into the low opening. "If you're bent on it," Joe cried, "I'm game, after what he's done to the young lady. It's my job. He's one of us, the perisher! But you heard that thunder. It's risky——"

"To hell with that!"

"*All* right! But get a pair of boots on, chum. There's not all that bleeding hurry. He don't know we're after him, does he? He don't know *I'm* here. We can't lose him, anyway. He's got to show a light. There's whole stretches of the Storm Relief where we'll see it a furlong away."

These arguments, though he scarcely grasped the sense of them, checked Cartwright. Joe released him to seize one of the sacks. Up-ending it, he shot on to the brick floor a medley of garments—rubber thigh-boots, jackets, wide-brimmed hats. Chaffinch began to empty the second sack. Cartwright took the pair of boots Joe passed to him. The latter, starting to unlace his shoes, looked up at Sir Bruton.

"Hear any more thunder, sir?"

"Another rumble. Sounded nearer." The Director squinted down at his senior assistant, who was also untying his laces. "Going along too, are you, Tuke?"

"Of course I am. I've never been down a sewer. And the more of us the better. The fellow will be desperate. Besides, we've got to know who he is, in case Miss Kittredge doesn't. She's been drugged. She may not be certain. Suspicion's no good. I see Chaffinch looking wistful," Mr. Tuke added, kicking off a shoe. "Now you're here, he can come as well. You can look after the girl. We'll leave you a lamp."

"Curiosity drowned the cat," Sir Bruton grunted. "As Cartwright says, the bloke's probably well away by now."

Mr. Tuke reached for a rubber boot. "He can hardly suspect we'd follow him, as Joe points out. And do you realize it's only five minutes since we started the hue and cry?"

To Cartwright, who heard this, it seemed incredible. Surely it was more like half an hour ago that they were running up Gloucester Terrace. He was clumsily pulling on one of the long boots; Joe, for all his apparent deliberation, was getting into his second. He drew it over his thigh, slipped on a shapeless blue jacket, replaced his cap by a crumpled hat, and began to edge past Cartwright to the opening in the wall.

CHAPTER III

CAVERNS MEASURELESS

WITH A tardy flash of commonsense, Cartwright was pulling a serge jacket on top of his own. Joe, lamp in hand, was crawling backwards into the aperture. He lowered his legs, hung for an instant bent over the sill, dropped at arms-length, and vanished. Above the rush of water, loud through the opening, his voice echoed up.

"Right!"

The youngest of the party by some fifteen years, Cartwright made easy work of the drop. He felt his ankles gripped; as he let go his hold, his feet were on a greasy step. Joe had backed yet lower into an archway. He shone his lamp upwards as the novelist waited to aid Mr. Tuke, whose legs, in their clumsy boots, now dangled from the sill. As he in turn dropped, Chaffinch's waders were following out of the opening. Leaving the lawyer, who had the second lamp, to deal with his chief clerk, Cartwright stooped into the arch. He went down two or three slippery steps. At the bottom, water lapping over his feet, Joe was peering out of the short tunnel, his lamp held behind him.

"Not a glimmer. He's turned the bend," he called back, and stepped out into the rushing stream. His voice came again. "Lift your feet . . . !"

Feeling his way down the final steps, Cartwright staggered under the tug of the torrent, which at once came almost to his knees. Treading cautiously, but finding solid brickwork underfoot, he saw over his shoulder Mr. Tuke emerge doubled from the arch, one of the wide-brimmed hats, a species of serge sou'wester, over his nose. He shone his lamp on the water, another hat poked forth, and Chaffinch plunged into the flood.

The noise of this at first seemed deafening. But a shout from overhead reached Cartwright, and he looked up, startled.

In the roof, a foot or more above him, light streamed through a hole—the ventilating shaft of evil memory. A powerful bellow boomed down.

"Good fishing, blast you!"

Joe was splashing sturdily ahead, lamp swinging, water flying and sparkling at every step. As Cartwright followed, he found time to give thanks for his boots and jacket. He had kept his head low, but they were in a brick tube so spacious that there was ample room to walk erect. The walls gleamed as if oiled. Joe's lamp, a few yards in front, cast a complete round bubble of light, his stumpy silhouette swaying in the middle of it. Four pairs of big boots made a prodigious splashing; the torrent rustled and frothed as it slid over the slimy bricks, down which the spray flung by this *cortège* trickled and glistened.

All this noise, beating about them in the tunnel, Cartwright found distracting. The mustiness of the air, now increased tenfold, seemed to stupefy him. A faintly foul smell infused it; it was oppressively close. Although the swift stream was with them, their progress was slow. Eddies and bubbles endlessly overtook them. The effort of keeping their feet on the slippery, concave bottom, of lifting the big boots through the flood, would soon become exhausting. This struggle against a formless hindrance, tugging and clinging like something sentient and hostile, went fittingly with all the rest of the nightmare now running to its end in an eerie subterranean world of waters and darkness.

For a while they all ploughed on without speaking, the sewerman wading ahead, a sturdy, reassuring figure. Then Mr. Tuke, close behind Cartwright, raised a loud matter-of-fact voice above the booming echoes.

"Rum experience, this. I wouldn't have missed it for worlds. Do you realize you're paddling in mildly historic waters? Somewhere in this muck there's a trickle that used to be the Westbourne. We must be getting near the Reaveleys' house now. Then we turn down under Lancaster Terrace. Joe's been coaching us on the map. I hope he's right about the fellow taking to what they call the Storm Relief. One could have too much of this. Apparently the Storm Relief's almost dry. Except when there's a storm, of course. Hence its name. And Joe isn't too happy about that thunder. If there's a downpour, I gather we shall have to nip on top p.d.q." Apparently little perturbed by this possibility, Mr. Tuke added in a cheerful shout, as if in reply to Cartwright's thoughts: "We needn't worry about his hearing us. He's evidently some way ahead, and making just as much noise."

"But who *is* he?" Cartwright shouted back.

"You have two guesses. Reaveley or Coverdale. He must be one of them. But which? And why? What has made Miss Kittredge a danger to either? She may be able to tell us. The odds seem to be on Reaveley, but they were together on this job, at one time, and Coverdale's still on it. We were fools not to think of asking what the job was."

Cartwright skidded on the greasy bricks. "Something to do with this damned place?" he cried.

Mr. Tuke confirmed the deduction. "L.C.C., M.D. See any manhole. In other words, Main Drainage. We knew about Coverdale being in the Chief Engineer's office, and Reaveley's talk about plumbing should have given us a hint." The lawyer splashed on for a moment in silence. Then he shouted again. "Well, the ghost's exorcised, anyway!"

"The ghost . . . ?" Cartwright repeated stupidly. The Hyde Park phantom was far from his thoughts just then.

The necessity to shout conveyed clearly a touch of exasperation in Mr. Tuke's reply.

"You heard Joe speak of a manhole opposite the Tube here? Just where the vanishing trick was done? That's how it *was* done, of course! That's why the ghost crossed the road diagonally. And not one of us saw it . . . ! We ought to be under the manhole soon. How often have you walked *over* it, on your visits to 7a? And thousands more? The pavements are dotted with them. I could kick myself . . . ! But not in these boots," Mr. Tuke added, with a return to the good humour which this adventure seemed to engender in him.

Cartwright digested this revelation as he splashed on. His eyes were on their guide, a few yards ahead, forging through the flood in his own globule of light like some gigantic water-spider in its air-bubble. He called back:

"What is this man Joe?"

"He's called a flushing ganger," Mr. Tuke shouted. "Name of Wilson. His job's maintenance. Clearing silt, seeing the brickwork's sound, general supervision——"

Whether or no he heard his name, Joe Wilson looked over his shoulder and put up a hand. He clapped it on his lamp, dimming the light. Mr. Tuke followed suit. Joe was moving more deliberately now, and more quietly.

With this screening of the lamps, Cartwright found he could actually see further ahead. In the misty air, the round bubble of light in front had been impenetrable. Now he detected a change in the dim perspective of tubular brickwork and turbid water. The great sewer was ceasing to be straight. It was curving to the right, to run beneath Lancaster Terrace to the line of Bayswater Road. Their quarry must have turned this bend just before they emerged from the manhole steps. They had now retraced their route underground; sixteen feet overhead was the end of Gloucester Terrace, and the door of 7a, and the car standing in the gas-lit street. . . .

Wits, as well as sight, were clearing. As in a kaleidoscope, chips of the puzzle—or of one puzzle out of many—were forming a pattern. This was the Ranelagh Sewer; Ranelagh had meant something to Kay, in connection with a forgotten story about Gervase Coverdale, whose job was main drainage. "It all goes down the drain," Squadron Leader Garroway had said to Coverdale; and then—"Nasty experience, eh? I'd rather run my risks above." And then Reaveley had interrupted, so that the story was never told. It was plain enough now where the nasty experience had occurred. There was nothing in this; but linked with it, by that ill-omened dinner party, was another untold story, of Coverdale's past: there was the finding of Corinne's green beret on the landing of the house in Craven Hill, of which Kay had told that afternoon in her account of the inquest. Was it to Craven Hill that Corinne fled on the Wednesday night? And what happened after . . . ? A development which so startlingly drew Coverdale into the mystery of that flight had seemed to lift a burden from Kay's mind, but there had been no time then to discuss it; and the man had played little part in the host of uneasy thoughts raised by the meeting at the Tukes' flat two days ago. The main theme on Sunday had been the ghost, now, it appeared, shown up for the trick it was. In that trick Reaveley must have been the chief actor. But was Coverdale in it too? Was that what Corinne meant when she flared up at a joke about her past, and taunted him with his own . . . ?

Cartwright had a feeling that in another moment vital pieces of the pattern would slip into place. But he was jerked out of his racing thoughts. Joe Wilson had stopped, and the trio behind was closing up with him. They were all in the bend of the sewer; the brown stream swirled round it, slapping their boots, drowning their movements as they trod more slowly and stood still. They could make out the dark glistening walls straightening again in front before shading into utter blackness.

The ganger called back to them. "He's in the Middle Level, or over it."

Swinging his lamp, he splashed forward.

Cartwright became aware that they were on a downward slope, slight but perceptible. The rush of water seemed louder and swifter; it grew deeper, creeping to their knees. He was very hot: sweat was running down his face. Yet they had travelled little more than a hundred yards since they dropped from the Subway.

Joe flashed his lamp upwards, playing it upon a round black hole in the roof.

"Air shaft. By the island in Lancaster Terrace, under the windows of that house you were ringing at."

Within a few yards the sewer was curving again, now to the left, eastwards. In the curve, in the right-hand wall, an opening gaped like a vast black mouth, and a second stream gushed out to mingle with the Ranelagh. Keeping on left-handed, his back to this confluent, the ganger bellowed back more information, lending to this grim nightmare of a chase the commonplace touch of a conducted tour.

"We're under Bayswater Road. This is the Middle Level. It runs on below Oxford Street and Clerkenwell Road to Old Ford. Joins the High Level there. Then it's called the Northern Outfall. Empties into the river at Beckton Works."

The tourists were themselves in a veritable river, flowing from west to east. It was round Cartwright's knees, and well above Joe's. Wider and deeper than the Ranelagh, the Middle Level carried the waters of other sewers far behind. The brickwork was slimily black; the air more foul and heavy. It was hard to realize that above their heads were the bright lights and noisy traffic of Bayswater Road.

Almost at once Joe was gesturing to them, and playing his lamp downwards. While they halted in the knee-deep stream, he waded on a few yards. The beam of his lamp, reflected from the water, revealed dimly another cave-like opening in the right-hand wall of the sewer. He seemed to peer into this; then he was waving the lamp, and again they were splashing on. The ganger was already pulling himself up on to a low barrier which stretched across the opening. The barrier rose a couple of feet above the flood; the brickwork sprang from either end to arch over his head. Heaving up his legs, he dropped on the other side. Only his head and shoulders showed beyond the barrier in a half-moon of blackness.

He shouted across to Cartwright. "This is the dam. It's dry this side. . . ."

The dam was of concrete, not of brick. With difficulty Cartwright hoisted himself off the greasy bottom, sat on the dam, swung his dripping boots, saw by Joe's lamp the welcome dry floor beneath, and slid down. Here, out of that echoing tunnel, it was suddenly strangely quiet. Only a few inches from them, the torrent they had left brushed softly against the concrete. As Mr. Tuke peered over the dam, looking like the Devil in a sou'wester, Joe put his face to Cartwright's, speaking in his normal voice.

"We're in the Storm Relief. Come rain, the Middle Level

overflows into here. That's what we've got to watch for, with thunder about. There's been no rise yet—the storm hasn't broke. Trouble is, we shan't know here when it *has* broke, not till it's over this dam. We'll know fast enough then, and it'll be the nearest manhole for us, pronto. By rights, we'd have a man on top, following us along. At the first drop of rain he'd bang a manhole cover three times. We'll have to watch out, that's all. There's plenty of manholes. No need to worry."

Cartwright, in his ignorance, was far from feeling worried. The struggle and strain were behind him, his feet were on dry ground, and he was impatient to take up the pursuit at better speed. His anxiety was for sight or news of the man they were pursuing. Except for the ganger's glimpse of him, they had not seen even a gleam from his lamp since he went underground. In a labyrinth of tunnels they were hunting blindfold.

"Suppose the fellow hasn't come this way?" he said.

"I'll take my oath he has!" Joe retorted. "Where'd he go, else? He thinks he's all right. He's had his fill of water, in them trousers! He'll be trotting along, drying off a bit, and then he'll begin to think of popping up in the park somewhere, where it's quiet and dark. He *could* be going up now—I'll show you—but where'd he land? Slap in the middle of Bayswater Road, by a bus stop. And him wet to the waist! Thinking he's safe, he'll not be such a fool. . . . Look, now. The Relief straightens out a few yards on, and runs like that half way to the Magazine. We'll see his lamp then, or my name isn't Joe Wilson. Well, we'll be going. Keep that light down, Mr. Tuke. I'll scout ahead."

For Mr. Tuke had now scrambled over the dam, and Chaffinch was astride it. Joe began to walk on. The floor sloped sharply from the dam; there were iron plates let into it, and a chain, and a trickle of water ran down. Otherwise the Storm Relief seemed as dry as a good cellar. It was another great brick tube, with a foot or two of clearance above their heads, and even by the dimmed lights Cartwright saw that the brickwork was clean, as if scoured. There was the familiar impalpable haze, but the air was fresher, barely tinged with the musty smell he felt would haunt his senses for days.

They trooped down the slope, lamps turned to the brick floor, the ganger some yards in front. A low archway, also of familiar design, opened on their right, and as Joe pointed to it Mr. Tuke murmured in Cartwright's ear:

"That must be the manhole he meant. Near the bus stop opposite the Tube station. Where the ghost popped down. We've seen it from above. We'd just come from there when we met you."

The flat slope had become concave, the incline itself far less pronounced, the trickling water a runlet, an inch or two deep. The big drain was levelling out, though always trending downwards. Since it was now a cylinder, the procession paddled in single file through the shallow water. Some atmospheric condition absorbed sound, and the small splashing they made was muffled. The lamps, directed to the rounded floor, left walls and roof in shadow; Cartwright could just discern the dry clean brickwork sliding by. Slender fibres, lying horizontally along the lines of mortar, could only be the ultimate roots of trees, which incredibly had drilled their way through; and he found time to remember that they were now beneath the shrubberies where Kensington Gardens join Hyde Park, by the pumping house and the Alcove.

He had just realized that the drain was curving, left-handed, when the ganger's light went out. Mr. Tuke instantly doused his. They all stood halted in darkness.

But for a moment only. As eyes grew accustomed to the murk, far, far in front another light shone.

CHAPTER IV

OUTRAGEOUS SPRINGS

It was at first no more than a dim pin-point far down the long straight tube of the Storm Relief. Like a firefly down a gun-barrel, so far away it looked, and so small, the ganger's shadow, as he moved, eclipsed it, all but the faintest aura around him, and the ghost of a reflection on the runlet of water in the straddle of his bow legs. He was shuffling backwards, and his hoarse whisper came to the trio behind him.

"I told you! There he is, the bastard. . . . !"

They were crowded at his back, peering over his shoulders. The light in front, Cartwright already realized, was not so distant as he had supposed. Bobbing and wavering, slowly receding, the pervading haze so dulled and diffused it that it seemed to float alone, like a corposant. The man who carried it was invisible.

Joe Wilson whispered again. "Now look. Our game is to follow him, keeping well back. If he twigs us, he'll run for it, and faster than what we can in these boots. With a good lead, he'll have time to force a catch further on, and get out. Or he'll dodge us—though he'll have to carry on to Knightsbridge if he tries that. He's past what they call the Syphon. You'll see it, on the right here—it runs back to the Ranelagh. There's nothing else bar park drains this side of Albert Gate. He could turn into the Piccadilly there, or down the Old Ranelagh. The dam'll be open, with thunder about. . . . *All* right, sir!"—for Cartwright, in his impatience, had unwittingly jogged him—"Take it easy! *He* ain't hurrying. He's not a couple of hundred yards ahead, though it looks more. . . . Now if he does what *I* think, and tries to get out on top here in the park, there's five manholes. One near where he is now, another north of the Magazine, two alongside the Serpentine—Mr. Tuke knows about *them*—and one just past the Dell, where the Old Ranelagh dam is. Our best chance to nab him'll be while he's getting a cover open, him not having a key. So when we see him going up, we'll run. . . . Now we'll get on. We can follow by his lamp, and use ours when he's round a bend. He can't hear us, not if we go careful. Sound don't carry much down here."

Vague against that remote foggy blur of light, Joe's shadowy form moved on again. In the haze of the close arid tunnel both sight and hearing indeed played strange tricks; his husky whisper had seemed at once netted and yet all around. It was plain enough, too, that the man in front was in no haste. The gently bobbing glow gave the measure of an easy pace. He had not even thought to look round; pursuit, in these clandestine depths, was wholly unsuspected. Perhaps, in the ganger's words, he was hoping to dry off a little, or he was delaying until the park above their heads should be emptied of all but its nocturnal fellowship, the vagrant companions of Wally Whichcord.

Eyesight, in a few seconds, adapting itself yet better to new conditions, the pursuers followed in his wake with surprising ease. The distant luminous ball gave them direction, its pale image in the trickle of water, flowing with them, led to it through the lustreless dark like a living thread. As they trod the water, or straddled it, the concave bottom guided their feet. The dimmest of shades to one another, lurching from side to side, lifting their big boots, planting them with care, often slipping or stumbling, but almost noiseless except for the faint creak of rubber, they plodded on. The will-o'-the-wisp ahead seemed to waver in time to their cautious steps.

So this last strange subterranean lap of the chase began; so, at the same deliberate pace, it went on. Intent on groping his way, half hypnotized by continual staring at that bubble of light far in front, Cartwright soon lost all sense of time and distance. Hours and miles might be going by. Plod, creak, plod, creak, muted plashings, darkness all round, the little golden ball always bobbing and beckoning—that was all. He was no longer overheated and sweating, but the close stale air was taking its toll in a headache. His earlier choking rage had steadied to a grim resolution. After a while, the writer's habit even asserted itself; though in anticipation his grip might be tightening on a throat, his fists smashing a face that was a compound of Clifford Reaveley's blondness and the swarthy Coverdale, another part of his mind was observing and recording. Observing, literally—for he seemed to be acquiring a vision like a cat's. A dimly seen gesture by the ganger, before they had trudged far, was not needed to show him a darker blot in the passing darkness which he identified as the adit of the Syphon, whatever that might be. Presently after, also on his right, another dim opening was even recognizable as a manhole tunnel. They were now at or about the point which the light had reached when first they saw it. In the meantime it had not stopped or paused; it still wavered ahead, at the same distance. Or was it now a little nearer? Was that why sight seemed keener? Were they creeping up . . . ?

Always behind sounded the muffled rubbery tread of Mr. Tuke and his chief clerk. Underfoot, thick rubber soles sometimes trod silt, gritty or slimy; where this was thickest, once or twice they scraped a slight ridge in the brickwork. And once something brushed Cartwright's ankle, there was a little flurry of splashing, and the ganger, checking an instant, whispered over his shoulder. "That's a rat. . . ." It was soon after this that Joe Wilson stopped abruptly, so that Cartwright bumped into him. The man seemed to be stooping, dabbling in the water, and the novelist became aware that this had widened and deepened. For the first time for many minutes, or hours, he remembered the thunder, and the purpose of the Storm Relief. But then, without a word, and without haste, Joe was moving on once more; and before long the rivulet had dwindled to a trickle again.

They were certainly gaining slowly on the invisible unknown, for suddenly, he was no longer invisible. In the disc of light, definitely brighter and larger, something moved, a shadow of a shade, swaying with it. No more, it seemed, than perhaps a hundred yards ahead, the misty rays reached back towards them. Cartwright fancied he glimpsed again, sidelong, the endless lines of pointing on the walls to right and left, and here and there a thread-like root. Joe Wilson was now a clear-cut silhouette; and as another manhole tunnel gaped, its arched mouth well defined, he suddenly halted again, and stood still. It was Mr. Tuke's turn to bump into Cartwright. With a jerk of his hand at the tunnel, the ganger whispered back:

"That comes up by the Magazine. Wonder where he's making for? Best let him get on a bit. The Relief turns along there, under the carriage road, and then runs behind the boathouses."

While they waited, eyes always on the receding light, Cartwright was trying to measure distances in the park overhead. To be near the Magazine, they must have come a good quarter of a mile from the Middle Level. They were more than half way to the Serpentine, and the eyot and the boathouses close to the spot where first Wally Whichcord, and then Corinne, had been dredged from its shallows. . . .

His thoughts jerked back. The light was altering shape, elongating, fading, dwindling.

"He's in the bend. . . ."

The last gleam was gone as the ganger spoke. He turned on his own lamp, screening it so that only a glimmer played on the toes of his boots and the rivulet rippling round them. Then he was moving on, faster now, straddling the water. At this awkward gait, like crabs, to lessen even the slight sounds of splashing, the others followed. Soon the drain was turning, in a wide curve to the left. Joe slowed up; the merest thread of light crept with him along the brickwork on that side. But for the faint creaking and scraping of boots, the occasional liquid murmur of water, unnatural silence reigned. Cartwright felt as though he were groping through a lifeless world. And then, the light was reappearing ahead, waxing, rounding again: Joe's lamp was out; again the dark funnel stretched before them, and the pursuit resumed its endless, monotonous course, the unconscious quarry keeping his easy pace, the hunters, in semi-darkness, plodding a hundred yards or so behind.

Endless it seemed; yet it must have been within a minute or two that the ganger hung in his cautious stride to throw another hoarse whisper over his shoulder.

"Tell Mr. Tuke that's the one what we started from this evening. By the Cockpit."

In the right-hand wall a third arched entry was darkly visible. Cartwright passed the message back, *sotto voce*, and in the same tone Mr. Tuke amplified it.

"The other vanishing tricks. Remember? Whichcord was roosting up on top near here. And after the second time, a fortnight ago, he stumbled on the truth. Literally. If he hadn't stubbed his toe, he'd be alive now. We'll never prove it"—Mr. Tuke's sibilant mutter was grim—"but one murder's enough for a hanging."

As Cartwright began to make some sense of this, the kaleidoscope spun again, and the picture of a long tale of fraud and crime and tragedy was shaping in his mind. But he was given no time to see it clearly, still less to knit it to other puzzles. Again his thoughts were shocked back to the present, as, in an instant, the slow tempo of this subterranean pursuit was changed.

A blaze of light was in his eyes. For so long a foggy glow, the lamp in front had been turned full on them. It shone steadily, dazzling. Whether a sixth sense had warned their quarry, or he heard some sound, it was at once evident that his lamp was more powerful than theirs, and that in the deceptive haze they had crept even closer on his heels than any of them suspected.

Joe had stopped; they all stopped, rigid. There was a pulsing moment when everything stood still. The white dazzle in their faces revealed every detail of the Storm Relief—the perspective of rounded brickwork, scoured and worn, white incrustations like salt, the foot-wide runnel of water, now a rivulet of fire. Afterwards, Cartwright remembered even noting that the drain was no longer a true round, but an oval.

The unnatural silence and suspense broke in a sudden pandemonium of sound and furious haste. Joe Wilson shouted and started forward. The blazing disc swept away and dimmed again. It was receding swiftly, swaying wildly. They were all in full cry after it, their own lamps lighted, boots churning the water. The tunnel rang with the hubbub; spray flew and glittered and spattered the walls, shadows, like vast demented bats, swooped over and round them. At once Cartwright strove to edge past the ganger, whose bow legs showed a good turn of speed, but he was hampered by the curving brickwork. His wet rubber soles slipped on it, and he fell back. A hundred yards ahead at first, no more, the chase was already gaining. The dark bent shadow, in its ball of light, seemed to fly down the endless vista.

It was breathless work in that close air. Cartwright, in his clumsy boots and extra jacket, was soon panting. Sweat broke out on his face. Through the din he could hear Mr. Tuke's heavy breathing at his shoulder. The lawyer, for his forty-nine years, was doing well, and Chaffinch was close behind him. A yard ahead, Joe scuttled and splashed in a jolting fan of light. Spray flew over them, and the noise seemed confounding. The brickwork streamed past; soon another low archway loomed and was gone. The flying shadow in front had not paused: it was still gaining, running like a madman.

Now the drain began to turn once more, right-handed. Cartwright made a fresh attempt to pass the ganger. Again he slipped, cannoned into Joe, and splashed heavily. And as he stumbled in the water, drenched to his waist, Joe himself had skidded to a stop. His voice rang out.

"*It's rising . . . !*"

They had all stopped, gasping, to stare at the water. It was over their feet. The ganger looked back.

"The rain's come! It's over the dam! Run for it . . . !"

He was off once more. They were all running again, sending the water flying. It was already too wide to straddle or sidestep. The light in front was racing round the bend. In their seconds' pause it had gained; it was still gaining on them. It was now a mere golden blur, reeling, shadowless. Then it vanished. . . .

But they were no longer pursuing. Hunted and hunters,

one and all were running for their lives. Amid the whirl of speed and sound and urgency, full understanding of this came slowly to Cartwright. He had little heeded earlier warnings; and though he knew the storm had broken, all that this meant was happily hidden from him. He did not know that from half north-west London—from Willesden and Kilburn and Paddington and Bayswater itself—brimming streets were pouring tons of water down into the Middle Level and over the dam behind them. He did not know that in such a cloud-burst the eight-foot Storm Relief could fill in a matter of minutes. But if he was ignorant of the full peril threatening, the ganger's voice and actions were imperative and infectious. Splashed and drenched, reeling and breathless, they were all running now as even anger and the heat of the chase had never made them run. Their quarry was forgotten. When they turned the bend, and once more the drain stretched straight before them, no light shone ahead; but Cartwright, for one, scarcely wondered why, or where the unknown they had hunted so far had got to. The need for haste was all he thought of. The rising stream was already above his ankles.

Realization had come. He had known fear in battle, the sickening fear of rent flesh and pain; but now he knew panic. He fought it down. They would get out; they *must* get out. They must come to the next manhole soon. Kay was waiting, perhaps conscious, suffering herself, fearing for him; and people were not drowned like rats because a little rain fell. . . .

In a moment he had a grip on himself again, though the flood was rising with extraordinary swiftness, and was now half-way to their knees, hampering and slowing them. It was flowing faster, swirling froth and bubbles past them. A yard and more wide, where it had been a trickle, their pounding progress through it sent waves up the curving walls. Water splashed in their eyes, ran down their faces, dripped and flew from their working arms. Something swept by, struggling, fighting to turn and swim against the current: Cartwright saw small red eyes gleam in the light of the lamp behind him. It was odd he should have been thinking of rats. He wondered if this vermin was the same they had met, surely hours ago. . . .

With a gush of relief that was the measure of his dread, he saw by the ganger's lamp another opening in the wall. The rushing stream was over the sill. But Joe did not even pause. He splashed on, his hoarse shout coming back in a series of gasps.

"Overflow . . . Serpentine . . . no good . . . only a few yards now. . . ."

The water was up to their knees. They were not running now, but ploughing heavily through it. The air was intolerably close; Cartwright's lungs seemed near to bursting, his heart pounded violently. He glanced over his shoulder, to find Mr. Tuke still close behind, and Chaffinch lurching in the rear. But there were, indeed, only a few more yards of this. The struggle and the nightmare were almost over. Once again the ganger's light revealed a tunnel entry. The swelling torrent eddied in and out of it, a third of the way up its low arch. Joe Wilson was stooping to go in.

With another revulsion of relief, Cartwright felt suddenly lighthearted. He turned in the thigh-deep flood to grin at Mr. Tuke. From under the flopping hat a croaking voice gasped back:

"What—a—night—we—*are*—having . . . ! No—go on!"

For the younger man was wading aside to make way. He persisted, and Mr. Tuke wasted no more precious time on civilities, but stooped to follow the ganger. There was a brief pantomime with Chaffinch, who merely stood still, too breathless to speak, and Cartwright went before him. The tunnel was full of light, but stifling, and flooded so high that he had another instant of sheer terror as he bent under the roof, his face not two feet above the water. Would there be room for them all in the shaft? What if Joe could not open the iron cover quickly . . . ?

The ganger was climbing the iron ladder. Mr. Tuke was in the brick shaft, straightening up, lighting the tunnel mouth with his lamp. Cartwright crept out, and thankfully stood erect. With Joe's big boots at the level of their shoulders, there was just room for a third in the narrow rectangular pit. Chaffinch emerged, to squeeze himself beside them. The water was half way up their thighs. A baulk of timber rose up one side of the shaft; it was marked in feet by bands of white paint, and while they waited Cartwright watched, with a sort of fascination, the dark gleaming flood creep up, inch after inch, to the three-foot mark. It lapped the white line, and covered it; it was now at their waists; and then there was a clash overhead, a second clang, as the ganger pushed the grating back, and his rubber boots were mounting again. A gust of fresh air swept down upon the three below, and heavy raindrops with it. Mr. Tuke was grasping the ladder, feeling in the water for the rungs. . . .

A few moments after, and they were all above ground, getting their breath, inhaling the cool air, water dripping from them, standing together under the light of a street lamp and in a downpour of rain. Thunder crashed overhead. A flash of lightning lit up the sodden tan of Rotten Row.

It was only then that Cartwright once more remembered the man they had been pursuing.

CHAPTER V

CONVERSATIONS IN A THUNDERSTORM

"ALL THE same, that's where he'll be," Joe Wilson said. "That's where he bolted to, and he can't get out."

When Queen Caroline took 300 acres of Hyde Park to make Kensington Gardens, and caused ten pools of the little River Westbourne to be drained and cleaned and linked together to form the Long Water and the Serpentine, the eleventh and smallest pool was left to become the centre-piece and ornament of what every Londoner knows as the Dell. Here the party of four now stood, again ankle-deep in water, but with the rain dashing down on them and thunder rolling round the dark sky. From the manhole by which they had reached the surface, in the footpath on the north side of the curious hump of Rotten Row, they had descended into the dip, climbed the railings of the Dell, and waded through the pool to its southern end, greatly agitating the ducks, long since retired for the night. Here, in the bank, beneath a dripping overhang of shrubs, the lamps revealed a low opening like a cellar window. Barred by an iron grating, its sill was almost at water level.

"It was put there in the old times," the ganger said, "for the overflow from the Serpentine. Nowadays this here pool'll trickle into it, if there's much rain, but that's all. Inside, it's as big as a room. It slopes down from here, and then there's a tunnel into the Storm Relief. The one what we passed just before we come up, which I hollar'd out to say was no good, 'cause you can't get out, along of these bars. When we saw *his* light go, he'd turned in here. He guessed we wouldn't risk it. We'd go on to the manhole. And there he is, the bastard! He can't get back into the Relief—it'll be half full by now, and up to the top of the tunnel. He's fair caught till the level falls."

Heedless of the lashing rain—they were already soaked—they stood in the dark pool and stared at the grating, lamps playing through the old, rusty bars on impenetrable blackness within. From what motives perhaps they hardly knew, they had shouted and called through the grating. But no voice had answered.

"What about the water from the Storm Relief?" Mr. Tuke said. "Won't it flood this place?"

"Given enough rain, it will," Joe agreed hopefully. "But it don't often happen. The floor rises inside, like I said, to this here outlet. The lower end, where the tunnel is, 'll be under water now, but up here it'll be dry. But if we have a real souser, and the water can't get away quick enough, then it'll be pushed up like, and through them bars, and into this pool, and the whole dip here'll be flooded for a bit, till it can drain off."

"In such an event, what will happen to our friend inside?" Mr. Tuke inquired with an air of detached curiosity.

"Likely he'll be drowned," said the ganger grimly. "Tit for tat. It's what he meant for the young lady."

They had not tried to lower their voices. It was natural that all should wonder whether the man hidden in the darkness there, perhaps just beyond those bars, could hear them. And so strong is the instinct to save human life, even for a gallows, that once more Mr. Tuke stooped to shout through the grating, and the others with him. But still there was no reply.

"Lying low, the bastard, and hoping to get out when the level falls," Joe Wilson said.

Mr. Tuke was moving his light across the vertical bars. "They are very corroded. Obviously antiques. Could he break through them, do you think? If he's who I think he is, he's a powerful man."

"Not without he's got a crowbar," the ganger replied confidently. "No, sir, he's safe for a good few hours now, even if the rain stops."

"What might be described as an *impasse*," Mr. Tuke remarked to Cartwright. "All we can do is to call at the police station in the park here on our way back. And are they going to mount a bobby on half the manholes in London? This Storm Relief alone, I understand, goes on under Sloane Square to Chelsea Embankment. Well, that's their headache. We've done enough for glory, and I'm as wet as the famous sponge. Wetter, because it wasn't."

With a last look, they turned their backs on the grating behind which a hunted man lurked, imprisoned until the sewers emptied, or overflowed to drown him. They waded out of the shallow pool, climbed the low railings, and began to trudge through the storm up the slope to the Serpentine Road.

It was a little later that Mr. Tuke said to Cartwright:

"You're getting a rough idea of things now, I suppose?"

"Some of them. The ghost, of course," Cartwright said. "And that *must* have been Reaveley. . . . A filthy trick!"

"Yes, the snapshot you saw shows how essentially alike he and young Demarest were, though nobody spotted it because of superficial differences of colouring and build. Hair-dye, and a false beard, and perhaps a touch of phosphorus paint, would be good enough in moonlight, with the victim already prepared to be deceived. As you say, it was a particularly cruel fraud."

"Was *Corinne* in it? I can't believe that!"

"I doubt if we shall ever know."

"That medium woman must have been."

"Oh, Madame Varché was in it, up to the neck. Since yesterday morning—dear me!" Mr. Tuke interjected, "it seems a long time ago—anyway, since then, when I succeeded in interesting the Assistant Commissioner, the police have been very active. Madame Varché was killed by a bomb in 1943, but they found her daughter. *She* remembers a caller who came several times to their house in the summer of '40. Her description fits Reaveley. According to her, he was passed off as an acquaintance her mother had made in the theatrical circles—not the highest, perhaps—in which both Madame V. and Reaveley seem to have moved. You yourself saw him about with an actor, though the ladies of the chorus were his chief interest. An expensive one. The daughter says her mother's circumstances improved about that time. Madame V. retired two years later."

The four men were walking along the Serpentine Road, beside the water. Except when a lightning flash lit up the dripping glades, it was pitchy dark: the rain fell in torrents, and the thunder rolled. All were soaked to the skin. They were on their way to the park police station, and thence to rejoin Kay Kittredge and Sir Bruton. Unless the girl had recovered consciousness, this pair was presumably still immured beneath Gloucester Terrace. The Director's figure, plus an unconscious woman, would be too tight a fit for the manhole. The two were in perfect safety there, Joe Wilson said.

"The moral aspect aside," Mr. Tuke went on, "it was a devilishly ingenious trick. I wonder whether some stage trap-door suggested it? Kames put his finger on it, and we never saw it, when he asked me if I supposed the ghost had gone through the pavement. Everything played into Reaveley's hands—even the raids and the weather. Remember what a dry year 1940 was? He had to have dry weather, as his wife knew, and as we know now. Then the raids cleared the streets, and there was no lighting. But he wanted a moon—he had to be seen just well enough to pass for his cousin's ghost. It would help the illusion, by the way, if he moved silently, and then he was going down a sewer, so he wore waders like these—not, as the witnesses supposed, the leather thigh boots they wear in the Navy. The rest of the trick was easy. He was still with the L.C.C. at that date, and he had the gear and a key for the manhole. He's a climber—he could swing himself down that shaft opposite the tube station in the second or two, while Mrs. Demarest was still across the street. It would be open, ready for him, but she couldn't see it in the shadows. It was no doubt oiled, though Wilson showed us how quietly you can open and close them——"

"The weather!" Cartwright broke in, his mind less on the mechanics of the trick than on these people he knew, or had known, his friends and Kay's, people one dined with, and met at clubs, now revealed as living all the time in another world of fraud and villainy. "Was *that* what Corinne meant, when she asked Reaveley if he was getting jumpy again?"

"I imagine that was what was in her mind," Mr. Tuke said. "If she was not in the fraud at the start, she must have known about it, or suspected it, very soon after. What was worrying her last Wednesday night, the cause behind the *crise de nerfs* and all the rest of it, was the resurrection of the ghost, after seven years. She would know it must be her husband. No doubt she tackled him about it, but he'd deny it, with one of his charming grins, and she was left wondering what he was up to. With Whichcord's death coming so soon after, I fancy she was more than a little uneasy."

Cartwright exclaimed again. "Whichcord! I'd forgotten about him. What a tangle this is!"

"We're unravelling it," Mr. Tuke said. "And what a book you could make of it. Damn this rain . . . ! Well, let's see what we can piece together about Whichcord. In those days Reaveley lived in Earl's Court, and, anyway, having gone underground in Bayswater, he had to carry on along the Relief to the south side of the park because of the railings. If he could climb them, it would look odd if he was seen. But he had every right to pop in and out of manholes. It was his job. No doubt he had a sack somewhere at that end, with a regulation serge coat and hat. Now Joe says they kept a close watch on the drainage system during air raids. A heavy bomb might go deep enough to crack the brickwork. Some did. Reaveley may have met a patrol coming along, in which case he'd turn back and nip up a manhole. As the patrol might come up too, or have a man on top, he'd take cover till the coast was clear. Do you remember passing back a message from Joe about a manhole near the Cockpit?"

"Yes, I remember." Cartwright, who had no hat, was passing a sodden handkerchief over his streaming hair.

"That was the shaft Reaveley used. We shan't go as far as that now, but it's on the grass strip just off this road, between the road and a path. It's not thirty yards from the Serpentine. That night Whichcord was under a plane tree a couple of hundred yards up the slope. He was probably dozing when Reaveley dodged up and took cover in a clump of trees at this end of the Cockpit. But he was awake when Reaveley came out a little later. There is an isolated ash between the plane tree and the manhole, directly in line with them both. As Reaveley passed behind the ash, he may have altered his direction slightly—anyway, he had the tree behind him for his last hundred yards, and so to Whichcord he seemed to vanish. The light was far from perfect, and again he'd take care to lower the manhole cover quietly. By the time Whichcord's curiosity took him down to investigate, Reaveley was well away in the Storm Relief again. As there was nothing beyond the ash but the Serpentine, Whichcord had some reason to believe in the ghost when he heard of it."

Mr. Tuke removed his serge hat to wring the water from it. They had turned up the path to the Ranger's Lodge and the police station. The rain still lashed down in gusts, but the thunder was passing away to the south.

"Now," Mr. Tuke went on, replacing his hat with a shiver, "now we jump seven years, to the night three weeks ago when Whichcord saw the ghost a second time. He was under his favourite tree again, or thereabouts. Details are lacking, because he is no longer available to supply them. But the ghost can only have been Reaveley once more, in another hired naval reefer and cap. That was a neat touch. It would scare off any Hyde Park regular, if one happened to see him. They haven't forgotten the old story—witness Mr. Jones, of whom you'll have heard from Miss Kittredge."

"But what was Reaveley up to this time?" Cartwright asked.

"That was what his wife wondered—and with reason, poor woman. He was rehearsing her murder."

"Good God . . . !" But almost at once Cartwright was adding: "Of course, I know now it was no accident, or suicide. But how did he? Yes, I begin to see that. . . . *And Kay?*"

"Let us be tidy," Mr. Tuke said. "Mentally, anyhow, if we do look like drowned rats. Let's finish with the luckless Whichcord. The manhole in question, along there by the

Cockpit, is set in concrete which rises an inch or two above the grass. You don't notice it, any more than you notice all the other manholes, gas, electricity, water, drainage, that stud our pavements and parks. But you might notice it if you tripped over it. From a phrase Whichcord used to his sister, that is evidently what he did. He stubbed his toe. This was a few days after he'd seen the ghost again, and he may have been nosing about, puzzling over the mystery. He looked at the manhole, which I dare say he'd seen before without consciously observing it, and the mystery was solved. Then he began to put two and two together. With his proprietory interest in the ghost story, and his sources of gossip in local pubs, no doubt he knew a good deal already about the new household at 7a Lancaster Terrace. If he didn't know about Reaveley's old job with the L.C.C., he soon found out. Because he happened to know our friend here, Joe Wilson, by sight, and what *his* job was. He ran Joe to earth, cooked up some story, and pumped him about main drainage and the Storm Relief, going over it all on a map. . . ."

"How did *you* get on to all this?" Cartwright put in.

Mr. Tuke sounded modestly pleased with himself.

"By doing a little nosing round on my own account, and then setting Chaffinch on Wilson's track. Chaffinch is a born ferret, and he found Joe in a few hours. We all met this evening, including Kames—*he* wasn't going to be left out of it—and when we ran into you we'd been tracing the Storm Relief overground, from the Cockpit manhole. It was beginning to be obvious how it had been used, and we were going down into the Subway to start there and work back. . . ." Mr. Tuke sneezed violently, scattering raindrops. "Damn and blast!" he said. "Well, you can work out Whichcord's little game, and what happened to him, for yourself."

"Blackmail . . . ?" Cartwright said. And then, more slowly: "And you mean he was murdered too? Didn't he realize the risk he was running?"

"He wouldn't realize it in the least," Mr. Tuke replied. "He had no idea he'd seen a rehearsal for a murder. All he suspected was some more hokey-pokey on the old lines, and *they* were what interested him. He looked forward to a nice little income for keeping his mouth shut about what happened seven years ago. Easy Street, as he put it. But he'd run into something much bigger. Reaveley, I should say, would be a dangerous man to blackmail, anyway, and with the murder of his wife in view, and his intended use of the Storm Relief, he daren't leave Whichcord alive. How he got rid of him, you can guess as well as I can. An appointment here, by the Serpentine, late at night—it would seem natural enough to Whichcord, who haunted the place after dark, and slept under trees—a sudden grip on his throat, over a scarf or something, to prevent fingermarks on the flesh, and in a few seconds, unable even to cry out, his head would be under water. And that would be that. Another police notice would go up. Nobody would worry much about a vagabond like Whichcord. And nobody did."

Shocked though Cartwright was, his thoughts had gone back already to the fate of a later victim, and to the repetition of the word 'rehearsal'. "But how . . . ?" he himself had asked, and he broke in with the question again.

"But Corinne . . . ? I still don't understand that. Did she come back to the house?"

"On this hypothesis," said Mr. Tuke, "she never left the house—alive, that is. While we were prattling in her drawing-room on Wednesday evening, her husband was drowning her in her bath—Eh?"

For again Cartwright had cried out, "Good God!" Then he said quickly: "Go on. . . ."

"How she left the house," Mr. Tuke went on, "we saw for ourselves to-night. Reaveley, in his naval rig, carried her down that fire-escape at the back, as Miss Kittredge was carried down an hour or so ago—that gleam you saw may have been the study light going out—and along the alley behind the bombed houses to Lancaster Street. It would be three or four in the morning, with no one about. Then a quick run across Gloucester Terrace, down into that thing called the Subway—it's the old Ranelagh Sewer, disused since they had to lower the level because of the District Railway—and so along our route into the Middle Level and the Storm Relief. Then up by the Cockpit, close to the Serpentine. No easy job, getting a body up one of those ladders, and perhaps something fell off. Reaveley's peaked cap, perhaps. Anyway, he seems to have had to go below again. So he put the body on a park seat, where it was least likely to invite inquiry, and where our Mr. Jones saw it. When he returned, he put the fear of God into Mr. Jones. After that, all he had to do was wade out, lay the body under water, and go home. Probably above ground, to save time. That would explain his going below to recover whatever he'd dropped. Then he waited for the sad news to arrive with the milk. He must have felt pretty safe. Special tests could distinguish bath water in the lungs from Serpentine water, but both are fresh, and the pathologist wouldn't make such tests unless she was given cause for suspicion. She wasn't——"

"And he'd have done that to Kay!" Cartwright cried. "My God, I hope he's drowning by inches now. . . ! But why? *Why* did he do it all? Why kill Corinne? Was it money?"

Mr. Tuke's shrug, invisible in the dark, sent raindrops trickling down his spine. He shivered and swore.

"Money. Or freedom. Or both. The police have already dug up information confirming the hint your friend at the ministry gave you. Reaveley was in a bad hole. He's been in the moneylenders' hands for years. They'd give him rope as long as he had expectations from his wife, but Mrs. Reaveley may have been talking seriously of another will, in spite of what Miss Kittredge says. We don't know what has been going on in that house. Miss Kittredge herself knows, or suspects, more than she admits. She is grateful and loyal, she rather likes Reaveley, when he isn't making eyes at her—which may be merely a habit—and she has been denying the evidence of her own senses. After all, except in jobs like mine, people try to see the best in others. . . . Personally, I have no doubt whatever that murder has been hatching in that house for some time, but——" Mr. Tuke paused to wipe the rain from his face before adding disconcertingly: "But whether it hatched out is still arguable."

Cartwright, blinking in the rain, stared at him.

"Have you forgotten the alternative candidate?" Mr. Tuke asked him. "All this popping up and down sewers, and re-creating the ghost, may only show intention. Did someone else have the same idea, or borrow it, and get in first? Who, in fact, is behind those bars in the Dell?"

"Coverdale?" Cartwright exclaimed. "Yes, I'd forgotten. . . . Of course, you talked of him, too."

Mr. Tuke sneezed again. "I hope these policemen have got some whisky," he said. "Well, now, our dark horse. All we really have against Coverdale is Mrs. Reaveley's remark about his past. What did she say?—'people who are lucky at finding things'. Whatever she meant, Coverdale took it badly."

"She might have meant anything."

"True. But it's always fun speculating. Something Joe Wilson said gave me an idea. He was telling us that they find all sorts of jetsam down in those sewers—handbags, purses, things discarded by pickpockets and the rest, and shoved through the gratings. Hyde Park seems to be particularly favoured for sharing out loot and disposing of unwanted or incriminating articles. Sometimes valuables get overlooked. A mate of Joe's found a diamond ring in the lining of a bag. He handed it over, but some of us might think twice before giving up a valuable and saleable piece of property found in such circumstances."

Cartwright had to laugh. "You ought to be a novelist," he said. "You have the essential imagination."

"I make very good long shots sometimes," Mr. Tuke retorted, with as much dignity as conditions permitted. "I merely throw this out as a thing a normally honest man might do. To many people, stealing by finding is not theft. And a man like Coverdale, if I've summed him up correctly, might even brag about it in intimate moments. But it might be awkward for him if it was later raked up in public."

They were approaching the Ranger's Lodge. Windows shone, blurred by the rain, for it was still early in the night—not much after eleven. Mr. Tuke went on:

"Coverdale, I should say, has a violent temper. Not one of our planners, perhaps, like Reaveley, but likely to lose his head in a rage. Then there's the beret found on his landing. That's evidence—of something. It may have been planted. The housekeeper obviously didn't think it had been there a week. It came out that visitors can go up without her knowledge. Didn't you say Reaveley was lunching at Lancaster Terrace on Sunday?"

Cartwright nodded. "And yesterday too. Kay told me."

"Then he was in the neighbourhood at a time when the doric Mrs. McWhirter would be in her basement—a point in favour of a plant. Did Miss Kittredge tell you anything else? About his behaviour yesterday, for instance?"

"No. She only spoke of him casually this afternoon."

Mr. Tuke was peering through the blackness and the tearing rain. The blue lamp over the door of the police station shone dimly. Cartwright, glancing back, saw Chaffinch and the ganger trudging behind, apparently in morose silence.

"Do you realize where Coverdale lives?" Mr. Tuke asked.

"Craven Hill, isn't it?"

"And Craven Hill is the next turning into Gloucester Terrace after Lancaster Street. Coverdale's flat is at this end. What runs under Gloucester Terrace?"

"Good Lord. . . !" Cartwright muttered.

"Yes, our dear old friend, the Ranelagh Sewer. And there's another manhole within thirty yards of Coverdale's front door. And, unlike Reaveley, he is still professionally connected with main drainage."

Far to the south, now, thunder still rumbled. Furious gusts of rain still lashed Hyde Park. Autumnal leaves danced and rustled and were torn from their branches. All over London roads were swimming, gutters were torrents; and underground the great drains were filling and roaring, hundreds of miles of rushing water, pouring in cataracts to the river and the sea. Behind bars, in the Dell, a prisoner still waited, while at his back the flood rose. . . .

Cartwright spoke suddenly. "But what had *Kay* done?"

"We shall soon know," Mr. Tuke replied. "Obviously our murderer was rattled. Whichever he is, the inquest must have shaken him. There were significant omissions, and Akers was very easily satisfied."

"What did you mean, at the house, when you said something about the *date*? You didn't like the date."

"Oh, well, to-day is the 13th, and the Ides of September, and an anniversary of the ghost's first appearance."

"Are *you* superstitious?" Cartwright said.

"Dear me, no." Mr. Tuke sneezed once more. "Hell . . . !" he said. "But most criminals are. They believe in omens, and lucky days, and what have you. I thought the conjunction of dates a little disturbing. One of my long shots."

Through the blackness more windows shone. A gush of light fanned out as the door of the police station opened, and a caped constable looked curiously at the bedraggled quartette approaching him.

CHAPTER VI

CONVERSATIONS IN THE SUBWAY

"IT REALLY began yesterday morning," Kay said drowsily. "I'd been to Peter Jones's to buy some black gloves, for the funeral. Mine were shabby. And in Sloane Square a man was coming up out of one of those manhole things in the pavement." She yawned. "I wish I wasn't so dopey. . . !"

"Don't talk, if you don't want to," said Sir Bruton.

"But I *do* want to! I want to wake myself up, and I can't walk. And I don't want to think. . . . *Listen* to that water! Oh, I wish Gordon—I wish they'd all come back!"

"They're all right."

In spite of the Director's confident tone, the thundering rush of water in the sewer beneath, booming up through the air-shaft against which he and the girl were sitting, and making the brick floor vibrate, caused him serious misgivings. And though he had dealt airily throughout with the adventure upon which the rest of his party had embarked, now more than an hour ago, it was with an obvious effort that Kay brought her mind back to her story.

"Well, as soon as I saw this man coming up like that, it all came back to me. I mean Gervase Coverdale's story—the one I couldn't remember. You say this is the Ranelagh Sewer underneath—that's where it happened. He was down in it when a sudden thunderstorm came on, like this one. He was nearly drowned. . . ." Kay caught her breath, and went on quickly: "And then I began to think. I'd quite forgotten what his work was, you see. But now that I remembered, I began to wonder. . . ." She put a hand on Sir Bruton's arm, her small face, a dim oval in the light of the single electric lamp, turned up to his. "Tell me. Corinne's death wasn't an accident, was it? Or suicide?"

Sir Bruton laid a large hand over her small one.

"Neither, my dear, I'm afraid."

Kay gave a shuddering sigh. "I've felt that for some days. And—well, somebody did drag me down here, didn't they. . .? But about Gervase. Once I started to remember, I thought of other things. He made a joke once about being able to go underground almost from his door. That's just along here, you know. I've forgotten what the point was, but the Serpentine came into it. I'd actually forgotten the whole thing. I say, I'm telling this very badly, aren't I?"

"You're doing fine, for an invalid," said Sir Bruton.

"I'm waking up, anyway," said Kay, who indeed seemed more alert. "I wish my head wasn't so muzzy still. . . . The point is, when I did think of all this, in the middle of Sloane Square, I felt so relieved. . . . I'd been afraid—I'd been wondering—about Clifford. It was a nightmare. . . ."

Sir Bruton failed to suppress a chuckle. "Relieved, eh? Not too lucid yet, but I get your meaning. You'd been wondering if Reaveley had a hand in your cousin's death, and then you remembered Coverdale's job, and jokes about the Ranelagh and the Serpentine, and you put your money on him?"

"Well, yes," Kay said. "I didn't know about Corinne's beret then, but I *had* wondered if she'd gone to his flat that night, as she did before. And—and——"

"And if there was a rumpus, and he shot her in the drain?"

"It sounds dreadful! But then there's this. . . ."

Her hand indicated the gloomy cavern of the Subway, its curving walls and roof barely seen in the feeble light. She shuddered, suddenly and violently, and Sir Bruton patted her hand, and swore under his breath.

"You're all right now," he said. "Only a few bruises and a sprained ankle. I'd get you out myself if I wasn't so fat. Now let's get on with your story. You were so bucked when light burst on you in Sloane Square that you had to rush home and tell Reaveley, eh?"

"He happened to be there. He'd come to lunch."

"And what did he say?"

"Not much. Pooh-poohed it rather, and asked me not to talk about it. He said I was being melodramatic."

"I bet he did. Less talk the better, for him. And you still didn't remember what *his* job had been?"

"But I never *knew*, till you told me just now!" Kay cried. "He never talked about what he did in those days. Neither did Corinne. I thought he'd always been an ordinary sort of engineer. You mean—he wouldn't want it to get about?"

"Well, he mightn't, you know," Sir Bruton said. "It's no secret, but it was a long time ago, and people forget. He mightn't, just now, want you talking all over the shop about the L.C.C., and his knowing all the sewers in London, not to mention bathing-caps and damp patches in cupboards. You were so relieved you told him about that too, I suppose?"

"Yes, I did. I felt ashamed. . . ."

"It *was* a damp patch, eh? That was Tuke's notion."

"Yes," Kay whispered.

"Did you mention Tuke was with you at the time?"

"No, I didn't. I didn't say when I found the cap."

"Tell him you hadn't asked the maids about it?"

"He asked if they knew how it got in the cupboard, and I said I hadn't spoken about it."

"Putting your head in the lion's mouth," Sir Bruton grumbled, and felt Kay shaking again. "There, there! We don't *know*, you know. It still may be either of them."

"But *Clifford*! It's so horrible to think of. . . !"

"Stow it. Tell me a bit more. About to-day. You say you felt queer after supper. What did you drink?"

"Claret," Kay said. "Clifford came back with me to lunch, after the inquest, and he opened a bottle, and made me promise to have some more later."

"Leave him alone with the bottle after lunch?"

"Oh, I suppose so. Yes. He was in the dining-room with the paper for a bit while I was in and out."

"And before he went, he packed the maid off?"

"He *suggested* it. I told you. To-morrow's her half day, but Clifford said we might bring people back from the funeral. He asked if I could let Parker go to-day."

"His idea, then. What time'll she be back?"

"She's supposed to be in by eleven."

"Hence the hurry, perhaps. Never mind——" For Kay had drawn a sharp breath. "Then what happened?"

"Gordon came in the afternoon. He couldn't stay. Then nothing happened till I was going to have supper, just before seven. I looked out of the window, and Gervase Coverdale was coming up the Terrace. I—I suddenly got in a panic," Kay said. "I'd been thinking about him all day, and . . . Anyway, I rushed to the telephone, and tried to get Gordon, but he was out."

"You didn't think of pretending *you* were out?"

"No, I never thought of it. Besides, I told myself I was being melodramatic, as Clifford said. And—and, anyway, why should Gervase harm *me*?"

"Yes, why?" said Sir Bruton. "Got anything up your sleeve? About Mrs. Reaveley's crack at his past?"

"Of course not," Kay cried. "I told Mr. Tuke. I don't know what Corinne meant."

"Well, what did the gent want?"

"To see Clifford. He seemed angry, and worried—about that beret. He swore he didn't know a thing about it. He said Corinne hadn't been to his flat for weeks."

"Was *he* alone with the claret?"

"Well . . . yes. It was on the table. I had to answer a phone call."

"Long enough. And soon after that you felt sleepy?"

Kay nodded. "I was in the study, reading. I suppose I just went off there. I don't remember anything more till I began to wake up here, and thought I was in a cellar, and wondered what the noise was, and why you were here. . . ."

The Director patted her vaguely once more, for she was beginning to tremble. He shifted himself uneasily.

"These infernal bricks are damned hard, eh? I'm not as fat as I thought. Might as well be in a cellar. And look at that water. We'll be flooded next."

The runnel of water down the centre of the brick floor had been steadily widening, for rain was pouring down the still open manhole and through the low tunnel into the Subway. They could hear the downpour beating in the shaft, though the receding thunder was now drowned in the rush of the torrent below. The mustiness of the air, forced up through the ventilating shaft and the window in the wall, was increasing. Kay, controlling her tremors, put a hand to her forehead as she tried to ease her own position. She was resting against a pad made of Sir Bruton's raincoat, Chaffinch's jacket, and the two sacks, but her ankle, sprained when she was dropped feet first down the manhole, was swelling and painful. She felt as though she were bruised all over. Peering a little fearfully into the blackness of the Subway, she exclaimed:

"Can't we try to get out? I'm much stronger, and not so dizzy. I can hold on to you, and hop. I'm sure I can manage a ladder. What time is it?"

Sir Bruton held his watch to the light. "Ten to twelve. No harm in trying, eh?—Hullo, hullo . . . !"

"They're back!" Kay cried, and, forgetting her ankle, tried to rise, but sank back with a little moan of pain.

For a faint voice could be heard, a disembodied shouting, muffled and unintelligible in the din of the water beneath, but coming from the direction of the manhole, thirty yards away in the shadows. Sir Bruton was getting to his feet. He knocked his head, and strangled one of his more rococo oaths. Then he was bellowing down the vault, and again they heard the muffled voice. It did not seem to be any nearer.

"If it isn't them, it may be a bobby or someone," Sir Bruton said. "I'd better see. If I can."

"Take the lamp," Kay cried. "I don't mind."

The Director's large form, in a haze of light, trundled, stooping, towards the manhole tunnel. The voice was still shouting, still muffled and far away. It sounded angry. Sir Bruton's bellow boomed and echoed again.

"Come down then, blast you!"

For it was plain to him by now that the owner of the voice was no nearer than the street above. Arriving at the low arched entry, he waved the lamp at Kay, invisible in the hazy darkness behind, and stooped to direct a terrifying shout through the tunnel, as through a trumpet.

"*Come on down!*"

The answering shout was intelligible. "Show a light!"

Sir Bruton shone his lamp into the archway. Feet scraped the iron ladder, and then someone was coming along the tunnel. A bent form emerged and straightened carefully, full in the light of the lamp; and the Director said in a flat voice: "Dear me! You are very wet, Mr. Coverdale."

Coverdale, in a dripping raincoat, soaked trousers clinging to his legs, stood dazzled by the light, his eyes screwed up in his florid face under a sodden hat-brim.

"Who's that?" he cried angrily. "What the devil do you mean, leaving the cover open, and no one on top? I'll report you for this. If someone falls down that shaft——"

"My fault," said Sir Bruton. He gave a sinister chuckle. "But there are extenuating circumstances, Mr. Coverdale. As I observed, you are very wet. Been wading?"

"*Who* is it?" Coverdale demanded, still peering. "I know your voice. I thought you were one of our men. What's going on here? Put that light aside. I can't see you."

Sir Bruton obligingly turned the light on his own face, which was particularly malignant at that moment.

"What on earth . . . ?" said Coverdale, and stood gaping. But he appeared more astonished than alarmed. Rain dripped from him. And before he could collect himself to speak, more voices sounded faintly in the street above, grew louder, and were succeeded by another shout down the manhole.

"Here come the troops," Sir Bruton said. "Well, sir, you haven't explained."

"Explained . . . ?" Coverdale's bewilderment seemed genuine. "Surely it's for you, Sir Bruton . . . What *is* up?"

"I meant your trousers. How did you get them so wet?"

Coverdale's temper took charge. "Is this a quiz? Walking in a downpour, if you must know! Splashed by buses. . . . Hell, man, it's sousing down! I'm on my way home. I want to get into dry things, as soon as you've told me what the devil you're doing here. Isn't that one of our lamps . . . ?"

There was a scuffling in the shaft. Someone else was coming through the tunnel. It was Cartwright, who in turn stood staring at the spectacle of the Director and Gervase Coverdale facing one another like angry dogs. Before he could speak, Mr. Tuke was creeping out.

"Back to the dear old home. . . ." Then he, too, was stooping forward and staring. "And look who's here! Well, that seems to settle it, Cartwright. The favourite wins. . . ."

But Cartwright had already lost interest. Away in the darkness Kay was calling. Without ceremony he snatched the lamp from Sir Bruton's hand, and ran to her.

Mr. Tuke, by the light of his own lamp, looked from Coverdale's scowling, dumbfounded face to the Director's still malevolent one. He went up to the latter and drew him aside.

"What a time we've had! Hyde and Seek in a plumber's nightmare. Well, it's all over, I think, bar shouting. Hypothesis One wins, as I said." He glanced back at Coverdale, who had just been joined by Chaffinch. Joe Wilson was emerging from the tunnel. Mr. Tuke lowered his voice. "Our friend's past seems to have nothing to do with the case. Did you get so far as to ask him about it?"

"No," Sir Bruton said, a thought regretfully.

"Yes, a pity. We can't now, I suppose. Another thing we shall never know. Not a tidy case, this. . . ." Mr. Tuke was racked by a sneeze. "And I've caught a frightful cold."

CHAPTER VII

THE *MORNING NEWS* LEAVES ITS READERS GUESSING

THE HYDE PARK GHOST?

ANOTHER DROWNING FATALITY IN THE PARK

(From the *Morning News* Staff Reporter, JAMES FENNE)
Wednesday.

"EARLY this morning the body of Mr. Clifford Eric Reaveley, of 7a, Lancaster Terrace, was found lying in two feet of water in the Dell, Hyde Park. Apparently Mr. Reaveley had been trapped in an old drain, designed as an overflow for the Serpentine, by the rise of water in the sewer below caused by last night's storm. This was the worst London has experienced for some years, 4.50 ins. of rain being registered in an hour at Hampstead. The pool in the Dell is connected with the drain, and so with the main drainage system, by an iron grating. As the rising water overtook him, Mr. Reaveley, a man of great strength, succeeded in forcing two bars of the grating from their sockets, but the effort must have exhausted him, and falling forward into the shallow pool he was drowned before he could recover strength to rise. At one time Mr. Reaveley was employed in the Chief Engineer's Department of the L.C.C., but it is not known how he came to be in the drain last night.

"In another column I have dealt with the adjourned inquest on the body of Mrs. Clifford Reaveley, who met a similar death in the Serpentine just a week ago, and readers will need no reminding of the fate of my old acquaintance, Wally Whichcord, in the same waters, two days earlier. Three drowning fatalities are now linked with the strange story of the Hyde Park Ghost, and in an exclusive interview a witness at yesterday's inquest, Albert Jones, tells how he was the fourth known person to see this ominous spectre. Who else has seen it? Does it still walk, and does Death, the Grim Reaper, still follow? Or have we come to the end of this trail of mystery and disaster? Time will show."

A CATALOG OF SELECTED

DOVER BOOKS

IN ALL FIELDS OF INTEREST

A CATALOG OF SELECTED DOVER BOOKS IN ALL FIELDS OF INTEREST

CONCERNING THE SPIRITUAL IN ART, Wassily Kandinsky. Pioneering work by father of abstract art. Thoughts on color theory, nature of art. Analysis of earlier masters. 12 illustrations. 80pp. of text. 5⅜ × 8½. 23411-8 Pa. $2.50

LEONARDO ON THE HUMAN BODY, Leonardo da Vinci. More than 1200 of Leonardo's anatomical drawings on 215 plates. Leonardo's text, which accompanies the drawings, has been translated into English. 506pp. 8⅜ × 11¾. 24483-0 Pa. $10.95

GOBLIN MARKET, Christina Rossetti. Best-known work by poet comparable to Emily Dickinson, Alfred Tennyson. With 46 delightfully grotesque illustrations by Laurence Housman. 64pp. 4 × 6¾. 24516-0 Pa. $2.50

THE HEART OF THOREAU'S JOURNALS, edited by Odell Shepard. Selections from *Journal*, ranging over full gamut of interests. 228pp. 5⅜ × 8½. 20741-2 Pa. $4.50

MR. LINCOLN'S CAMERA MAN: MATHEW B. BRADY, Roy Meredith. Over 300 Brady photos reproduced directly from original negatives, photos. Lively commentary. 368pp. 8⅜ × 11¼. 23021-X Pa. $14.95

PHOTOGRAPHIC VIEWS OF SHERMAN'S CAMPAIGN, George N. Barnard. Reprint of landmark 1866 volume with 61 plates: battlefield of New Hope Church, the Etawah Bridge, the capture of Atlanta, etc. 80pp. 9 × 12. 23445-2 Pa. $6.00

A SHORT HISTORY OF ANATOMY AND PHYSIOLOGY FROM THE GREEKS TO HARVEY, Dr. Charles Singer. Thoroughly engrossing non-technical survey. 270 illustrations. 211pp. 5⅜ × 8½. 20389-1 Pa. $4.95

REDOUTE ROSES IRON-ON TRANSFER PATTERNS, Barbara Christopher. Redouté was botanical painter to the Empress Josephine; transfer his famous roses onto fabric with these 24 transfer patterns. 80pp. 8¼ × 10⅞. 24292-7 Pa. $3.50

THE FIVE BOOKS OF ARCHITECTURE, Sebastiano Serlio. Architectural milestone, first (1611) English translation of Renaissance classic. Unabridged reproduction of original edition includes over 300 woodcut illustrations. 416pp. 9⅜ × 12¼. 24349-4 Pa. $14.95

CARLSON'S GUIDE TO LANDSCAPE PAINTING, John F. Carlson. Authoritative, comprehensive guide covers, every aspect of landscape painting. 34 reproductions of paintings by author; 58 explanatory diagrams. 144pp. 8⅜ × 11. 22927-0 Pa. $5.95

101 PUZZLES IN THOUGHT AND LOGIC, C.R. Wylie, Jr. Solve murders, robberies, see which fishermen are liars—purely by reasoning! 107pp. 5⅜ × 8½. 20367-0 Pa. $2.00

TEST YOUR LOGIC, George J. Summers. 50 more truly new puzzles with new turns of thought, new subtleties of inference. 100pp. 5⅜ × 8½. 22877-0 Pa. $2.25

CHILDREN'S BOOKPLATES AND LABELS, Ed Sibbett, Jr. 6 each of 12 types based on *Wizard of Oz, Alice,* nursery rhymes, fairy tales. Perforated; full color. 24pp. 8¼ × 11. 23538-6 Pa. $3.50

READY-TO-USE VICTORIAN COLOR STICKERS: 96 Pressure-Sensitive Seals, Carol Belanger Grafton. Drawn from authentic period sources. Motifs include heads of men, women, children, plus florals, animals, birds, more. Will adhere to any clean surface. 8pp. 8½ × 11. 24551-9 Pa. $2.95

CUT AND FOLD PAPER SPACESHIPS THAT FLY, Michael Grater. 16 colorful, easy-to-build spaceships that really fly. Star Shuttle, Lunar Freighter, Star Probe, 13 others. 32pp. 8¼ × 11. 23978-0 Pa. $2.50

CUT AND ASSEMBLE PAPER AIRPLANES THAT FLY, Arthur Baker. 8 aerodynamically sound, ready-to-build paper airplanes, designed with latest techniques. Fly *Pegasus, Daedalus, Songbird,* 5 other aircraft. Instructions. 32pp. 9¼ × 11¼. 24302-8 Pa. $3.95

SIDELIGHTS ON RELATIVITY, Albert Einstein. Two lectures delivered in 1920-21: *Ether and Relativity* and *Geometry and Experience.* Elegant ideas in non-mathematical form. 56pp. 5⅜ × 8½. 24511-X Pa. $2.25

FADS AND FALLACIES IN THE NAME OF SCIENCE, Martin Gardner. Fair, witty appraisal of cranks and quacks of science: Velikovsky, orgone energy, Bridey Murphy, medical fads, etc. 373pp. 5⅜ × 8½. 20394-8 Pa. $5.95

VACATION HOMES AND CABINS, U.S. Dept. of Agriculture. Complete plans for 16 cabins, vacation homes and other shelters. 105pp. 9 × 12. 23631-5 Pa. $4.95

HOW TO BUILD A WOOD-FRAME HOUSE, L.O. Anderson. Placement, foundations, framing, sheathing, roof, insulation, plaster, finishing—almost everything else. 179 illustrations. 223pp. 7⅞ × 10¾. 22954-8 Pa. $5.50

THE MYSTERY OF A HANSOM CAB, Fergus W. Hume. Bizarre murder in a hansom cab leads to engrossing investigation. Memorable characters, rich atmosphere. 19th-century bestseller, still enjoyable, exciting. 256pp. 5⅜ × 8. 21956-9 Pa. $4.00

MANUAL OF TRADITIONAL WOOD CARVING, edited by Paul N. Hasluck. Possibly the best book in English on the craft of wood carving. Practical instructions, along with 1,146 working drawings and photographic illustrations. 576pp. 6½ × 9¼. 23489-4 Pa. $8.95

WHITTLING AND WOODCARVING, E.J Tangerman. Best book on market; clear, full. If you can cut a potato, you can carve toys, puzzles, chains, etc. Over 464 illustrations. 293pp. 5⅜ × 8½. 20965-2 Pa. $4.95

AMERICAN TRADEMARK DESIGNS, Barbara Baer Capitman. 732 marks, logos and corporate-identity symbols. Categories include entertainment, heavy industry, food and beverage. All black-and-white in standard forms. 160pp. 8⅜ × 11. 23259-X Pa. $6.95

DECORATIVE FRAMES AND BORDERS, edited by Edmund V. Gillon, Jr. Largest collection of borders and frames ever compiled for use of artists and designers. Renaissance, neo-Greek, Art Nouveau, Art Deco, to mention only a few styles. 396 illustrations. 192pp. 8⅜ × 11¼. 22928-9 Pa. $6.00

THE MURDER BOOK OF J.G. REEDER, Edgar Wallace. Eight suspenseful stories by bestselling mystery writer of 20s and 30s. Features the donnish Mr. J.G. Reeder of Public Prosecutor's Office. 128pp. 5⅜ × 8½. (Available in U.S. only) 24374-5 Pa. $3.50

ANNE ORR'S CHARTED DESIGNS, Anne Orr. Best designs by premier needlework designer, all on charts: flowers, borders, birds, children, alphabets, etc. Over 100 charts, 10 in color. Total of 40pp. 8¼ × 11. 23704-4 Pa. $2.50

BASIC CONSTRUCTION TECHNIQUES FOR HOUSES AND SMALL BUILDINGS SIMPLY EXPLAINED, U.S. Bureau of Naval Personnel. Grading, masonry, woodworking, floor and wall framing, roof framing, plastering, tile setting, much more. Over 675 illustrations. 568pp. 6½ × 9¼. 20242-9 Pa. $8.95

MATISSE LINE DRAWINGS AND PRINTS, Henri Matisse. Representative collection of female nudes, faces, still lifes, experimental works, etc., from 1898 to 1948. 50 illustrations. 48pp. 8⅜ × 11¼. 23877-6 Pa. $2.50

HOW TO PLAY THE CHESS OPENINGS, Eugene Znosko-Borovsky. Clear, profound examinations of just what each opening is intended to do and how opponent can counter. Many sample games. 147pp. 5⅜ × 8½. 22795-2 Pa. $2.95

DUPLICATE BRIDGE, Alfred Sheinwold. Clear, thorough, easily followed account: rules, etiquette, scoring, strategy, bidding; Goren's point-count system, Blackwood and Gerber conventions, etc. 158pp. 5⅜ × 8½. 22741-3 Pa. $3.00

SARGENT PORTRAIT DRAWINGS, J.S. Sargent. Collection of 42 portraits reveals technical skill and intuitive eye of noted American portrait painter, John Singer Sargent. 48pp. 8¼ × 11⅛. 24524-1 Pa. $2.95

ENTERTAINING SCIENCE EXPERIMENTS WITH EVERYDAY OBJECTS, Martin Gardner. Over 100 experiments for youngsters. Will amuse, astonish, teach, and entertain. Over 100 illustrations. 127pp. 5⅜ × 8½. 24201-3 Pa. $2.50

TEDDY BEAR PAPER DOLLS IN FULL COLOR: A Family of Four Bears and Their Costumes, Crystal Collins. A family of four Teddy Bear paper dolls and nearly 60 cut-out costumes. Full color, printed one side only. 32pp. 9¼ × 12¼. 24550-0 Pa. $3.50

NEW CALLIGRAPHIC ORNAMENTS AND FLOURISHES, Arthur Baker. Unusual, multi-useable material: arrows, pointing hands, brackets and frames, ovals, swirls, birds, etc. Nearly 700 illustrations. 80pp. 8⅜ × 11¼. 24095-9 Pa. $3.75

DINOSAUR DIORAMAS TO CUT & ASSEMBLE, M. Kalmenoff. Two complete three-dimensional scenes in full color, with 31 cut-out animals and plants. Excellent educational toy for youngsters. Instructions; 2 assembly diagrams. 32pp. 9¼ × 12¼. 24541-1 Pa. $4.50

SILHOUETTES: A PICTORIAL ARCHIVE OF VARIED ILLUSTRATIONS, edited by Carol Belanger Grafton. Over 600 silhouettes from the 18th to 20th centuries. Profiles and full figures of men, women, children, birds, animals, groups and scenes, nature, ships, an alphabet. 144pp. 8⅜ × 11¼. 23781-8 Pa. $4.95

SURREAL STICKERS AND UNREAL STAMPS, William Rowe. 224 haunting, hilarious stamps on gummed, perforated stock, with images of elephants, geisha girls, George Washington, etc. 16pp. one side. 8¼ × 11. 24371-0 Pa. $3.50

GOURMET KITCHEN LABELS, Ed Sibbett, Jr. 112 full-color labels (4 copies each of 28 designs). Fruit, bread, other culinary motifs. Gummed and perforated. 16pp. 8¼ × 11. 24087-8 Pa. $2.95

PATTERNS AND INSTRUCTIONS FOR CARVING AUTHENTIC BIRDS, H.D. Green. Detailed instructions, 27 diagrams, 85 photographs for carving 15 species of birds so life-like, they'll seem ready to fly! 8¼ × 11. 24222-6 Pa. $2.75

FLATLAND, E.A. Abbott. Science-fiction classic explores life of 2-D being in 3-D world. 16 illustrations. 103pp. 5⅜ × 8. 20001-9 Pa. $2.00

DRIED FLOWERS, Sarah Whitlock and Martha Rankin. Concise, clear, practical guide to dehydration, glycerinizing, pressing plant material, and more. Covers use of silica gel. 12 drawings. 32pp. 5⅜ × 8½. 21802-3 Pa. $1.00

EASY-TO-MAKE CANDLES, Gary V. Guy. Learn how easy it is to make all kinds of decorative candles. Step-by-step instructions. 82 illustrations. 48pp. 8¼ × 11. 23881-4 Pa. $2.50

SUPER STICKERS FOR KIDS, Carolyn Bracken. 128 gummed and perforated full-color stickers: GIRL WANTED, KEEP OUT, BORED OF EDUCATION, X-RATED, COMBAT ZONE, many others. 16pp. 8¼ × 11. 24092-4 Pa. $2.50

CUT AND COLOR PAPER MASKS, Michael Grater. Clowns, animals, funny faces...simply color them in, cut them out, and put them together, and you have 9 paper masks to play with and enjoy. 32pp. 8¼ × 11. 23171-2 Pa. $2.25

A CHRISTMAS CAROL: THE ORIGINAL MANUSCRIPT, Charles Dickens. Clear facsimile of Dickens manuscript, on facing pages with final printed text. 8 illustrations by John Leech, 4 in color on covers. 144pp. 8⅜ × 11¼. 20980-6 Pa. $5.95

CARVING SHOREBIRDS, Harry V. Shourds & Anthony Hillman. 16 full-size patterns (all double-page spreads) for 19 North American shorebirds with step-by-step instructions. 72pp. 9¼ × 12¼. 24287-0 Pa. $4.95

THE GENTLE ART OF MATHEMATICS, Dan Pedoe. Mathematical games, probability, the question of infinity, topology, how the laws of algebra work, problems of irrational numbers, and more. 42 figures. 143pp. 5⅜ × 8½. (EBE) 22949-1 Pa. $3.50

READY-TO-USE DOLLHOUSE WALLPAPER, Katzenbach & Warren, Inc. Stripe, 2 floral stripes, 2 allover florals, polka dot; all in full color. 4 sheets (350 sq. in.) of each, enough for average room. 48pp. 8¼ × 11. 23495-9 Pa. $2.95

MINIATURE IRON-ON TRANSFER PATTERNS FOR DOLLHOUSES, DOLLS, AND SMALL PROJECTS, Rita Weiss and Frank Fontana. Over 100 miniature patterns: rugs, bedspreads, quilts, chair seats, etc. In standard dollhouse size. 48pp. 8¼ × 11. 23741-9 Pa. $1.95

THE DINOSAUR COLORING BOOK, Anthony Rao. 45 renderings of dinosaurs, fossil birds, turtles, other creatures of Mesozoic Era. Scientifically accurate. Captions. 48pp. 8¼ × 11. 24022-3 Pa. $2.50

JAPANESE DESIGN MOTIFS, Matsuya Co. Mon, or heraldic designs. Over 4000 typical, beautiful designs: birds, animals, flowers, swords, fans, geometrics; all beautifully stylized. 213pp. 11⅜ × 8¼. 22874-6 Pa. $7.95

THE TALE OF BENJAMIN BUNNY, Beatrix Potter. Peter Rabbit's cousin coaxes him back into Mr. McGregor's garden for a whole new set of adventures. All 27 full-color illustrations. 59pp. 4¼ × 5½. (Available in U.S. only) 21102-9 Pa. $1.75

THE TALE OF PETER RABBIT AND OTHER FAVORITE STORIES BOXED SET, Beatrix Potter. Seven of Beatrix Potter's best-loved tales including Peter Rabbit in a specially designed, durable boxed set. 4¼ × 5½. Total of 447pp. 158 color illustrations. (Available in U.S. only) 23903-9 Pa. $10.80

PRACTICAL MENTAL MAGIC, Theodore Annemann. Nearly 200 astonishing feats of mental magic revealed in step-by-step detail. Complete advice on staging, patter, etc. Illustrated. 320pp. 5⅜ × 8½. 24426-1 Pa. $5.95

CELEBRATED CASES OF JUDGE DEE (DEE GOONG AN), translated by Robert Van Gulik. Authentic 18th-century Chinese detective novel; Dee and associates solve three interlocked cases. Led to van Gulik's own stories with same characters. Extensive introduction. 9 illustrations. 237pp. 5⅜ × 8½. 23337-5 Pa. $4.50

CUT & FOLD EXTRATERRESTRIAL INVADERS THAT FLY, M. Grater. Stage your own lilliputian space battles. By following the step-by-step instructions and explanatory diagrams you can launch 22 full-color fliers into space. 36pp. 8¼ × 11. 24478-4 Pa. $2.95

CUT & ASSEMBLE VICTORIAN HOUSES, Edmund V. Gillon, Jr. Printed in full color on heavy cardboard stock, 4 authentic Victorian houses in H-O scale: Italian-style Villa, Octagon, Second Empire, Stick Style. 48pp. 9¼ × 12¼. 23849-0 Pa. $3.95

BEST SCIENCE FICTION STORIES OF H.G. WELLS, H.G. Wells. Full novel *The Invisible Man*, plus 17 short stories: "The Crystal Egg," "Aepyornis Island," "The Strange Orchid," etc. 303pp. 5⅜ × 8½. (Available in U.S. only) 21531-8 Pa. $4.95

TRADEMARK DESIGNS OF THE WORLD, Yusaku Kamekura. A lavish collection of nearly 700 trademarks, the work of Wright, Loewy, Klee, Binder, hundreds of others. 160pp. 8¾ × 8. (Available in U.S. only) 24191-2 Pa. $5.95

THE ARTIST'S AND CRAFTSMAN'S GUIDE TO REDUCING, ENLARGING AND TRANSFERRING DESIGNS, Rita Weiss. Discover, reduce, enlarge, transfer designs from any objects to any craft project. 12pp. plus 16 sheets special graph paper. 8¼ × 11. 24142-4 Pa. $3.50

TREASURY OF JAPANESE DESIGNS AND MOTIFS FOR ARTISTS AND CRAFTSMEN, edited by Carol Belanger Grafton. Indispensable collection of 360 traditional Japanese designs and motifs redrawn in clean, crisp black-and-white, copyright-free illustrations. 96pp. 8¼ × 11. 24435-0 Pa. $3.95

CHANCERY CURSIVE STROKE BY STROKE, Arthur Baker. Instructions and illustrations for each stroke of each letter (upper and lower case) and numerals. 54 full-page plates. 64pp. 8¼ × 11. 24278-1 Pa. $2.50

THE ENJOYMENT AND USE OF COLOR, Walter Sargent. Color relationships, values, intensities; complementary colors, illumination, similar topics. Color in nature and art. 7 color plates, 29 illustrations. 274pp. 5⅜ × 8½. 20944-X Pa. $4.95

SCULPTURE PRINCIPLES AND PRACTICE, Louis Slobodkin. Step-by-step approach to clay, plaster, metals, stone; classical and modern. 253 drawings, photos. 255pp. 8⅛ × 11. 22960-2 Pa. $7.50

VICTORIAN FASHION PAPER DOLLS FROM HARPER'S BAZAR, 1867-1898, Theodore Menten. Four female dolls with 28 elegant high fashion costumes, printed in full color. 32pp. 9¼ × 12¼. 23453-3 Pa. $3.50

FLOPSY, MOPSY AND COTTONTAIL: A Little Book of Paper Dolls in Full Color, Susan LaBelle. Three dolls and 21 costumes (7 for each doll) show Peter Rabbit's siblings dressed for holidays, gardening, hiking, etc. Charming borders, captions. 48pp. 4¼ × 5½. 24376-1 Pa. $2.25

NATIONAL LEAGUE BASEBALL CARD CLASSICS, Bert Randolph Sugar. 83 big-leaguers from 1909-69 on facsimile cards. Hubbell, Dean, Spahn, Brock plus advertising, info, no duplications. Perforated, detachable. 16pp. 8¼ × 11. 24308-7 Pa. $2.95

THE LOGICAL APPROACH TO CHESS, Dr. Max Euwe, et al. First-rate text of comprehensive strategy, tactics, theory for the amateur. No gambits to memorize, just a clear, logical approach. 224pp. 5⅜ × 8½. 24353-2 Pa. $4.50

MAGICK IN THEORY AND PRACTICE, Aleister Crowley. The summation of the thought and practice of the century's most famous necromancer, long hard to find. Crowley's best book. 436pp. 5⅜ × 8½. (Available in U.S. only) 23295-6 Pa. $6.50

THE HAUNTED HOTEL, Wilkie Collins. Collins' last great tale; doom and destiny in a Venetian palace. Praised by T.S. Eliot. 127pp. 5⅜ × 8½. 24333-8 Pa. $3.00

ART DECO DISPLAY ALPHABETS, Dan X. Solo. Wide variety of bold yet elegant lettering in handsome Art Deco styles. 100 complete fonts, with numerals, punctuation, more. 104pp. 8⅛ × 11. 24372-9 Pa. $4.50

CALLIGRAPHIC ALPHABETS, Arthur Baker. Nearly 150 complete alphabets by outstanding contemporary. Stimulating ideas; useful source for unique effects. 154 plates. 157pp. 8⅜ × 11¼. 21045-6 Pa. $5.95

ARTHUR BAKER'S HISTORIC CALLIGRAPHIC ALPHABETS, Arthur Baker. From monumental capitals of first-century Rome to humanistic cursive of 16th century, 33 alphabets in fresh interpretations. 88 plates. 96pp. 9 × 12. 24054-1 Pa. $4.50

LETTIE LANE PAPER DOLLS, Sheila Young. Genteel turn-of-the-century family very popular then and now. 24 paper dolls. 16 plates in full color. 32pp. 9¼ × 12¼. 24089-4 Pa. $3.50

THE RIME OF THE ANCIENT MARINER, Gustave Doré, S.T. Coleridge. Doré's finest work, 34 plates capture moods, subtleties of poem. Full text. 77pp. 9¼ × 12. 22305-1 Pa. $4.95

SONGS OF INNOCENCE, William Blake. The first and most popular of Blake's famous "Illuminated Books," in a facsimile edition reproducing all 31 brightly colored plates. Additional printed text of each poem. 64pp. 5¼ × 7. 22764-2 Pa. $3.50

AN INTRODUCTION TO INFORMATION THEORY, J.R. Pierce. Second (1980) edition of most impressive non-technical account available. Encoding, entropy, noisy channel, related areas, etc. 320pp. 5⅜ × 8½. 24061-4 Pa. $4.95

THE DIVINE PROPORTION: A STUDY IN MATHEMATICAL BEAUTY, H.E. Huntley. "Divine proportion" or "golden ratio" in poetry, Pascal's triangle, philosophy, psychology, music, mathematical figures, etc. Excellent bridge between science and art. 58 figures. 185pp. 5⅜ × 8½. 22254-3 Pa. $3.95

THE DOVER NEW YORK WALKING GUIDE: From the Battery to Wall Street, Mary J. Shapiro. Superb inexpensive guide to historic buildings and locales in lower Manhattan: Trinity Church, Bowling Green, more. Complete Text; maps. 36 illustrations. 48pp. 3⅞ × 9¼. 24225-0 Pa. $2.50

NEW YORK THEN AND NOW, Edward B. Watson, Edmund V. Gillon, Jr. 83 important Manhattan sites: on facing pages early photographs (1875-1925) and 1976 photos by Gillon. 172 illustrations. 171pp. 9¼ × 10. 23361-8 Pa. $7.95

HISTORIC COSTUME IN PICTURES, Braun & Schneider. Over 1450 costumed figures from dawn of civilization to end of 19th century. English captions. 125 plates. 256pp. 8⅜ × 11¼. 23150-X Pa. $7.50

VICTORIAN AND EDWARDIAN FASHION: A Photographic Survey, Alison Gernsheim. First fashion history completely illustrated by contemporary photographs. Full text plus 235 photos, 1840-1914, in which many celebrities appear. 240pp. 6½ × 9¼. 24205-6 Pa. $6.00

CHARTED CHRISTMAS DESIGNS FOR COUNTED CROSS-STITCH AND OTHER NEEDLECRAFTS, Lindberg Press. Charted designs for 45 beautiful needlecraft projects with many yuletide and wintertime motifs. 48pp. 8¼ × 11. 24356-7 Pa. $2.50

101 FOLK DESIGNS FOR COUNTED CROSS-STITCH AND OTHER NEEDLECRAFTS, Carter Houck. 101 authentic charted folk designs in a wide array of lovely representations with many suggestions for effective use. 48pp. 8¼ × 11. 24369-9 Pa. $2.25

FIVE ACRES AND INDEPENDENCE, Maurice G. Kains. Great back-to-the-land classic explains basics of self-sufficient farming. The one book to get. 95 illustrations. 397pp. 5⅜ × 8½. 20974-1 Pa. $4.95

A MODERN HERBAL, Margaret Grieve. Much the fullest, most exact, most useful compilation of herbal material. Gigantic alphabetical encyclopedia, from aconite to zedoary, gives botanical information, medical properties, folklore, economic uses, and much else. Indispensable to serious reader. 161 illustrations. 888pp. 6½ × 9¼. (Available in U.S. only) 22798-7, 22799-5 Pa., Two-vol. set $16.45